INTERNATIONAL ACCLAIM FOR

The Underpainter

"Urquhart is one of Canada's most accomplished and interesting writers."
— *Edmonton Journal*

"Original and dazzling, radiant and quietly perceptive, Urquhart's new novel delights the senses even as it astonishes the mind. . . ."
— *London Free Press*

"A lyrical novel with a deep, unsentimental connection to ordinary life. . . . [Urquhart's] language is vivid enough to take your breath away."
— *Boston Globe*

"Urquhart explores the ability to love and the failure to love; the visual pictures and images of humanity beneath the surfaces on which art is created. *The Underpainter* is a savory read."
— *Flare*

"Urquhart's evocation of time and place shimmers with clarity. . . ."
— *Publishers Weekly* (starred review)

"Urquhart has written a novel whose narrative power matches her delicate artistry with words . . . lodges in the mind and heart forever."
— Montreal *Gazette*

"Richly textured prose, and an intricate, many layered structure."
— *Sunday Times* (U.K.)

"A rich, multi-faceted story, skillfully told."
— *San Francisco Chronicle*

THE UNDERPAINTER

JANE URQUHART

M&S

Canadian Cataloguing in Publication Data

Urquhart, Jane, date
The underpainter

ISBN 0-7710-8664-4 (bound)   ISBN 0-7710-8654-7 (pbk.)

I. Title.

PS8591.R68U52   C813´.54   C97-931044-X
PR9199.3.U76U52

We acknowledge the financial support of the Government of Canada through
the Book Publishing Industry Development Program for our publishing
activities. We further acknowledge the support of the Canada Council for the
Arts and the Ontario Arts Council for our publishing program.

Cover and text design: Kong Njo
Cover painting: *Three Weeks Last Wednesday Two*
by Emma Hesse, 1996, oil on panel

Typeset in Centaur by M&S, Toronto
Printed and bound in Canada

McClelland & Stewart Inc.
The Canadian Publishers
481 University Avenue
Toronto, Ontario
M5G 2E9

1 2 3 4 5   02 01 00 99 98

For Tony Urquhart,
whose spirit is visible in art, in life

For Amy Quinn,
who discovered the letters, and knew

For Ellen Seligman,
with affection and gratitude

"Although an even north light is preferable in the greater number of cases, direct bright sunlight is sometimes useful in examining blacks and other very dark colours."

— RALPH MAYER,
The Artist's Handbook of Materials and Techniques

The woman is standing near the window in the downstairs front room of a log house on the north shore of Lake Superior.

It is the winter of 1937.

She is wearing a grey tweed skirt and a checked woollen bush jacket. Her dark-blonde hair is pulled back from her face and hangs in a thick braid almost to her waist. Despite the fact that she has kept her fires — both in the Quebec heater in this room and in the stove in the kitchen — burning all night, it is cold enough that she can see her breath. In her hand she holds an unopened envelope with the words "Canadian National Telegram" printed on it. Her head is bent and her shoulders are slightly stooped as she stares at this folded and glued piece of paper.

To the left and to the right of the house in which she stands lies a series of similar homes built for the miners who arrived in this place in the 1860s. Since the penultimate closure of the silver mine in 1884, all but a few of these dwellings are abandoned in winter. In recent decades they have been used as summer residences only by certain adventurous families from the small twin

cities of Port Arthur and Fort William, which are situated
sixteen miles to the west but cannot be seen from here because a
limb of the huge, human-shaped peninsula of rock, known as
The Sleeping Giant, hides them from view.

This unconscious granite figure is famous. In the summer,
tourists driving the gorgeous north shore of Lake Superior stop
their cars and stare across Thunder Bay at his reclining body.
Passengers who have travelled on the Trans-Canada train can
bring his physique to mind long after mountains and prairies
have faded from memory. He is twenty miles long, this person
made from northern landscape, and, in 1937, no roads as yet have
scarred his skin. According to the Ojibway, who have inhabited
this region for hundreds of years, he was turned to stone as punishment for revealing the secret location of silver to white men
greedy enough to demand the information. He will lie forever
obdurate, unyielding, stretched across the bay.

The little settlement of Silver Islet Landing, where the
woman lives, occupies a site on his anatomy sometimes referred
to as "the toe of the giant."

During the brief summer season, bonfires bloom nightly on
the small offshore islands she can see from her front windows.
Swimmers dive from the dock near the large clapboard building
that acts as a hotel and a store. Steamers, which provide the only
transportation to the spot, ply back and forth from Port Arthur;
the narrow track near the shore is filled with running children.
Occasionally games and entertainments take place on the sand
beach at the end of the lane. There is often laughter, and sometimes singing.

By mid-September, stillness and quiet are reinstated, the summer population having returned to the schools and industries of daily life. One old government official, who is responsible for the maintenance of two lighthouses and for the sporadic winter postal deliveries, remains in his house near the dock. And the woman remains in her cabin a little farther down the shore. By the time the world begins to frost, and then to freeze, even the memory of the summer activity seems unreal, as if it had been a mere performance and she a witness — not even a member of the audience but a stranger in the wings.

When these houses were built, almost eighty years before, the need for shelter was so pressing that the mining company was forced to use unseasoned timber, which had warped in odd directions over the course of the first year. On frigid January mornings, the miners, their wives and children, had awakened to the sight of miniature snowdrifts on the floor and ragged open spaces between the logs. The gaps were swiftly filled with anything that came to hand — socks, knitted hats, treasured table linen from the Old Country. Eventually the houses gave up the struggle, settled, and became stable. Only then were the upstairs walls plastered and whitewashed. On the ground storey the logs remained — and still remain — exposed in the parlour and the kitchen.

Once when the woman was driving a nail between the timbers to hang a picture that I had given her — a picture of herself in her summer garden — a chunk of caulking gave way and an embroidered handkerchief, edged in lace, fell like a message out of the wall.

She is standing near the window beside a rough log wall. The unopened telegram in her hand appears to have already darkened with time, darkened in comparison to the white snow around her house, the brightness of sun that enters the room.

She pushes a tendril of hair behind her ear, a strand that has escaped the braid. This strand contains some threads of grey. She stares at the envelope, then lifts her head to watch the departure of the mail sled, its driver and team of noisy dogs, to watch it glide over the snow-covered ice and disappear behind Burnt Island. For several minutes she wants to refuse the message she has not yet read. The world around her is quiet and fixed, frozen and beautiful. She does not want the scene disturbed. Even the tracks of the sled irritate her; they have scarred the white surface, they have soiled the day.

The woman's winters are long and bright and silent. Just before nightfall the landscape blossoms into various shades of blue. Few events interrupt the tranquillity; a storm, maybe, or the delivery of supplies, or her own infrequent journeys over ice, around Thunder Cape, into Port Arthur. She has come to rely on the predictability of the season, its lengthiness, its cold. She doubts she would be able to understand a life without it.

She crosses the room and lifts the lid of the Quebec heater, which she holds at the end of the lever for some time as if not quite certain why she has taken this action. For a moment it looks as if she will toss the telegram, unread, into the fire. But this is not what she wants. When she replaces the lid, there is the sound of cast iron striking cast iron, a sound so familiar to her she barely hears it.

Sitting on the chair nearest the stove's heat, she carefully opens the envelope. It falls to her lap. She reads the contents.

Almost immediately she decides to leave. In her father's long-ago abandoned room upstairs, she takes his ancient mining clothes from the closet, shakes the dust from the overalls, and removes her jacket and skirt. She covers her feet in several layers of socks and steps into his boots, his overalls, then puts on his large down-filled parka. This is the costume she occasionally wears when she is outdoors in winter, though she knows it to be somewhat ridiculous on the body of a woman entering middle age. Outside her door she reaches for the skis leaning against the outer log wall, places them side by side on the paper-dry snow, tightens the leather straps over her father's boots, and sets out.

Just before she passes, like the mail sled an hour ago, between the mainland and Burnt Island, she turns to look back at the shore, back at the house she is leaving behind her. There is no differentiation, in this season, between water and land. A delicate wisp of smoke is escaping from her chimney, though she has added no wood at all to her fire this morning.

It is six and a half miles to Thunder Cape, a large spearhead of land rising thirteen hundred feet and clearly visible across the frozen bay. She will spend the night with the couple that keeps the lighthouse there. Tomorrow she will ski sixteen miles across Thunder Bay to the modest lakehead city of Port Arthur.

—◇—

All of this is a very long time ago now, forty years at least. A very long time ago and purely hypothetical on my part. I did not see her leave her house, ski towards Thunder Cape, turn to watch the thin trail of smoke emerge from her chimney. I did not see her shake the dust off of her father's underground clothes or strap the skis to his large boots.

The telegram she carries in her pocket, or has left behind on the kitchen table, or has thrown into the trash, the telegram I never saw but know for certain she received and read, has told her that I, Austin Fraser, am waiting in Port Arthur, in a fifth-floor hotel room, hours of distance away.

I

THE LAKE EFFECT

Each afternoon now, when I have finished with my work, memory beckons me into the street, insists that I walk with her in the snow. These are the things she wants to see: the cloud of my own warm breath obscuring my face, my uncertain steps, the small round wounds my steel-pointed cane makes as it impales the dangerous ice. She wants me moving slowly, feebly, around and around the one residential city block that has become my shrunken world. She wants to see me circling in the cold, going nowhere.

Even though there is nothing in me that wants to court the past, it fills my mind, enters my painting. The *tock, tock* of my cane striking ice is like the noise that beads make as they click together on a string. It is the sound of memory at work, creating a necklace of narrative.

There is nothing in passion, really, except the sense that one should open one's self to it. In many ways it can be as cold as

anything else. Years ago in Silver Islet I would leave the painting I was working on in the upstairs room of Sara's house, leave
it facing the window, hoping that overnight some of the Great
Lake Superior might move into it, or some of Sara's dreams,
though she slept in the back room and her window faced the
rock, the cliff. Perhaps something of what remained of the offshore mine might make itself felt on the canvas. At the time, I
was travelling in my experience along a cusp of acceptance.
Being not yet known to myself or others, I continued to be
interested in the figure and in landscape. I had been fascinated,
you see, by the actuality of the north; its rocks and trees and
water. Interested in Sara, the woman who lived there. It was
during what would be my final summer at Silver Islet Landing
that a stylistic change caught my mind, pulling me from
realism towards the concept of formal ambiguity. This freed
me, or so I thought, because, unlike a figure or a landscape, a
concept can be carried anywhere. So I gathered up the embryo
of this idea, along with my clothes and brushes and canvases,
and took it with me first to New York and then some years
later I took it here, to this vast modern house in Rochester, the
city of my birth.

I never saw Sara again after that – except from a very great distance – which may explain why part of me still feels it is possible that she might want to insinuate herself back into my life, my
painting. But what an addled old man I am to let such foolish-
ness enter my thoughts. The woman who comes to mind is
wearing that short-sleeved house dress with the buttons down

the front and the pockets over the hips. Even in the dead of winter I see her with her legs bare and her dark-blonde hair hanging in a thick braid down her back. And — even more impossible — she is only thirty-five years old, whereas Sara would have been in her seventies. And hairstyles, clothing, fashion have changed so completely.

I myself have not for a long time been prey to the whims of fashion, although admittedly it had some influence over me in the past. Political fashion, aesthetic fashion, spiritual fashion, even, I suspect, emotional fashion; that sense that one should let whatever comes along seize the heart.

The fashionable modernist architect who built the cavernous house in which I live, for instance, believed that absolutely nothing should be added to indoor spaces, nothing at all except light. He wanted everything else kept out: furniture, colour, paintings, fabrics — and even his beloved light was allowed entrance only after it had passed through glass. How he would have hated my shelves of painted china, insisting that all this clutter interfered with the "idea" of his work. He was a great advocate of ideas. I live in the most eastern of his long, spare, prairie-style houses. It suits me very well.

I received the news from Canada last week. Special delivery. The mailman must have knocked — there is no buzzer — he must have knocked, received no answer, slipped the letter through the slot. I am very hard of hearing now, and have few visitors, so I am not attentive to the possibility of arrivals at my door. Who knows how long the cream-coloured envelope had been on the floor of

my vestibule before my housekeeper, the ever-present, irrepressible Mrs. Boyle, emerged from the basement laundry room and
picked it up? She had handed me the ordinary mail earlier in the
day and I had dealt with it as I usually do by consigning most
of it to the trash after setting aside the bills, which I always send
on to the accountant. She flung the envelope in question down
on the desk that occupies one corner of my studio. "Special
delivery," she said.

I crossed the room. I unfolded the letter, which told me of
Sara's death and the astonishing news that she had left the house
to me.

This small log house would have been Sara's only possession. It seemed impossible that anybody else, even me — no, particularly me — could take ownership. I wanted nothing to do
with it.

Mrs. Boyle had been hovering nearby, pretending to dust but
anxious no doubt for information I had no intention of giving
her. "You've gone all ghastly," she said. "What on earth is the
matter?" I assured her that I had certainly not "gone all ghastly,"
that I had simply been surprised by a legal letter concerning
some property near Port Arthur, a small city on the north shore
of the Great Lake Superior.

"I have absolutely nothing at all to do with it now," I said. "I
haven't been anywhere near the place for over forty years."

I rose from the desk, left the studio, and walked through the
house to the vestibule. From the closet there I removed my hat,
coat, scarf, and cane. Then I sat down on the bench near the
door and struggled with my galoshes — I am eighty-three years
old, and bending in any direction has become a problem.

As I unbolted the heavy front door, I heard Mrs. Boyle shouting at me from the kitchen. Something about cold and wind. I pretended not to hear her and stepped outside.

The first time I saw Sara she was holding a large broom, sweeping, her body twisting around the object as if she were dancing with it. Later I drew the broom with great care, great precision, right down to the last bristle. I drew even the inconsequential rose on the label that was wrapped around the base of the handle. Sara's back was to me – I hadn't yet seen her face – and the curve of her spine was visible through her cotton uniform. She was sweeping the verandah of the hotel that had once housed businessmen and speculators from American cities, but that now catered to tourists who wanted the view from Lake Superior's north shore. She worked, in season, at the hotel and lived year-round in the small log house that her father had left her.

The house she has now left to me.

Had she not been working at the hotel I might never have seen her at all, though perhaps we would have passed each other on the track they called, and likely still call, The Avenue, when the lake, the vast inland sea, would have had all of my attention. Or she might have been walking behind me as I strolled towards the end of the settlement – a crescent moon of mostly uninhabited miners' houses around a subtle bay – and would have slipped inside her door, disappeared, before I turned around.

As it was, I was sitting in one of the wooden rockers on the verandah, drawing the offshore mine situated on the island for which the townsite was named. It was 1920, the first and last year

of my father's connection with that fundamentally extinct operation, just before he took himself and what was left of his
money permanently back to the States. I was drawing the mine
for my father, the last resident American speculator in the hotel,
though I would rather have been concentrating on the rocks, the
trees, even the hotel itself. But he had asked this one favour of
me and I had agreed.

Through the cotton of her uniform I could see her strong,
slim back, her shoulder blades shifting as she moved the broom.
As her head was held in a slightly tilted position, I could see the
long tendon on the side of her neck and one vein there, pulsing.
She appeared to be trying to cover every square inch of wooden
floorboards with the bristles of the broom, but there must have
been a narrative running somewhere in the back of her mind, a
narrative that did not, as yet, involve me. What was she thinking
during those last few moments of innocent labour before I disturbed her life?

I could see the slight curve of muscle in her upper arm,
could imagine the sharp edge of a graphite pencil capturing the
motion, the gesture. Freezing it.

And yet, watching her, her unselfconscious grace, I wanted
to interrupt the task, to add my own presence to the image. I
wanted to hear her voice, and I wanted to hear it speaking to me.

"Would you like me to move?" I asked, already rising from
the rocker. I wanted her to turn around, to face me.

She stopped sweeping then, pivoted, pushed a strand of hair
back from her forehead and regarded me with surprise, as if she
hadn't known that anyone was there at all. Her eyes were on me
now. I could see her prominent cheekbones, her expressive mouth.

"Oh, no, sir," she said, "you can stay right where you are for as long as you like."

Each day now, when I return to the house after my walk, the letter is lying, just as I left it, folded neatly on the table in front of the chair, glowing in a shaft of the famous architect's authorized light. I do not pick it up to finish reading it. I refuse to know the details of her death, how long it took to find her, whether there was pain. No one but Sara, you see, could have lived at Silver Islet year-round any more. The old government official must have died years ago, and now, at the end of each summer, there will be no one out there at all.

Tomorrow I will begin the underpainting for my next picture. I will paint Sara, the inherited house, the fist of Thunder Cape on the horizon, the frozen lake, her hands, the Quebec heater, the slowly fading fires. I will paint the small-paned window, the log walls, a curtain illuminated from behind by winter sun, the skein of grey I never saw in Sara's hair. Then carefully, painstakingly, I will remove the realism from it, paint it all out.

This afternoon when I left the house there was fresh snow, few footsteps on the sidewalk, and only one set of parallel lines left by a car that must have passed less than ten minutes before. I began to walk, as I always do, around the block. When I had completed this tour six times, I noticed that my tracks in the snow made it look as if a number of people had been walking behind me, following me on my promenade. I did not miss the significance of this.

I have travelled this route many times before. By the time you have reached my age, everything has repeated itself at least once. The Silver Islet house was not my first inheritance, for example. And Superior was not my first north shore.

I was born in 1894, in Rochester, New York, a city of ravines and canals, rivers and waterfalls, inventors and industrialists, preachers and psychics; a city so chock-full of the turmoil connected to rampaging waters and vicious cycles of weather that the Gods sought revenge by making it, ultimately, famous for giving almost everyone the ability to create fixed images, the ability to stop action in its tracks. George Eastman had already opened his State Street factory by the time I entered the world, and, by 1900, he was distributing his Kodak Brownie camera from coast to coast: a fitting beginning to the current century.

At the tail end of the last one, while I played on the floor with my toy soldiers and tried to avoid outings with my mother, my future teacher, Robert Henri, returned to America from France. According to my friend Rockwell Kent, Robert H. burst into the studios of New York City, preaching the idea of visual art as a response to the life and to the energy of the world, shouting the names Renoir, Cézanne, Pissarro as if they were vegetables he was desperately trying to sell at market.

My own artwork at the time focused on a series of military campaigns waged by stick soldiers wielding stick swords. America, I believe, was at war with Spain; there must have been talk of Teddy Roosevelt's Rough Riders. And then there was my Louisiana-born grandfather, on my father's side, who had fought for the Confederacy during the Civil War and who visited us for a week or so once a year. Sometimes, to my great delight, he would deliver the "rebel yell" at the dinner table in our otherwise dark and solemn household, between courses, making my mother jump in her seat and causing my father, who was not the least bit inclined towards spontaneous outbursts, to swear under his breath.

While Robert Henri was for the first but not the last time hectoring his students, insisting that, like his adored Cézanne, they paint the landscapes of their own continent and the streets of their own cities, I was attempting to discover a way to avoid contact with the streets and landscapes of my own neighbourhood. My mother was unusual; a gifted Gothic narrator and not at all interested in facts. But she was strictly accurate when it came to setting, and researched her material well. Drawn to the sublime in nature, she particularly admired high vantage points – look-offs, I called them – and, as a result, she was impressed by the great number of chasms and gorges that cut their way through the city we lived in. It was her fondest wish that I be delighted by these geological oddities as well.

As a young child I was always looking down into landscape, never across it or along it. In church the congregation droned, "I will lift up mine eyes unto the hills, from whence cometh my help." I had never looked up at anything, except for architecture, and even that was mercifully low in those days. Moreover, the depths into which I would have had to descend in order to watch rocks and vegetation climb skyward were filled with tombstones, on the one hand, and murderous rapids, on the other. The Genesee River rampaged angrily through the centre of town generating the power that drove the industries of our prosperous city fathers. Darkly romantic pillared and gargoyled tombs created valleys of death out of the series of ravines that became Mount Hope Cemetery. The long footbridge crossing the Genesee and the serpentine avenues that wound around and above the huge, deep graveyard were my mother's favourite destinations. I feared and hated both places. I was certain I would be drawn down to death one way or the other as, holding my mother's hand and decked out in my sailor suit and straw hat or wrapped in layers of quilted clothing, I approached these lofty spots.

When I mustered the courage to complain, my mother assured me I was fortunate to have access to such spatially interesting scenery. Daughter of a market gardener from Hilton, a hamlet situated in the uncommonly flat lands ten miles or so from the centre of town, nothing, she maintained, could please her more than to look from on high into landscapes both wild and dangerous. A fear of heights, she told me, was nothing more than a fear of depths. She, however, feared predictability, boredom, and certain distant, fixed horizons. Flat land, she said, was like a dull story; one where you were able to determine the middle and the end right at the beginning. Large bodies of water were different in that you never quite knew what they were going to do even when they were frozen, and that alone made them

interesting. We talked about such things on our promenades, or
rather she talked about them. I said very little. I was just a child.

I now realize she was quite a lot like my friend, the painter
Rockwell Kent. She should have been given a boat and a sail
and set adrift to bump up against one steep, forbidding shore
after another, though the monotony of the long journeys from
departure to landfall might have put her off his style of adventure. Still, they had much in common and, had they ever met,
Rockwell might have fallen in love with her. He was a man
obsessed by dangerous landscapes, by women, and the north.
He stopped travelling only long enough to begin painting; he
stopped talking only long enough to start writing; he stopped
womanizing only long enough to attempt to repair his disintegrating marriage. His brain, like his painting, was controlled by
polar forces. The north was with him always, regardless of where
he hung his hat. By the time I was nine and setting forth on what
would turn out to be my last series of walks with my mother,
Rockwell would have already survived the vagaries of the eccen-
tric Abbott Thayer's freezing outdoor school, would have been
enrolled in Robert Henri's life class for two or three years.
Having been born at the tail end of the century, it seems to be
my destiny to walk into the finale of every drama I encounter. By
the time I met Rockwell, by the time I met Robert Henri . . . but
I am getting ahead of myself. Suffice it to say that I missed the
Armory Show, modernism's notorious début in North America,
by one year, though now I don't regret this for a minute.

———◦———

My father left our ordinary house on Atkinson Street each morning promptly at 8:15 in order to walk to George Eastman's State Street factory where he worked as a clerk. As a child I was quite taken both with the factory itself — seven storeys high! something to look up to — and with the objects that emerged from it. Cameras. Photographs. Images still and calm and dependable. I assumed that my father was responsible for these reliable pictures, despite the fact that there were only two photographs in our house: the first showed my parents thin and grim in their wedding clothes; the other was of me as a baby, silly and girlish in my christening gown. We owned a Kodak Brownie camera — everyone in Rochester did — but my mother forbade its use. "They stop things," she would announce whenever the subject of cameras arose. "They interrupt the normal flow of events. Furthermore, they eliminate things. If I take a photograph of this," she would say, pointing to a beer factory across the Genesee River, "I obliterate this and this." Even now I can see the way she gestured as she spoke, her arms sweeping back and forth, conjuring the rest of the world, the world that a photograph might have obliterated, the world of the stampeding river, the world I was afraid of.

Father told me much later that she had begun her walks to the river and the cemetery while I was still in my pram. In the beginning these outings were, as far as he could remember, sporadic and made some sense to him in that babies should be "aired." By the time I was six, however, the journey had become a daily routine. Regardless of the weather, pressing household chores, invitations to ladies' teas, my own feeble objections, we set forth. If it were raining, my mother would carry a huge black umbrella. If it were snowing, she would bundle me, and herself, in scarves and mitts and quilted coats. Only severe illness, hers or mine, could keep her home. I was severely ill as often as possible, loving the quiet of my room, my books and toys spread around me on the pale-blue blanket, the "Land of Counterpane" so gorgeously described by Mr. Stevenson in my favourite poem. Essentially, my greatest ambition at the time was to be a sickly child, as sickly as the author in question had been. But just as soon as the thermometer from Mr. Taylor's instruments factory indicated that I was well again, off we went, over the roaring river, to the edges of the valley of the shadow. "Yea, though I walk through the valley of the shadow of death," the congregation chanted, "I will fear no evil . . . thy rod and thy staff they comfort me." I was convinced the revered rod was Mr. Taylor's thermometer, comforting me, keeping me from shadowed valleys, causing me to love the word "fever."

Mother claimed we were related to Mr. Taylor, but then Mother claimed we were related to all of Rochester's prominent citizens. "Just you and me," she would say conspiratorially, "we are related by blood to Mr. Taylor. Not your father, he is not related to anyone."

I was too young at the time to remind her that my father was, of course, related by blood to me.

According to my mother, when she was a child her distinguished relatives had driven her in their magnificent cabriolets to the much more fascinating water and beaches of the Great Lake Ontario, which was closer than you might think to the flat lands around Hilton. They had gone to the lakeshore in all kinds of weather, and it was this that must have instilled in her the idea that outings were good for children. Sometimes there was ice, she explained, and then there would be ice boating and skating. The ice was white near the shore, then grey, then darker grey. It turned black just before it disappeared into the liquid, inky churn of Great Lake water. It resembled an oversized polished ballroom floor and, as one grew older, one danced upon it arm in arm with a partner. I could barely imagine this. For me, ice was something that appeared overnight, startling and silver on the bare limbs of trees near a waterfall, or hung like angry, dripping fangs over the gorge through which the Genesee River tumbled.

Rockwell Kent would tell me years later that he loved ice, insisting that it was more interesting than mere soil; that it created itself out of available, sometimes invisible materials, then disappeared again; that it had a mind of its own.

He would have worshipped my mother.

It is no surprise to me now, given the abysses in the surrounding geography, that men famous for mail chutes and elevators should have flourished in my native city. James B. Cutler and L. S. Graves, respectively. Mother claimed that we were related to both of these gentlemen, as well as to a certain Jonathan West, who had invented a celebrated kind of water meter. The accomplishments of the great men of our city, all of whom were apparently related to us, figured largely in the words my mother chose to describe the landscapes through which we wandered.

"Down you'd go," she once said, staring from a bridge that spanned the frothing Genesee. "Down you'd go, just like a love letter in a Cutler chute."

Another time, when we were walking around the top edge of the graveyard, she announced darkly, "These paths curve, this way and that, just like one of Henry Strong's whips flung down in the grass." I wondered what these long whips would be used for and what kind of large animals they might be meant to subdue.

At Mount Hope Cemetery we stood under arbours and sat on stone benches. We paused to admire the impressive mausoleums of one alleged relative after another. We examined marble statuary — marble that was sometimes brought all the way from Italy, my mother told me — and which ranged from small urns to realistically rendered life-sized family groups.

"That certainly is a good likeness of cousin Reginald's dog," Mother would say, looking fondly at a marble beast curled at the feet of a bearded marble entrepreneur who was himself seated comfortably in an armchair on his own tomb. "Its name was Mergatroyd."

I don't believe I have ever been intimately involved with a woman as young as my mother was then. She had married my father at sixteen and had been — if one did not take into account our afternoon outings — more or less housebound ever since. As far as I knew, she had no friends; even her own parents, my grandparents, were dim, shadowy people who never appeared in our house and whose small clapboard house in Hilton we rarely visited. Whether they disapproved of the marriage, or were themselves disapproved of by my father, I wasn't ever to know. His own family was far away in a place called Baton Rouge. I had met only my Confederate grandfather, who came to visit once a year.

It was a claustrophobic world that, more than my mother's

flat, pedestrian girlhood, may have explained her need for imaginary relatives and dramatic scenery. I remember the darkness of the house during the day, the murky lamps at night, the silent suppers and punctual bedtimes. My mother and I had little in common with my father; as she had said, he was, at least in the metaphorical sense, related to no one. She and I, however, were related to the alternative worlds connected to childhood. Pretty and delicate, bored and prone to fantasy, she was, I suppose, just a little girl. I became her playmate; her sometimes unwilling playmate. By the age of nine I adored her and was perplexed by her; coveted and occasionally felt smothered by her company.

Most people, I understand, remember only bits and pieces of any particular day in their childhood. Only certain static images, much like the photographs my mother so disapproved of, cut through the recalled atmosphere of being six or nine or five years old. I am not, as I have pointed out, so fortunate. Robert Henri maintained that the wondering eyes of a child see everything, but when childhood has passed, much of what they have seen is lost. I carried everything I saw on a certain day in 1904 with me into adult life, either because of what happened later or perhaps in spite of what happened later. Yet this visual intensity is still only a matter of optics. I can see the way the snow moved through the neighbourhood, the colour that the cold placed on my mother's face, the icy, shining wires swinging in the wind, snowdrifts against the outer walls of mausoleums, but I cannot see myself, the boy I was then; at least, I cannot see his face. And there are no photographs. My mother would never have allowed photographs.

It was late January. I was nine and in school by then, but that didn't prevent my mother from insisting on the walks; often she would be waiting at the gate when I emerged from the school door. But this was Saturday, a holiday from that particular humiliation, a day that I would have preferred to spend drawing my now fully fleshed-out soldiers waging their fully fleshed-out battles. And colouring them. Poster paint had entered my life.

The previous night an ice storm had coated everything in silver and we had awakened in the morning to a tinsel world.

When we left the house my mother exclaimed at the beauty. "This is what happens," she said, "when you live in the north. Everything can change in the most magnificent way, completely, overnight." We were walking slowly because of the ice underfoot. "We live as far north as possible," she said. "Aren't you glad?"

She had either forgotten, or was choosing to ignore, Canada.

"We are northerners," she said proudly. "We like the cold."

Huddling in my woollen coat against the increasing chill of the wind, I wasn't quite sure that I agreed with her, but I dared not voice my opinion.

"Our river runs north," she announced as we inched our way over the slippery footbridge. I was trying not to think of the river, the long, deep distance between me and its swift current. "The north is the birthplace of spiritualism," my mother continued cheerfully. "The north is where spiritualism lives." She paused, admired the view from the end of the bridge, then added, "Thanks to my great-aunts, your great-great-aunts, the famous Fox sisters."

I was treated to a full description of the Rochester Rappings, the knocking and pounding from the beyond that, according to my mother, had visited these ladies at all times of the day and night. Mourners lined up for blocks to keep appointments with the famous Fox sisters because they could put absolutely anyone in contact with the spirit of absolutely anyone else, provided that the person to be contacted was thoroughly dead. I imagined white ghosts with hammers lying beneath wooden floors, angrily demanding attention from the living. But my mother corrected me when I told her this. The mourners, she said, cherished such bangs and thumps, such requests for attention. And the ghosts themselves would knock and rap only if one or more of her great-aunts were present in the room. The ghosts, she assured me, were very fond of her great-aunts, who were dead themselves now and had been for some time.

"Do *they* rap?" I asked. "Does everyone?"

My mother laughed then, put her arm around me and pulled me close. "I've never thought of that," she said.

I loved her. I remember loving her. I think. No, I'm certain of this. In my early childhood she was my whole world.

By the time my mother and I had reached the graveyard it had begun to snow for the second time: soft, gentle flakes, large enough to be examined on a mitten.

"No two are alike," my mother said. "But then no two of us are alike either, even if we are related."

Later, Rockwell would develop the same theme. He was a great believer in the relentlessness of character, of originality. You could not get rid of it, he once told me, even if you wanted to.

There have been times when I have wanted to.

As we moved deeper into the graveyard, my mother reminded me that her great-uncle, the Reverend Pharcellus Church, delivered the inaugural address when Mount Hope Cemetery was opened in 1830, praising its magnificent views, its "bottom lands" and "abrupt declivities." It had been his favourite spot for a stroll in his declining years, and now, seventy years later, it was ours.

"He was an admirable man," she told me. "You should be proud to be related to him. I was going to name you Pharcellus when you were born, but your father wouldn't hear of it. He wanted something more southern, so we settled on Austin."

Even at nine years old I was grateful for this.

We watched the bottom lands and abrupt declivities fill with snow for quite a while, long enough to see the slate and stone roofs of house tombs in the valleys become covered with white as we crept along the icy paths above them. Then, just as we reached the centre of this fearsome place, the old oak trees began to whine and creak as the wind shifted, increased in velocity, and stirred up a blizzard more blinding than any I had experienced in my short life.

"I think we'll have to wait this one out," my mother sang above the storm. "I believe we will have to take shelter."

We were standing near a mausoleum that looked like a miniature cathedral. My mother squinted at the lettering above the door and said, "I'm certain cousin Slattery won't mind."

She scraped the snow from the threshold with her boot, pushed open the protesting wrought-iron doorway, and beckoned me inside.

No one had been to visit cousin Slattery for a long time, I decided, when my eyes had adjusted to the gloom. His checkered marble floor was neither swept nor washed, all his flowers were dead, and Jesus, who had fallen from the cross, lay smashed upon the altar. A pointed stained-glass window at the rear of the room was broken and missing one or two panes; a good thing, I thought, since this allowed some light and air to enter the structure.

"It appears," my mother said disapprovingly as she looked around, "that cousin Slattery was a papist." We were Episcopalian, a denomination whose name I had never been able to pronounce. I had no idea what a papist was, and when I asked, my mother's subsequent descriptions of saints and martyrs led me to believe that the famous Fox sisters must have been papists as well. We had settled ourselves down on prayer stools, the needlepoint upholstery of which had decayed long ago, and dried bits of straw were pushed out of them by our weight. My knees came up to my chest in such a position, my mother's almost to her chin. Outside, the squall wrapped itself around our little dwelling, and I imagined it flinging itself into the declivities we could no longer see.

I don't know how long we stayed in cousin Slattery's chapel, but most likely, though it seemed like forever, it was little more than an hour. Squalls, such as the one that raged through Mount Hope Cemetery that day, rouse themselves to a great fury, then evaporate, a function in this region of what is now called "the lake effect." I do remember, however, that at some point I became cold and began to complain. I remember too that when my mother took off her coat and wrapped it around me, the heat of her body was trapped in the cloth, and I could feel this warmth, even through the quilting of my own coat, and it comforted me.

It was shortly after this day that my mother died of scarlet fever, a disease with a beautiful name. Oddly, there was never a hue with this designation in an artist's paint box until at least the 1940s, and then it was called quinacridone scarlet, the cumbersome first word smashing the brightness and delicacy of the second. Still, almost any time I used red in a painting I would think of my mother as I uncapped the tube. Cadmium, vermilion, Venetian, madder, alizarin crimson all brought our walks in Mount Hope Cemetery to mind, despite the fact that she is not buried there but sleeps instead in the little graveyard of Hilton.

It saddens me to think of her in Hilton, with flat fields stretching out on either side and neither marble statuary nor extreme geography to honour her brief life, decorate her death. But Lake Ontario is nearby, and it was of this frozen lake that she spoke as she lay delirious and dying. She believed that she was skating far out on the bay; she believed that there was someone on the shore calling her back. "I can't come in," she said over and over. "I've gone too far and the ice is turning black." Filled with energy until the instant of her death, her hands groped among the bedclothes as if she were looking for something in the dark, something she would recognize by touch. I, recovering from scarlet fever myself, was barred from her deathbed, but, looking through the keyhole and listening at the door, I knew she was trying to find me, that I myself was on the shore she couldn't return to. I called and called, silently of course, though sometimes I whispered her name.

It is alizarin crimson that I now associate with my mother, her life, the disease, her death. A colour so unreliable it could practically be called fleeting, it disappears in less than thirty years. No amount of varnish can protect it. Turn it from the light and it still fades with a determination that is almost athletic. And yet it is the most beautiful of the reds; dark, romantic, and fragile, it is an outburst of joy among the other colours on the palette, though chances are the artist will live to see it weaken, deteriorate, and finally vanish. It is impossible to keep.

In my child's mind, the colour of the disease was a band of red on the ice my mother spoke of, and I could see her, actually see her, move across it to the place where the ice turned from grey to black, until finally I could see her enter the inky waters of the Great Lake.

She had joined all of her relations. She had gone as far north as she understood it was possible to go. She was never coming back.

Once again it is not far from my door to Mount Hope Cemetery, not far to the ravines and tombs that so fascinated my mother, and, I suppose, it won't be long before I will join all the other residents of this city who have increased the population of the graveyard's heights and depths. Returning to Rochester could have been viewed as the initial stage of a journey towards the graveyard gates: the first plodding steps of an old elephant going home to die. But, in fact, it was the availability of a piece of property that brought me back to my native city. Ten years before, I had bought the house built by the famous modernist architect, the house in which I now live. Long and low, spacious and angular, it is completely out of character in this neighbourhood of mock Tudor revival and large, ornate nineteenth-century houses. Like this architect, I find that the upholstered furniture and useless gadgets, the kept things that decorate most houses, depress me. I need space around me, and light. Air. Like him, I want a lot of emptiness between me and any object in a room.

I am a civilized man by nature. Despite the reality that at my age pure enjoyment seems to require more strength than I possess, I like my creature comforts. A soft bed, a warm bath in a spacious tub; clean, wide rectangular windows, spotless white walls. For this reason I hired Mrs. Boyle, to whom I speak as little as possible, though, unhappily, this does not prevent her from speaking to me. When she leaves in the evening she takes the noise of the world with her, and I find myself alone with one of her casseroles in the kitchen, smoking and swearing and wishing I were in that other kitchen, with the Great Lake thundering outside and me cleaning my brushes near the sink. The kitchen I have just learned that I now own. But I refuse to take anything from the world now. I will continue to live in a modernist work of art with a housekeeper and ghosts; uncomfortable ghosts who form attachments to neither calm white architecture nor quiet residential streets. Ghosts whose only reason for being here is to haunt me.

Decades ago, between the ages of twenty and forty, I was in the gathering period of my life, filling myself to the brim with subject matter until I was forced to overflow onto the picture plane, onto the canvases Sara so often posed for. I was an accumulator, a hoarder. I trespassed everywhere and thieved constantly. I believed that I would always be younger than those around me; that I was connected to the history of that to which I was related, never to its conception. I was a student of Robert Henri's at a time when his celebrated career — even as a teacher — was coming to a close, a time when his earlier pupils, or at least those of the much-admired Ash Can School, had become more famous than he, and they, in turn, were being submerged by the advance of cubism after the Armory Show. I met Rockwell Kent when he had already lived the lives of ten men, had fathered children, had had affairs, had lived and worked in the Far North. Even what I was to learn of Sara's story leaned towards the past, not the present: the mine disintegrating below the lake and everything in her father's house kept and cherished like relics. As I saw it then, each life I touched had found its focus and was existing in a kind of aftermath. I think of my friend George Kearns when I first glimpsed him. He was hardly more than a boy, but the ease with which he strolled around his shop, his cherished China Hall, gave the impression that it had been, for a very long time, the centre of his world. In contrast, there was me; my relationship to any place, any surroundings, was always awkward and self-conscious. Yes, then there was me, dismissing relationship so casually.

This large, famous white house in which I live — this house that suits me so well — was neither built by me nor for me. Now, in its open spaces, behind its oversized panes of glass, I am haunted by robbed histories, stolen goods. Each day in the studio I play with colours, build up textures, experiment with white, distort the subject matter underneath, while the ghosts press their faces, their lives against the doors and windows, trying to make me stop.

I missed the Armory Show by one year.

I participated in neither war.

I never travelled farther north than the opposite shore of Lake Superior.

I avoided love.

Eventually all of my work, even that which is now in private collections, will go to institutions where it will be consigned to walls or banished to basements. It matters little to me which location posterity chooses. What matters is the China collection; the bright objects gradually filling the glass shelves on the south wall of this otherwise mostly empty room. Who will want it? Who will treasure it? Who will place it in the correct light? It has taken so much time to put even part of it together, so much meticulous effort. A task not made any easier by Mrs. Boyle nattering about the probability of my eyes being ruined by too much close work and too much reading. I have a small library, just a few shelves of books, really, books containing information about manufacturers, marks, certain celebrated potters and designers. Sometimes I remove a volume from the shelf for no particular reason at all, let it fall open on my lap randomly, and stare at a photo of an eighteenth-century piece, a piece so rare that George Kearns could never even have imagined possessing it. Sometimes in my mind I see myself presenting it to him. A gift. I never, in all the time I knew him, gave George a gift.

Perhaps it could be a wedding present, for him and Augusta. Ghosts at a ghost wedding. And me the wedding guest who slew the albatross.

But I accept no invitations of any kind, am visited only by the past. And George and Augusta were never man and wife.

"You should get out with people more," says the socially minded Mrs. Boyle. "Stop fussing around with all those poisonous paints. You only keep starting over again anyway. If you saw

people once in a while, maybe you wouldn't make so many mistakes. Maybe you'd actually finish one of those pictures."

Pictures. Mistakes.

As I said, I take nothing from the world now.

All the water in this city runs urgently towards the north, hurries towards the Great Lake with the name of a Canadian province. The city itself, however, looks east and west from the two sides of the Genesee River, as if its citizens had one day decided to curl inward rather than admit to the existence of another land, an opposite shore with rivers and farms and cities of its own.

The country across the lake never really takes shape in the collective imagination here. Cold, distant, separated by enough water that the curve of the earth makes it invisible, the far shore disappears swiftly from the memory — despite excursions, or even complete summer vacations there — as quickly as a trip to an amusement park might, after daily life is resumed. The impression left behind is as vague and fleeting as the various intensities of light over the lake, which change before they fully register in the mind, before anyone with watercolours and a brush is able to capture them on the paper in his hand.

I was seventeen in 1912, when my father made enough money on Canadian mining stocks to begin to take more seriously the country that the lake concealed. An acquaintance, a section manager at the Eastman factory, had persuaded him to invest in a property north of Lake Superior, and, unlikely as this may seem, his money doubled and then tripled. My silent, sober father, much, I think, to his own amazement, proved to have financial talent. He had not remarried. For a time after my mother's death he had no social life to speak of, and was therefore able to spend his evenings poring over his accounts and stock-market quotations – his own special game of solitaire. Often at night I would fall asleep listening to him add sums aloud as he sorted papers filled with numbers, papers which themselves made a comforting sound when he moved them, like a soft breeze in a grove of maples.

Ours was a tidy, ordered, and not unhappy existence. The interior of the house seemed to have physically changed with my mother's absence, the warm, sometimes claustrophobic quality I associated with my early childhood having departed with her, even though not a single piece of furniture, not a curtain, not a doily had been changed or removed since her death. My father and I moved in our separate predictable orbits, and trusted the regularity of each other's habits. He did not inspect me as my mother had each day before I left for school, and rarely commented on my behaviour or my achievements. He would scan my school reports in the most cursory of ways, was neither pleasantly surprised when I was at the head of the class nor greatly disturbed if my grades began to falter. He did not, you see, insist upon relationship. Emotion was almost entirely absent from the contact we had with each other — which is not to say that he was unkind to me or that we had no feelings for each other. I, in turn, was comfortable with his lack of intrusion. It seemed to me that the rooms we lived in had become spacious, that light and wind entered easily through the windows. Occasionally sounds reached us from the outside, from the real world. My father liked birds, I remember, was glad if an unusual species appeared in our yard; a Baltimore oriole, for instance. Sometimes we talked about things like that.

Immediately after my mother's death, my father moved out of the bedroom they had shared, slept instead in a small, cell-like room at the far end of the hall. I had always believed that the large bedroom was my mother's place anyway — her dressing table, her wardrobe full of long, dark-coloured clothing — and so my father's change of sleeping quarters had little effect on me. For a while, when I was still quite a young child, and when I was certain my father was not near, I would quietly enter the abandoned room, approach the dressing table, and play with my mother's music box. I would twist the metal key at the bottom of the small instrument, listen to the Minuet in G until the music slowed, then began to falter, then ceased altogether with one last, sad plucked note. Once, just as I carefully folded down the hinged lid of the box, I felt two large arms encircle me. My father lifted me away from the dressing table and collapsed on the bed with me on his lap. I looked in the mirror, the same mirror that had so often held my mother's image, and watched with a kind of horror as my usually restrained father wept awkwardly into my neck. I knew better than to try to squirm out of his embrace at this moment, but as I felt tears stinging my own eyes, everything in me wanted to do so.

My father released me eventually, rose and, without saying anything at all, walked quickly from the room. We never spoke of the incident.

Years later something else remarkable and disorienting happened. I returned one day from high school to find my father pacing like a penned dog across our small entrance hall. It was four o'clock in the afternoon and he was never back from the office before six: routine, of course, was the engine that drove our lives. But his presence in the hall at such an hour shattered all that; it was completely out of character. I was as shocked as I would have been had I found him standing naked on the lawn.

When I asked him why he wasn't still at work, he looked up in a startled sort of way, as if he were surprised at *my* appearance, or as if he didn't recognize my voice, my face. He opened one hand, palm upwards, shrugged and said, "No more work for me, I . . . we are ridiculously rich. I won't ever need go to work again."

We stood facing each other in a small, square, useless space, physically closer than we had been since that afternoon in my mother's room, staring into each other's eyes as we never had before. I remember he held his hat in his hand, as though not quite sure whether he was arriving or departing.

The word "rich" was so foreign to me I barely understood its implications. "Are you certain?" I stammered.

He nodded slowly. I noticed his mouth was quivering, his skin ashen. The pattern of his life, I realized even then, had been smashed. He had the appearance of a man in the midst of a great emergency. I half expected him to call an ambulance, or the police.

"Silver," he said. He was still looking directly into my eyes, his expression almost angry. "Some godforsaken place in Canada called Cobalt."

"Cobalt," I echoed. All I could see was a particular shade of blue.

If I had been, at the time, interested in portraiture, I should have wanted to capture my father as he looked then. Much later Robert Henri would teach me that the features of a face incline towards the one expression which "manifests the condition of the sitter." But there was more than that in my father's face. Instinctively I knew that I was seeing him on the brink between all that he had been and all that he would become. It was there with us in that modest hall, balanced between us for a moment in the late part of an autumn afternoon.

It was very quiet. My father passed his hat from hand to hand, and, once or twice, he opened his mouth and cleared his throat as if there were something else he wanted to say to me. Then the angle of his vision altered slightly, almost impercepti- bly, and I realized he was withdrawing, looking past my shoul- der towards his new life.

"I have school work," I muttered.

I became terribly aware that I had no idea what we would say to each other in the hours between four and six, hours during which I had, until now, occupied the house alone.

"Of course," he replied. He placed his hat on the hall table, then shuffled aside to let me pass. We separated to go to other rooms in the house. As I climbed the stairs, I could hear his foot-steps in the kitchen. It seemed to me then that my father had taken the decision to keep walking, walking away from his previous self.

There are any number of ways to lose the people who make up the fabric of one's life. Sometimes the alteration is slow, internal, almost invisible, so that one does not notice until years later that the other has been gone for half a decade. Sometimes the person one has become attached to changes so radically it is as if he or she has died, to be replaced by someone else altogether. In the next few months my father's personality altered dramatically, and permanently, as he burst into a world I would never understand. He spent his days in the offices of brokers and promoters; the serenity of our evenings vanished as his non-business hours became filled with committee work relating to hospitals and museums. Women entered his life, coaxed him away to lengthy dinner parties in the neighbourhood where I now live. He started to purchase expensive clothes.

For a brief period at the beginning of all this, he began, inexplicably, to speak. As if money were the key he needed to unlock language, he confessed details he had previously withheld. He would climb the stairs late at night, shake me awake, and talk about the past: his childhood, his journey from the south to the north, his first glimpse of Mother, their marriage, her increasing strangeness after they had set up housekeeping. He remembered the oddest things: how the roped wood of a banyan tree trunk outside his childhood home interlaced like the decorated borders of a medieval illuminated manuscript; a Pullman porter he had spoken to on a train called *The Orange Blossom Special*; the mauve hue of gaslight in the fog outside the Rochester Temperance Hall where he and Mother had met. She had been working, he said, for less than a year in a garment factory near the river, and he prided himself on having rescued her from all that. I was hungry for the information he was giving me, and often, after he had padded away to his own room, some of it would work its way into my dreams, where the stiff young couple in my parents' wedding photo would relax and laugh and embrace.

Then, as abruptly as it had begun, this interlude ended, and although my father continued to talk, it was only of the present. I came to understand that by telling me about the past, he had been removing it; that I had been a kind of receptacle into which he discarded his old self so that there would be room for the new person he was becoming. A well-swept, clean, and empty space for the present, for the dinners and meetings and boardrooms, the new world to which I had no access.

I hated this. I wanted the familiar routine, wanted my father to leave the house promptly at 8:15 and return promptly at 5:45. I wanted his quietness, his solitary whispering, wanted either the comforting rustle of his papers or his words about the past just as I was sliding into sleep. As he spun noisily away from me, I gradually began to distrust entirely the motivation behind the delivery of words. I stopped talking, responding, dove deeper and deeper into myself, the world of my drawings, until I was out of the house as often as possible, recording waterfalls and ravines on pale sheets of paper, just as I believed my mother had hoped that I would.

My father, in the middle of his life, was transformed from a shy clerk into a jolly, boisterous, and, in the end, overconfident, almost foolhardy entrepreneur. He who had never related to anyone was suddenly relating to everyone. Except me. I related only to the paper, to the pencil in my hand, to the tangle of lines that trapped a sampling of energetic water under my fingers, the contour following the edges of rock.

At the beginning of the summer of 1913, my father told me we were heading north to spend the summer on the other side of the lake, and, for the first time in our lives, he and I stepped on board the ferry that travelled, weather permitting, back and forth across the forty-mile distance from shore to shore. He had bought, sight unseen, a small lakeside summer property in the Canadian town of Davenport. The air, he had been assured by the realtor, was much purer there, the water cleaner and more suitable for bathing. Moreover, the summer social life, the parties held by wealthy Americans in large lakeside summer homes, would be, my father believed, my ticket of entry into that world. I had completed my first year of classes at the Rochester Art Institute and was making some casual friendships among the painters, musicians, and actors who were part of the limited cultural élite of my city. Rather than Canada, I would have preferred New York, or Chicago, or a trip to Europe. Or, failing that, I would have preferred to remain in Rochester. Still, I boarded the boat with as much good nature as I could summon and, once we had cast off, walked moodily around on deck in a manner I thought suitable for a person of artistic temperament.

Ten years later, Rockwell Kent and I would discuss the glamour of a north shore, how everything opens and clears there, sky, various winds, water; how light lingers long after it should in summer, as if trying to announce something vital that has been overlooked or refused. But none of this came to my eighteen-year-old mind as I attempted a watercolour of the pastoral, lush Ontario shoreline. What intrigued me instead was how a landscape could look both manicured and uninhabited at the same time. There was something in me then, some love of both solitude and order, that responded immediately to what I was seeing. But as we drew closer to Davenport, my elation began to diminish. Stilted and small, the town seemed to be lacking in potential. Lining the shore were huge, white American summer homes, perfect examples of the kind of immodest display of wealth that I, an art student with socialist leanings, felt ought to be disapproved of. I decided right away that I would have nothing to do with the mannered society that would undoubtedly fill the drawing rooms and croquet lawns of such places. I would stand alone, endure the summer.

There was something else. Until that moment, turning north had involved lake and sky and emptiness for me, but now I was under the impression that everything was askew — the shore, the sun, the hills all appeared to be facing the wrong direction, and my mind kept wanting the trees that climbed the slopes behind the town to be submerged, the breakers to roll away from the beach. In later years, as I have intimated, it would be the north shore of any body of water that attracted me, but, at eighteen, I was still innocent of the kind of obsession that attraction demanded. I spent my first few days in Davenport sulking on the porch of our summer house, staring out over the lake towards my abandoned city, and resenting my father's repeated and unsuccessful attempts to get me involved in badminton parties and other such nonsense. Sometimes I walked on the beach, but the sand filled my shoes and socks, and I was too self-conscious to remove them, so I plodded back to the house and closeted myself in my room, which, compared to the golden light on the vast expanse of water, seemed dark and small. I tired of such behaviour eventually — I was eighteen after all — and when my father finally left me alone to pursue his absurd badminton parties, I walked out the back door and began to explore the town.

How to describe the colonial world that flourished in the streets leading away from manicured American lawns? Union Jacks heaved in the wind from the lake, Queen and King streets intersected in the centre of town, Victoria Hall and Albert Street celebrating the intersection. The British Hotel looked imposing and prosperous. The first bank I saw was called The United Empire, and the moving-picture theatre went by the name of The King George. There was often a concert in progress in the band shell in the town park given by what I would later come to know as the Davenport Garrison Artillery Band. Their uniforms looked like a cross between those worn by soldiers during the Boer War and pictures I had seen of English policemen.

I have lived for years in two large American cities. I have spent winter vacations in French and Italian villages, and fifteen summers on Lake Superior's north shore, yet few of these places impressed themselves on my visual memory to the extent that Davenport has – a place where I spent only two summers, a place to which I returned less than a dozen times in the years that have followed. If I close my eyes I can see even the most irrelevant details of the summer town: the weeds in the kitchen garden that my father and I neglected. Places in the park – near the band shell or the dance pavilion – where the grass was worn thin. A striped awning shading a shop entrance. Lit windows viewed from the beach at night. But my mother was right about the danger of fixed images. I want none of this. A pebble from a Great Lake shoreline, a coin with a leaf and a king embossed on either side, a shard of porcelain – the smallest thing is capable of driving you mad if you are unable to forget it. I am like an old museum filled with relics no one is able to identify any more. But there it is. George Kearns is a particularly tenacious ghost, and Davenport was George's home town.

I went back to Davenport a few years ago, slipped into town like a thief. I hadn't been there since a brief and, in the end, brutal visit in the winter of 1937, and yet it was the memory of the serene summer of 1913 that afflicted me: a reflexive, backwards glance to the time when I was eighteen and George was twenty, and both of us were innocent.

Little had changed in the town. No, if I am to be truthful, I must say that everything had changed. The ferry terminal was abandoned. Neither *The Maple Leaf* nor the *Northern Star* travelled the waters back and forth to Rochester: the country where I lived was apparently seeking its playgrounds elsewhere. Kearns's China Hall had also vacated its premises, and, when I looked through what had been George's shop window, I saw coils of rope, boxes of nails, cans of paint. Not that it made any difference. Cursed by recall, I could bring to mind every shining piece of precious bone china George had lovingly placed on the shelves of the China Hall during the course of that long-ago summer. That and how my own face and body had looked then, reflected in his window glass.

The ground floor of my father's house on the beach was now being used as the office and the dining room for the unattractive modern motel that filled the space where the garden had been. Orange plastic chairs stood in front of sliding-glass entrances. Disgusted by the sight of these, I walked towards the lake, turned my back to the water, and stood for a few minutes on the sand, looking up at the miraculously unaltered verandah, remembering the young man who had brooded there. Then I left the place and walked across the park.

The dance pavilion had been torn down years before, and I was almost relieved at first to discover that I could not remember where it had been situated. A large expanse of grass where there were no mature trees, however, disclosed its site, and as I walked towards this place I recalled views of the night lake from windows and balconies, the music of The Baltimore Rhythmaires, youthful couples gliding over a hardwood floor. The irretrievable prewar calm.

We believe that the whole planet rotates at once, but, in fact, it seems to me each entity in it turns on its own private axis, independent of the larger dawns and sunsets. I wondered about this vanished building. How and when it had begun to depart from the forward momentum of social history. I wondered how many sad old musicians had picked out the tune of the last dance, and when and if they knew that they, the dance floor, the scattered dancers, had all become irrelevant.

As I have become irrelevant.

Then I walked back to my car, climbed in, and drove east on the King's Highway Number Two, towards the end of the lake, towards the bridge that would take me back to my own country. My own state.

It wasn't long after that I added a canvas to what the critics would later call my *Erasures* series. It was the third painting I had attempted in my new style, the first two being entitled *Concealed Animals* and *The Sawhorse*, respectively. By the time I was finished, there was just the faintest trace of a building in it. A year later, I noticed that the shape of the roof and the dark blue of the lake were coming through the layers of white, but I solved that problem by scraping and repainting. I always wait at least two years before releasing a painting, placing it in the public eye, so that I am able to correct chemical impurities such as the one I've just described. It's rather like waiting for cement to harden, or for a newly constructed house to settle.

The summer of 1913 in Davenport, Ontario, Canada. The chalky vermilion of the brick walls I passed when I walked, the bubbles in the clean, bright glass of the small-paned windows, and all the gardens but ours weeded, raked, perfect. As I said, I began to explore the town, and I met George Kearns.

It was a hot afternoon, the park and the beach were full of noisy children, their mothers and aunts; the main street was practically deserted. I was walking west on King Street, the central thoroughfare of the town, when I saw a young man in a long white apron leaning in the doorway of a shop on the opposite side of the street. I noticed him first because he was about my age and then because of his extraordinary beauty, his blond hair shining like a lamp under the sun, the relaxed curve of his body against the door frame. Then I noticed that he held a sketchbook in one hand and a pencil in the other.

Even a person totally uninterested in art will approach another who is making a drawing, as if this strange activity of attempting to reproduce the perceived world is one which needs to be supervised, monitored. Or perhaps it is the intensity of the draughtsman's focus that lures complete strangers to his side; some kind of primitive desire to impede a relationship this intimate between subject and renderer. Having myself been the object of such interference, having felt the drawing dissolve beneath my touch at the approach of an observer, I nevertheless crossed the street and casually broke the young man's concentration. Smiling, puzzled, he looked up. He never did manage to master the distancing skills I had developed early in life; he never could keep the world at bay. How young and fresh his face was. Perhaps mine was as well.

He had been drawing Victoria Hall, he told me, because he wanted to paint it on a china vase. Beside him was that window I've spoken of, the window of the China Hall. He explained he was wearing an apron because he was sometimes called upon to help out in his father's neighbouring grocery store, which he could enter by passing through a door in the east wall of his own china shop. I felt that this white apron separated him from me entirely; as indisputably as the fact that he painted on china, a pastime of which I, a serious student of art, disapproved. I leaned on the other side of his door frame and we began to talk. I imagine it was a summer choice between George and his world and the superficial world my father was trying to coax me into that determined our friendship. But that day we spoke only about the heat, about drawing pencils and watercolour paper, about sable and camel-hair brushes. In the course of the following week I stopped at the China Hall to see George whenever I was out walking.

Quite early on, perhaps immediately, I could see that, though I was a few years his junior, George found me intriguing. And I, of course, was attracted to his interest, having never before been so admired. He had the amateur's fascination for the arts, and a strong belief, which I did not dispel and probably encouraged, that he was in the presence of a genuine practitioner. I scoffed at the designs on incoming shipments of tableware, lectured him shamelessly about real art while he smiled good-naturedly on the other side of the counter. Only once, I remember, did he interrupt me. He had been reaching for something high up on a shelf, his back to me so I couldn't see his face. "It's the only thing I can do," he said, "in this place."

On Sundays we borrowed the old horse and delivery wagon from George's father and made our way slowly into the hills that arced on the northern horizon and that one could see from the centre of town. Once we arrived in a spot where there was shade for the horse and a view for us, George would remove two old wooden chairs from the vehicle, settle himself into one of them, and begin to draw wildflowers and pastoral scenes while I paced back and forth along the lane searching, unsuccessfully, for signs of chasms and falling water. I was uncomfortable with the docile atmosphere of summer pastures so sometimes I drew George, or the horse and wagon. I spent much of the time commenting on George's drawings, which were proficient if somewhat sentimental for my taste. I was pleased and inflated by what I considered to be my ability to instruct him and with his readiness to accept my instruction.

But, try as I might, I could never turn him from his china painting. He always brought along a cardboard folio in which to press certain plants and flowers that interested him and that he would use as references for his designs. This was a practice I sneered at as much for its girlishness as for its unsuitability to the making of what I believed, then, to be "real art."

I told him this, told him no one would get away with such nonsense at art school, then asked him bluntly why he didn't go to art school if he was so interested in drawing.

"I can't imagine that," he said. "A school for nothing but art."

"Don't they have them here then?" I asked. "Are there none at all in Canada?"

"None for me," George said. I thought he was being protective, evasive in his answer. It had simply never entered my mind that a family, dependent for its income on a grocery store and china shop, might not have sufficient money to send a son to the city to play with paints and crayons. Only one son's education could be paid for in his family. His older brother, I later learned, had gone to law school.

"Besides," he continued, "I like china. I like the business. It gives me time to think and something to look at while I'm thinking. I can read in the shop. I can order things from England and France." He squinted at the poplar tree he had been drawing. "It's really not so bad."

I glanced at his perfect face – a face more fine-featured, more youthful-looking even than my own – his blond hair and moustache, his fine skin. I tried to imagine a life filled with saucers and teapots, account books and cash drawers, and was utterly unable to do so.

But I could imagine what George would be thinking about in the yellow light of early afternoon, the slow, quiet hour in the shop, what he would be thinking about while he unpacked shipments from England and France and set up his fragile displays. It was already halfway through the first summer. Yes, I would have known what he was thinking about because he had already taken me to the pavilion. I had already seen the way he responded to Vivian.

About twenty years ago, before I began my current series of paintings and while I was still living in New York, I worked on ten small abstract paintings called *Objects in a China Hall*. I was beginning to put together the collection by then, though for many reasons it had taken me eight years to make the decision to do it. Each time I added a new piece to the shelves I had built for this purpose, I would draw it and then paint it on a one-foot square canvas. I would walk around the studio for hours at a time with a Sèvres teacup mere inches from my eyes, then try to capture on canvas what I had seen. I was experimenting with visual intimacy, moving the object closer and closer until proximity obliterated meaning as I always suspected it would; the patterns – flowers, birds, garlands, swags, or whatever – exploding and blurring on the surface of the paintings. The series was meant to be a memorial to George, to the delicate, breakable cosmos that had surrounded him. But, in the end, the paintings – a wasteland of colour – didn't work. I could never determine the right format for them. Squares were not appropriate, and when I experimented with the shaped canvases that were in fashion then, they fought with rather than mirrored the curves of saucers and bowls.

But I've put all that away. There is ample storage in my modernist basement. "Go forward with what you have to say," Robert Henri once told me, told all of us who listened – mesmerized – to every word he uttered. "You are new evidence, fresh and young."

Well, I am old evidence now. There is no testament that has not been tarnished by age.

Entire kingdoms of objects have disappeared from the planet, it seems, but not from my visual memory, my eidetic malediction.

Think of all the gear associated with the horse-drawn carriage, the winter sleigh; all the straps and bits and bells, the reins and shoes and blinkers. Think of the wrappers for razor blades decorated with bearded men, a tin container for coal oil, the paper rolls for player pianos, spats, moustache cups, a square box sporting a huge red blossom from which music spills. This century has been one particularly concerned with disappearance, elimination. What ever happened, for instance, to the pale-yellow tickets from the pavilion, summer 1913? Five cents a dance.

I would stroll up from our beachside house in the early evening and meet George in front of his locked store. Even from a block away I would be able to see his frown, know that he was preoccupied. Vivian Lacey would have been the focus of his imagination for the better part of the afternoon, the possibility of her appearance that night ringing like an adamant bell in his mind, until he would have been unable to hear, to see anything else.

As we crossed the park he would become more and more silent, finally not talking at all except to reply monosyllabically to random requests I was making for information — facts I hoped would fill the void I could now feel developing between us. He never looked at me when he answered, and I know now that to speak would have meant his breaking through the dark, painful music that he took with him to the dance, to Vivian. But at the time I simply noted with surprise and mild anxiety that there was an odd kind of absence that the mere idea of a woman can create in a man like George, as if, lifted by the evening breeze, he was left floating somewhere, far out over the lake.

Once we were inside the pavilion his mood would mutate; he would become garrulous, almost coarse, punching the shoulders of the young men he knew, referring to me as his "Yank pal," all of this a shoreline of angry energy around the deep lake of the inexplicable suffering that, even then, related to Vivian. Claiming that women liked Americans best, he insisted that I dance with every girl he spoke to, though many of them were several years older than I was and all of them blushed with embarrassment. Sometimes when I miserably blundered through dance steps I was only just beginning to learn, I would see George looking towards the door, his face strained, as if he wished to break from this artificial interior of coloured lights, loud music, and paper scenery, as if he wished to be out in the meadows, or back in his cluttered China Hall, alone, with moonlight shining on the platters.

Then Vivian would appear – her dark, upswept hair, her perfect, gleaming teeth. She would approach George, who would be forcing himself to study the opposite wall, and seize his arm, tugging him towards the centre of the floor. The dance that ensued was one of the oddest I have ever witnessed; the whole room turned to watch it. Vivian led George through the steps, positioning his limp arms, one on her shoulder, the other on her hip, and then moving her own right hand rhythmically from his back to the nape of his neck, lifting it now and then to caress his hair or lightly touch his lips and cheeks. She was like a light flickering near him, a brush painting his features. All the time they were dancing, she laughed, chattered. He remained stiff, impassive; moving, or being moved, from static pose to static pose. His expression was grim.

I thought, at first, that he hated her.

At the end of the dance she released him, a pet bird with whom she had tired of toying, and stepped from partner to partner, treating each with the same bright, yet oddly detached attention. I was amazed by her beauty – there was no one there like her – but I was even more astonished by the fact that she chose her own partners, often even paying for the dance tickets herself, while the other girls sulked shyly in corners waiting to be chosen.

Vivian never waited for anything. She was always in perfect control.

It wasn't until the end of the summer that I managed to persuade George to talk about her. By then, however, I had gathered

information from some of the other young people my age I had
come to know around town. Vivian was new in Davenport, I was
told, had arrived the previous autumn with her mother, who was
choir director at the Presbyterian Church. Vivian played the organ
there and sang, had, in fact, made a name for herself all over the
province as an amateur musician. But that wasn't all; she and her
mother rented themselves out as entertainment (The Lacey
Girls), and it was rumoured that they had played the northern
mining towns – the dance halls as well as concert halls. There was
an air of scandal about them, softened somewhat by their connection with the church. The father, it was said, remained in Toronto,
where he ran a boarding house. The mother apparently had great
ambitions for her daughter, kept her home most evenings when
they weren't performing to practise scales. She was allowed to go
out only on infrequent nights. I thought this explained Vivian's
desperate gaiety, her need to harness every partner in the room.

George and I were painting in watercolour on a Sunday afternoon after a Saturday night during which Vivian's appearance
had reduced most of the young men in the room to a collection
of servile suitors and had caused in George a melancholy anger
so fierce it was palpable and so prolonged it was changing the
shape of the whole afternoon.

"What is it about that Vivian woman?" I asked, breaking a
taboo I knew perfectly well was in place. She had chosen to
dance with me once or twice during the previous evening. I was
pretending that I wanted to know more about her, but I really
wanted to know more about George.

"What do you mean?" he snapped. "What about her?"

"Why does she make you so angry?"

"She doesn't make me angry." George banged his small tin paint box shut. "Why should she make me angry?"

"That's what I'm asking you."

George stood, picked up his chair, and tossed it in the back of the wagon. He walked around the vehicle and slouched beside the old horse, stroking the soft part of the animal's nose for several minutes. Then he turned, walked past me, and collapsed into a sitting position on the ground near the edge of the hill. I could tell by the movement of his curved back that he was breathing heavily, almost as if he were gasping for air.

I had begun to walk towards him when he put his arm out to one side to discourage me from coming any closer. "The truth is, I'm terrified of her." From where I stood his voice was barely audible.

"I mean nothing to her," he whispered. "I become invisible whenever she enters a room." I stepped in front of him so that I could see his face.

George said nothing, but let the extended arm fall to his side, a gesture of surrender. Still, he did not look at me for longer than a fraction of a second, keeping his gaze fixed instead on the horizon of the distant lake.

"George," I began, "she's just a woman. There is nothing about her —"

He interrupted me. "Fate," he said, "destiny. I'm connected to her somehow, but she's not connected to me . . . not at all."

"Oh, come on," I said, laughing, unable to envision fate or destiny playing any kind of role in the life of a man in a white apron, a man operating a china emporium. I bent to pick up the drawing that George had absently brought with him to the edge of the hillside and that was now about to be carried off by the wind. I was still smiling, but I stopped when George looked at me oddly and I realized there were tears in his eyes.

I knew nothing of passion then. Two decades would have to pass before I would be able to recognize it when I was in its company, and, even now, I am not certain that I ever let it slip beneath my own skin. Still, after I had looked at George's face that August afternoon, something briefly altered in me and I was able to turn and see the summer landscape as I never had before. It was almost evening, the fields that lay before us were richly lit, as if the sun that had poured itself into the earth all day, all season long, were now being released through bark and foliage. Fields of grain, elm trees, sumac bushes, pine groves became sources rather than reflectors of light, the soft shapes of hardwood lots seemed as full of sky as the banks of cumulus clouds that floated above them. Even the rail and stump fences, the cairns of boulders assembled a century before were charged, radiant, their awkwardness a shining memorial to the labour of the men who had built them. This was the first time I had been moved by the tranquillity rather than the violence of nature, the first time I felt the scene before me to be one of perfect harmony. I had never before suspected it was possible that landscape — this impression — might be a compensation for misery, for loss.

The lake was bright blue, sparkling below us. Two or three white sails were visible near the harbour. On the other side lay my own country, my own city. I looked again at George, who had remained seated, his back bent, his arms on his knees, his face dark with emotion.

"I'll be going back soon," I said, handing him his uncompleted drawing.

He looked at the piece of paper for a moment, then crumpled it in his fist, threw it towards the view. He rose to his feet and smiled. "There's always next summer," he said.

A few years later, when both Robert Henri and Rockwell Kent were making their philosophies known to me, the former was quite vague and the latter absolutely clear on the subject of passion. Robert H. would have admired my tranquil vision, would have nodded with approval as I described it. Conversely, Rockwell would have instructed me to turn my back on the scene, to seize the tail of the northwest wind, to travel into storm and chaos, with the assurance that brightness and clarity would follow. He was a man who craved the catastrophe of experience. "The impossibility of one life," he would rage, shaking his fist at the sky above MacDougal Street, "against the brilliance, the possibilities of everything alive in it!" Almost anything was capable of carrying him off: women, islands, politics, weather, his own thundering heart. He once said to me, quite seriously, "Get drunk, Austin, have a love affair. It would be a tragedy to die and discover that you hadn't completely used up your body."

Robert H., on the other hand, spoke of states of being, long hours with materials and tools available and ordered, the hand ready to capture the image. To his mind, there was no experience more important than the art that was produced by it.

Robert Henri was my teacher; Rockwell Kent my friend. They both took their leave of me one way or another. No, I should be honest here. It is I who spend long hours in the studio trying to take my leave of them.

On our last walk to the pavilion that summer, George offered me a swallow from the flask he was carrying in his hip pocket. I accepted but pretended to drink more than the few drops I allowed into my mouth. I hadn't had much experience with alcohol.

He was unusually talkative for a Saturday night with Vivian's appearance imminent, asking many questions about The Art Students' League in New York, since I had decided to spend my academic year in that city. At one point, I remember, he told me, half in jest, that I would be a great artist one day, and asked me to remember him when I was.

"I'll still be painting on china," he said, his tone flat, difficult to interpret.

"Because you want to," I reminded him.

"Yes," he said, "that's what I want to do."

The autumnal moon was beginning to rise over the lake, its orange shape distorted, as if pregnant. The Baltimore

Rhythmaires were playing an upbeat melody as we walked towards the octagonal pavilion. By this time I knew so many of George's friends that they called and waved to both of us as we approached. I had stopped moping weeks ago, was now aware that I was unhappy that the summer was ending.

Just before we were to enter the building, George pulled me aside and offered me a cigarette. When I refused, he lit one himself, inhaled, threw his head back and blew smoke towards the darkening sky. Then he looked around him warily before he spoke.

"Tonight I won't dance with her at all," he said. "Tonight I will dance with everyone else. I will not dance with her, even once."

"She'll ask you," I said. "You know she always does."

"I'll refuse her." He ground the cigarette into the dust with his foot. "I'll refuse her," he said again. "I won't dance with her." George looked towards the pavilion. "She talks . . . she talks about nothing."

"She must say something if she talks."

"No . . . nothing, she says a lot of nothing. I could be anyone. Anyone else at all."

"But she is all you think about when you come down here."

I was beginning to understand that he was drunk. The whisky, the emotion. It occurred to me that he didn't resemble in any way the quiet, sanguine young man who stood behind the counter in the China Hall, as if when he had taken off his apron at six in the evening, he had removed a layer of his own skin, leaving him raw, edgy, vulnerable.

"It's all I think about," he said, "but I don't want to see her, have her talk about nothing, dance with her."

"I'm going in," I said. "Are you coming?"

"In a minute," he said and lit another cigarette. "By the way, I've always wondered — how did your father make all his money?"

I was a bit taken aback. "Something about mining stocks. Silver."

"So you'll be able to be an artist then, for as long as you want."

"I don't think my father's too keen on it. But more than likely he doesn't really care one way or the other."

"She likes it that your father has got money. She told me that."

"Wait a minute," I said. "She's never had anything to do with me. She doesn't even glance in my direction."

But I was misinterpreting George. "No, listen," he said. "That's who she is, what she talks about. She thinks about status constantly — can't wait to get away from here. She wants to be somewhere more important." He pulled the flask from his pocket. "You go on ahead, I can't go in there yet."

When I walked out onto the dance floor with a girl whose name I've forgotten now, I saw Vivian spinning in the arms of one of George's friends. She wore high heels and a blue linen dress that reached to her ankles but exposed her wonderful throat. She smiled and nodded to me, then said something to her partner, who rocked with laughter. I felt my face redden. One always wanted Vivian's approval.

George came through the door a few minutes later and stood near the wall with his hands in his pockets, staring hard in her direction. Then he shook his head like a beaten animal and began to walk straight across the floor, his eyes focused on the opposite side of the room. He brushed by Vivian, his hip and shoulder making brief contact with her body, and continued purposefully towards the lakeside of the building. The screened door slapped back into place after he passed through it.

Vivian had been thrown slightly off balance. She stumbled, stopped dancing, and looked at the door for four or five seconds, just the hint of a question passing over her face. Then she turned again, laughing, towards the young man she had chosen earlier in the evening.

This morning I awoke to the sound of water gurgling in the troughs and dripping like slow rain from the hundreds of icicles hanging from the eaves. The sky is clear, however, the sun dazzling, but the melting snow has created such pools in the street outside my window that each time a car passes, it is obscured by a brilliant cascade of water. The January thaw is always a surprise, a kind of invasion. Short-lived, it will be forgotten in a week, overshadowed, upstaged by one of our blizzards. But while it lasts it will disturb me. Films of moisture covering hidden ice will make my walks slow and difficult. If I were to fall now I would break like porcelain, and then there would be hospitals and medical people – another kind of invasion – and then, undoubtedly, there would be death.

Early this morning I dreamed of Sara's wrist bones, her wrist bones and the back of her hand . . . the ligaments there, the knuckles. The hand was lying in a narrow band of sunlight, resting on a table near a window. Because of the sunlight I could see the fine golden hairs on her skin and the intricate grain of the wood. I could see the creases at the joint where her hand had bent back and forth over the years. But it was the bump on the outer side of the wrist that held my attention in the dream, and I thought suddenly that all the other bones in her body must hang like pendants from this spot. I know, now that I am awake, that it was the lower end of the bone called the ulna that was intriguing me, the outer edge of the hinge that is the wrist. The sun, of course, would be coming in through her father's window, and the table on which it fell would be the one that had always been in his room. If I were to go there now, what would I do in that room, how would I use that table? But I have no need to go there. The accuracy with which I can recall Sara's anatomy, the anatomy of that room, is frightening enough.

Could George, I wonder, have reconstructed Augusta Moffat bone by bone, tendon by tendon, vein by vein? Had he ever drawn her? I never even asked, believing I was indifferent to all his art, whether it was on china or paper. And I was for a long time unclear about the relationship between him and this woman who had entered his life after the Great War. Had I been indifferent to it as well? By the time Augusta had become a part of George's life, I was adrift in my own, paying little attention to his letters, a semi-stranger during my then-infrequent visits. Augusta was a shadow on the wall of George's early middle life, or at least that is how I saw her, until later when the shadow gained substance, and she defined all our lives.

As I looked at the wrist bones in the dream, I could hear the sound of Lake Superior through a slightly open window. I could hear Sara's clock ticking steadily in the kitchen below. But what I really heard was just these icicles that I see before me now, slowly diminishing, dripping onto the lawn.

The following summer my father returned to the verandahed house on the other side of Lake Ontario and I returned with him, somewhat less reluctantly this time, but still uncertain as to what a summer spent far from what I considered then to be intellectual stimulation might have to offer. My father stayed in Davenport for just a few days, however, before heading farther north to examine mining properties in which he had invested, trusting, and as it turned out correctly, that the threat of war in Europe would cause his stocks to rise. I was to be left alone in the summer house, after a year of New York City, a year of art classes with Robert Henri.

Everything about the city had been charged with significance for me. Each stray cat, each garbage pail, the laundry swinging on lines strung between the sooty tenement walls. I loved the unceasing breathing hiss of the metropolis, the texture of the pavement, the sidewalk beneath my feet. For the first few months I had trouble sleeping, concerned that I would overlook some important aspect of the life that continued to churn all night around me. Often I would find myself at the window at two or three in the morning, mesmerized by an interchange taking place below me on the street: an explosive argument between lovers, a fist fight between two lurching drunks. The city was unmasked in ways I had never imagined possible; its nerve endings quivering a fraction of an inch beneath its surfaces. Though I spent hours and hours observing these flagrant acts of exposure, I was unable to participate, to enter the fray of experience.

I was a tourist then. I sense that I have remained a tourist. My recollection is that if I wasn't in my room in Greenwich Village or in Robert Henri's life studios at The Art Students' League, I was standing in the air or moving underground. The crossed iron bones of the Hudson and Harlem and East River bridges and the labyrinthian passageways of the new subway tunnels fascinated me. During the decades just prior to my arrival in New York, armies of labourers had knit the city together with threads of steel — tracks and girders and cables — and I was able to pass under and over rivers, to walk on the Brooklyn Bridge above the tarred roofs of factories, then slip beneath the surfaces of streets as if I were a needle, anonymous and shining.

And then there was my teacher, Robert Henri. A tall man with a surprisingly small face, he was filled with the kind of certainties that bolstered my own reticence. Before I left the city for the summer, he had spoken to me about the value of solitude, had warned me about disappearing into others, letting their voices echo, pollute singular, clear thought. He had instructed me to contain my own reactions, to express my feelings to no one, nothing, except to the paper or canvas. "Each sensation is precious," he would lecture. "Protect it, cherish it, keep it. Never give it away. You must develop that balance which allows all of the world to come in to you and only that which you have expressed in your art to move back out again into the world. When you are alone, without the distraction of community and affection, this will be easier to achieve."

My teacher had no way of knowing that neither community nor affection played a significant role in my life. His words merely gave me permission to remain aloof. This lofty promoter of American art with the affected French last name had sanctioned the voyeurism that had become, already, such a vital part of my personality.

I remained alone in the summer house for eight ritual hours each day, drawing the still life of driftwood, bottles, and apples I had set up in the kitchen, or making watercolour sketches of the changing sky, the undulating water as I knew Constable had done. I was capable at that time of becoming overwhelmingly sad for no reason, or of experiencing a surge of pleasure so great I would have to run on the beach for an hour in order to return to a state of calm. I was certain I was learning my own heart, my own senses, and perhaps I was. The walls of the house were lined with cedar. There was the fragrance of that and the feel of polished pine boards beneath my bare feet. A trail of sand from the beach followed me everywhere, as if I were shedding exhausted cells and replacing them with new ones, electric with sensitivity. In the mornings a breeze from the lake and a rectangle of sun moved through the window and crossed the floor towards my bed to wake me. The first thing I heard was the long exhalation of the breakers as they touched the offshore sandbars then crawled up the beach.

I remember quite clearly how I would lay out my paper and sketchbooks on the table of a room overlooking the lake, how I would gather my pencils and brushes like bouquets in my fists and place them in jars all over the window sills. The sound of the lake was always in the rooms I walked through, and sun and the trembling shadows of poplar leaves. There was still a child in me who appeared only when I was alone, and often I found myself playing in the sand below the verandah steps or collecting interesting pebbles near a shelf of limestone at the east end of our lakefront property.

I was almost happy.

I must have spent some time examining my body in mirrors because I can recollect it distinctly, the long, tight arms and legs, the smooth, browned skin, and the dark mass of hair on my head and at my groin.

It is the memory of that previous, younger body that causes the shock in me now, each night when I undress for bed.

Despite my commitment to seclusion, I visited the China Hall one day shortly after our arrival. I was anxious to see George, eager to describe my time in New York to one who I knew would be a receptive audience. It was early evening; the store had just closed for the day.

I stood outside the large window and for a moment looked through the glass. How inflated the term "China Hall" seemed now that I was gazing into its interior. It was not much wider than the cigar store farther down the street and only half again as long. The shelves that covered the walls from floor to ceiling were crammed with every kind of imported and domestic china: tea sets, dinner sets, chamber pots, foot baths, pitchers, spittoons, ornamental figures, basins, vases, jardinieres, and bowls. Here and there amidst the painted china I noticed the dull sheen of a silver-plated serving tray or candlestick, as George had decided to sell these items as well. The whole effect was rather like a busier than usual impressionist painting, but one executed

in richer, more vivid hues than the customary pastels. In retrospect, I would say that Vuillard's wine and mauve colours might
have accurately caught the atmosphere of the place. I can
imagine that particular French painter adding the figure of a
china merchant to his rendering of the interior, that and the collection of shadows that gathered at the back in the spot behind
the counter where George often sat at his turntable, one small
lamp illuminating a piece of china he was decorating.

I watched my summer friend for a moment or two before
knocking on the door to get his attention. He was sitting on a tall
stool, cradling a large piece of china in his lap — a compote or
covered dish of some kind. On the counter in front of him I
could see little pots of enamel paint and three or four delicate
brushes. He was alternating between running his hands over the
shape of the compote and reaching tentatively for a brush that he
would then hold in his fingers for a few moments before returning it to the counter. A book and a magazine lay open to the left
of the brushes. Behind him, on a shelf, were several large pieces
of white china — urns, platters, pitchers — with what appeared to
be the beginnings of paintings on their surfaces. Around him was
an air of such intense absorption that it seemed to annul the riot
of colour made by the jumble of china all over the store.

As I tapped on the glass in the door, George started, jumped
to his feet, and the piece on which he had been working slipped
from his lap and shattered on the floor. My apologies, when he
let me in, took the place of the greetings I had planned.

He laughed then and pointed towards the shelf near which
he had been seated. "Don't worry," he said. "I have lots of white
bodies now, some I've already begun to paint."

"White bodies?" I lifted my eyebrows and grinned.

"Undecorated porcelain," George explained earnestly. He had either missed, or was choosing to ignore, my amused expression. He touched one or two of the scantly painted plates with his fingertips. "I always seem to want to work on several at the same time."

When I knelt down to help him collect the fragments for the trash, I saw that he had already begun to paint the compote. There was part of a woman's face on one of the shards; an eye, the outline of a cheek, the curve of a sensuous mouth.

"You were painting a woman," I said, "and now I've ruined it."

"It was already spoiled," he said. "It wasn't working."

"You should paint faces on a flat surface," I told him. "And you should work from a model."

George was using a whisk and dustpan to gather the smaller pieces. "Where am I to get a model?" he asked.

I looked at the passersby beyond the window. "Anyone can be a model," I said. "Anyone at all. It is line and shape you are trying to explore. You learn all that working with a model."

At this time, my only knowledge of female form had come from Robert Henri's life class; shop girls and aspiring actresses posing for extra cash. They had never seemed quite real to me, though sometimes at night they walked into my dreams in the most intimate of ways. Robert H. had told us it was the artist's response to the subject, not the subject itself, that was important. He rarely spoke to the girls except to tell them when to break the gesture he had prescribed. I had seen more than one young woman begin to tremble and grow pale under the effort of holding a twisted, difficult pose for more than half an hour when our teacher had forgotten to allow her to rest.

George was silent, the dustpan poised, a large hand at the end of his wrist.

"At least with a model you would have something to observe and respond to. Then what you do would be more important."

Fragments were pouring, a miniature avalanche, from the dustpan into a tin wastebasket.

"How do you know this isn't important," he said finally.

In spite of the noise, I heard the sentence he spoke. More of a statement than a question, I am not certain it was really meant for my ears.

We walked down the length of the shop, opened the door, and stepped outside. The whole summer stretched before us like the main street where the China Hall stood, a street that was essentially a slow, moderately congested section of a central highway leading somewhere else. I watched while George lifted his arm above his head and began to crank an iron handle, watched the canvas awning over the window pull in on itself, fold after fold after fold.

Now and then during the time that I knew him, George would tell me about the larger industry connected to the decoration of china, about windowed rooms full of men and women painting Minton or Spode, not only in England and Europe but even in Canada, in cities that lay within a day's journey of Davenport. Toronto and Montreal each had large ateliers where some of the china was given a particularly Canadian flavour. Typical landscapes from each of the provinces were popular along with detailed renderings of specific flora and fauna. I laughed when George told me about one old woman who had spent her life painting beavers on soap dishes and another whose speciality was children frolicking in snow, a series entitled Boules de Neige. George, who at this time had never left Ontario, could, in his imagination, move through his country, landscape by landscape, because of the provincial plates so often displayed in his shop. Nova Scotia, he said, was fishing boats; Quebec, winter scenes with sleighs; Saskatchewan, sheafs of wheat and grain elevators; British Columbia, groups of mountains, and so on. Peculiarly Gothic-looking provincial legislatures and the spires of the Ottawa Parliament Buildings often appeared on cups and saucers. The whole collection gave me the impression that George's was a toy country; one to be played in, and played with, but one to be locked away with the dolls when you reached a certain age.

More familiar to me was the ever-present Blue Willow pattern. You could open a kitchen cupboard anywhere in the western world at that time and be confronted with at least some pieces of this blue-and-white china. Broken bits of it washed up on the beaches of the Great Lakes, dogs lapped water from it, it attended bridge parties and meetings of the various women's institutes, cake was offered on it at funerals and weddings. There were wash bowls and ashtrays, platters and chamber pots, biscuit jars and celery dishes, salt shakers and spooners. Bowls of it were filled with rose water, tubercular patients spat blood into it. It occupied three full shelves in George's China Hall.

Years later, on a winter night, I would drink whisky from it while Augusta Moffat and I waited for George to walk in from the cold.

But George first drew my attention to it on this summer evening in 1914, after he had closed the shop. He stood right in the centre of the China Hall holding a common bread-and-butter plate, handling it with such care I assumed that it was a valuable antique. He would not yet have met Augusta, though physically they might have been less than ten miles apart. I imagine she might have been standing in a kitchen doorway on the farm watching her brothers wrestle on the lawn, watching them train for the violence no one knew they would encounter. Or maybe she was walking through the evening light into the village, talking in her mind to an imaginary friend. I will never know. All I was able to see then was George's two pale hands and the piece of ordinary kitchen china they held.

"It's all there," he said. "The two birds with their wings out-spread. It's as if they are preparing to enter an embrace. And then there is the path, the bridge. . . ."

I saw only a kitchen dish.

"A world . . . a complete world."

In the slanting light of the June evening, I could see that George had changed over the period of the preceding fall and winter. There were dark circles under his eyes and fine lines over the tops of his cheekbones.

"And loss," he said. "The landscape of the Willow pattern is one that speaks of absence."

At that time I had not often thought of landscape as a code for something else. "What is absent?" I asked, peering at the plate. "How can anything be missing from a scene this crowded?" I was convinced that the picture on the plate, with its laughable pagodas and improbable bridges, was created in direct opposition to the laws of composition.

"The lovers," he said. "The lovers are gone."

"Dead, I suppose." I was child enough of my mother, and of the nineteenth century, to be able to interpret willows.

"No," said George quietly. "They are just gone; gone from each other and from everything else."

How terrible, I thought suddenly, is the grinding dailiness of George's life. How pathetic that he should have to spend his days contemplating kitchen china. There was a kind of horror in it, a futility. I almost disliked him at that moment, for my own certainty was that nothing at all was ever going to happen to him. The shop seemed smaller, narrower than it had just moments before. I became aware of a staleness in the air.

Moments before, I had watched George mechanically collapse the striped fabric that protected his store window. Fold after fold after fold.

When did the awning begin to fray, I wonder, and who, in the end, was instructed to take it down?

It seems that Sara has left me the contents of the house as well as the log structure and the land it stands on.

"And the contents," the document read, "to dispose of as the recipient sees fit." Those words — "contents, sees fit, dispose of" — have been rattling around in my head all day, plaguing me, tumbling about with images of the objects they refer to. I imagine auction sales, Sara's belongings displayed, picked over, taken away by strangers. This legacy was a deliberate act of cruelty on her part, I'm convinced of this. She knew I would be unable to cope, that I would drown in the vast sea of the past imprisoned by that house; Sara's past and that of her father.

I have not thought about the objects in her house for a long time; not since I painted several of them some years ago in a series I entitled *North Shore One*, *North Shore Two*, *North Shore Three*, and then one large single painting I called *Coastlines: Land's End and Cape Cornwall*. It always intrigued me that in her memory Sara carried impressions of the geological formations of that distant country's edge. Though she had never left Canada and had rarely, for that matter, even ventured as far as Port Arthur, she could describe the coastal paths of Cornwall as if she walked there daily, as if she had inherited a complete map of memory from her father at birth along with the shape of her hands and the colour of her eyes. And when she spoke about the ragged cliffs, the engine houses of the mines, the church in the village of St. Just, I could see every pebble on the track, each cog on the wheels of the hideous machines, though I had not yet developed what would become an almost prurient interest in the freight of her father's experience, the sad history of a transplanted Cornish miner.

There was little enough of Cornwall in the log house on the shore of Lake Superior, and yet Sara insisted that its coastline had been around her always as long as her father was alive and even, it would seem, after he was dead. Though I never asked her to, she detailed his walks each day to Botallack Mine, his descent into the underworld on the strange lift they called the man engine, various appalling accidents, the countryside littered with standing stones and chimneys and pierced over the centuries by thousands of mine shafts. The little grey houses in the villages. The fishing boats offshore. She spoke about all of this when she was posing and I was rendering the shadow of her instep or following the line of her neck with my pencil or the edge of a piece of charcoal. At the time, I hardly believed that I was listening, and yet here it is now, this distant, unseen country in my mind.

The unfairness of this, the unfairness of me having to keep these images, these crashing waves, these bursting churchyards, these rituals of farewell, as young men like her father departed for the New World. As if in revenge for my selectivity as a taker,

Sara always gave me everything when all I really wanted was the colour of her skin, the shape of her flesh on the canvas, and any extraneous information that would make those shapes, those hues more resonant. And pleasure too. Yes, I wanted that as well.

I was not unaware of her daily life, but felt it prudent to keep myself as far from it as possible. She rose at six and, after drinking coffee from the aluminum pot that I would find on the stove when I arrived at eight, she would leave the house and walk to the hotel to serve breakfast to the tourists. Naturally I saw her there — often she served me — but I paid no more attention to her than I would have to any other waitress. I had assigned this woman in her yellow uniform and white shoes the remote lodgings in my psyche reserved for her unknown (at least to me) winter self. I was courteous and formal and, after the first few encounters, she was as well. After breakfast, she and the other waitress cleared and washed the dishes, swept the dining hall and porch, and began to prepare for lunch. The cook's name was Sammy. He had worked in lumber camps and mining camps and his father had known Sara's father. But everyone knew everyone else in that part of the north. It was nothing special. I was never in the dining hall at lunchtime, having taken a picnic with me to Sara's house or sometimes to the shore in order to sketch. By the time she had served lunch and washed up afterwards it was about two o'clock. Then she untied her apron, hung up her uniform, and returned to the house.

I must have watched for her from the kitchen window because there she is in my eidetic cinema walking away from the hotel towards the row of miners' cabins. Her hair, her skirt, and a thin silk scarf she has tied around her waist are all being tossed to one side by the breeze from the dark lake. There are the poplar leaves shivering in the sunlight, and sun candles on the water. Dust. It must have been a dry summer. And a warm one. Her arms are bare. She is wearing delicate sandals.

I had approximately three hours alone with her (except on her days off, when I had all day), three hours only before she stepped out the door again and walked to the hotel to serve dinner; to serve dinner to me and the other paying customers. Very, very occasionally we met at night, but there didn't seem to be much point to this as I rarely painted in artificial light. Usually I stayed in my room and read, or I wrote letters to my friends in New York. Sometimes I dropped a card to George, who had returned to Davenport after the war and who still kept the China Hall. I went to bed early and slept well, except during those nights of high winds and large waves. Lake Superior, a huge inland ocean, really, could work itself up into a terrible commotion, a commotion that entered my dreams. Once I dreamed I saw Sara's body revolving in the foam beneath unfamiliar cliffs and, believing she was dead, I woke up weeping like a child and hating myself. I stood up then in utter darkness, left the hotel, and walked beside the thundering water to the log house, used my key, and crept into her bed. She knew who I was, even in her sleep. I don't like to think of that now; my name on her lips, the sound of it so near. It was one of the few times we'd awakened together — mid-morning — on a day when she wasn't working. I remember I said, "We have slept for a long, long time."

She laughed and rolled towards me, hugging me with her arms and legs. The uproar had passed and sunlight from the water was trembling on her ceiling, her walls. There was something remarkably fine and strong about her. The shadows that muscle definition created on her arms and inner thighs and along her abdomen when she lay on her side, these small basins were regions where I often rested my hand, my cheek. And now, late in the morning, the watery sunlight ran down and across the geography of her body as if she were lying in a bright, shallow river. Me swimming there beside her. I was not fully awake. I broke open in the face of this vitality, this brilliance, the shining strength of the beautifully constructed bones of her face. I could scarcely look at her. Finally, the room, my own body, my own language disappeared, and all I was able to do was say her name.

I was shaken by this, so shaken that I dressed soon afterwards, walked into the room where I normally worked, and began to collect my sketchbooks, my pencils. Claiming that I wanted to work outside on drawings of the shoreline, I left Sara alone for the remainder of the day. Robert Henri had said to me that what one was after when drawing or painting the figure was not so much the particular characteristics of the model but rather what the artist's visual sensations were when looking at her. He insisted that one should take from the visual that which attracts the actual eye, and then the mind's eye. I was becoming a master of selectivity. I was able to discard frivolous stimuli at will.

Sometimes I find that I am angry with poor old Robert H., though he was never in his life as successful as I have been and he has been dead for a very long time. Sometimes I find myself walking through the bright, empty rooms of this house, cursing him aloud as if he were standing before me and I were preparing to confront him. He had never been to Canada and yet carried on about the north as if it were alive in him, as if he were an authority. I have notebooks and notebooks full of the things he told me. What a public speaker he was, what a pontificator!

"Art is a result!" he announced glibly once. "It is the record left by those who have truly lived their lives. Those who have genuinely lived their lives will leave behind the stuff that is incontestably art."

He once told me — or told the class, I can't remember which — to be wary of too much talk. Talking almost incessantly himself, he nevertheless instructed us to keep our innermost thoughts private until they could be expressed visually. Silence, he maintained, preserved the deeper current of the personality, "and the deeper current," he said, "carries no propaganda: the shock of surface upheaval does not deflect it from its course." That being the case, I asked him — I'm fairly certain it was me who asked him — what difference could our talk, our own variety of surface upheaval, make to these more profound currents? He replied by saying that he was referring to the noise of the world. It was enough, he said, to have to penetrate the noise of daily life; God forbid that we should add to it. He pointed towards the street. "Running beneath all that daily life," he said, "you will find the deeper current, but only if you are quiet and still and wait for it to reveal itself. The same for the deep current you carry in here." He thumped his chest with one fist, somewhere near where his heart should have been.

This would have been sometime in 1915 or 1916, when George was already away at war. But then it wasn't my country's war, was it? It wouldn't be my country's war for another two years and, even then, only the adventurers would choose to go overseas.

My teacher taught us to stand in wonder in front of the world while overlooking altogether the world's response to us; unless, of course, that response were an acknowledgement of our own innate superiority, our special vision.

Lake Superior. How strange that Sara lived beside a body of water, a body of deep currents, bearing that name.

Robert H. taught us, taught me, that unless it could be turned into art, absolutely nothing was worth my time. "Art is a kind of mining," he said. "The artist a variety of prospector searching for the sparkling silver of meaning in the earth."

I think of my own father, and men like him. Men whose wise investments tore open the wilderness, penetrated the earth, moved mountains, and who ultimately were responsible for creating the furious machines that would eventually be used in the wars.

How right Robert H. was. About art. About success, ambition. The greed. The exploitation at the expense of nature and humanity. And, in the end, sometimes the beauty.

He was a wonderful teacher.

There is always a moment of wholeness, recollected when the world is torn, raw-edged, broken apart, a moment when the tidiness, the innocence of landscape – sometimes of the society that created the landscape – allows you to predict with accuracy the discord to come. The flawless summer of 1914 presented just such an opportunity for this kind of prescience. But in Davenport, the world around me was concentrating on its own freshness, its own youth. A sense of heightened animation was everywhere. People laughed and embraced on street corners, the beach was full of visitors, weather did not interfere with the growth of crops on the surrounding farms. Business, according to George's father, had never been as brisk.

From Dominion Day onwards, the ceiling of Davenport's dance pavilion was tented with flags – the Union Jack, the Red Ensign – and the talk before, during, and between dances was always of war. A forty-mile excursion across a shared Great Lake had brought me so close to Europe and its conflicts that, at times, even during my hours of withdrawal, it was difficult to remember that that particular continent and its adjacent imperial island were still thousands of miles away. George and his friends began to appear in uniform on Saturday nights, looking smug and mature after hours spent marching with their militia units. Words like Serbia and Belgium, places I barely recalled from grade-school geography, sprang easily to their lips. Girls with bright eyes, shining hair, and crisp new dresses were as restless as the young men they danced with, anxious for a declaration of open hostilities abroad, confident that their opinions were shared by the crowd.

Vivian was nowhere among the dancers. I had not seen her once since I'd returned.

When I asked about her, a shadow trembled briefly across George's face, as if a swift bird had passed between him and the sun. Then his expression became absolutely neutral. "She's gone," he said. "She left for Europe with her mother. They sailed months ago."

"Ah well," I said, wanting to reinstate an air of complicity between us, "if you're sent over you'll be able to see her. Though I suppose if it comes to that, her mother will have brought her back by then."

"There is no fear of me seeing her," he said. "I don't want to see her."

"What about fate . . . destiny?" I was almost teasing, then saw his face darken, but not soon enough. I was drawn to the minor drama of the oblique relationship, was using words as if they were cheap, lacking in power.

It was a gorgeous day. George and I were walking on the

diagonal path that bisected Davenport's lakeside park into two neat isosceles triangles. The lake was gleaming, a hundred bright sails on its surface. "I expect I'll be killed in the war anyway," George said. "I expect that is what will happen." He spoke these words almost cheerfully, as if he did not wish to disturb the lightness of the day, the beauty of the morning.

Everything around us was in perfect bloom; everything had been raked and swept and cultivated by people devoted to horticultural societies and town fairs where glossy vegetables and sleek horses won blue ribbons. Nothing had yet disturbed this picture. No one had the slightest understanding of irony. There was no need for it. In the decades that approached the summer of 1914, honour and loyalty had yielded satisfactory rewards. If you fed and groomed the horse, hoed and watered the garden, in all likelihood at some time or other you would be presented with a prize. I refused to take seriously George's statement about death. The only drama I could imagine for him would be romantic in nature, minor; interesting only in the vaguest of ways but, above all, well ordered.

"This war may never happen," I said. "And if it does, it will end almost immediately. You'll be back in no time."

We were almost at the King Street end of the park when George stopped, turned towards me, and announced that he had made out his will, that I was to inherit his china collection.

The half-painted vases and urns that stood on the shelf behind his counter came instantly to mind. I laughed and thanked him. There was irony in my voice, but as I've said, this was a place where irony was not understood. Yet.

"You could finish painting the vases, I suppose," he said,

"but it would be best if you saw the whole collection so that I could explain it to you."

"You're not going to leave me with everything in the store?" I said nervously. I envisioned an entire afternoon in the shop, George enthusing, pattern after pattern.

"The store is my father's," he reminded me.

All along King Street we walked in the shade of the large old sugar maples that have now all but vanished from towns and roadsides on both sides of the border.

"I'm talking about my own collection – you've never seen it – I keep it in my room." George paused then, waiting for some comment from me, I imagine. When I remained silent, his voice softened, became almost apologetic. "I suppose," he said, as tentatively as he might have had he been going to ask me to make a large sacrifice on his behalf, "I suppose you really should see it."

We were heading in the direction of the China Hall. It was Sunday morning and all of the shop windows we passed were covered by dark-green shades. I believed that what George was suggesting had nothing to do with the possibility of death, that he merely wanted to show me his treasures, and I still think I was partly right about this. George would survive the war, though he would be gone for a long, long time. There was an eagerness about him that morning that was compelling. I knew I would have to view whatever it was he kept in his room.

"All right," I eventually said, sensing that one way or another I was going to have to endure this punishment. "Let's see it."

In the clarity of the low, raking light, each building we passed seemed polished, scrubbed, and utterly deserted. Nothing moved except the odd cat and our own wavering reflections in the large glass fronts of the closed shops. George had spent the previous night at my beachside house so that we could get up at five on a Sunday morning to paint the sun rising behind the lighthouse. It had been, and still was, a morning of absolute calm, the lake a bowl of light under a pale-blue sky, the horizon erased. I had felt, on the beach, as if we were standing on the edge of the world with nothing but a gorgeous emptiness in front of us. "The water needs wind to define it," George had said. There had been no wind.

Like almost everyone else in Davenport, George's parents were at church. We let ourselves in by the back kitchen door, walked down the dim hall, past the quiet parlour, and climbed the stairs. This was my first visit to the rooms above the China Hall. The master bedroom, when I glanced at it, appeared formal – almost funereal. I thought of my own parents' large, shadowed room, how my father had refused to sleep there after my mother died, her brush and comb and music box still displayed upon the dressing table. George's room was almost spartan in contrast to his parents'. A uniform of the Davenport Heavy Battery hung from a clothes hook like an effigy on the wall.

"The collection," he announced, gesturing towards a book-case on the other side of the room.

There, behind hinged glass doors, was a scant assortment of china. Not much really – bread-and-butter plates painted with scenes from Izaak Walton's *The Compleat Angler*, a couple of dessert dishes that George referred to as "Dickens ware," a vase with a Canterbury pilgrim trudging along an empty track, and five brooches with orchids painted on them.

"These are the real treasures," George said, picking up one of the brooches and handing it to me.

"How so?" I turned the piece of jewellery around and around in the palm of my hand.

"Dewsbury may be the greatest living artist."

"Dewsbury," I repeated stupidly.

"A painter for Royal Doulton's Nile Street factory." George gazed out his east-facing window as if he could see all the way to London. "I'll buy his landscape vases when I have more money."

I examined the miniature painting for a few more moments, mostly for the sake of politeness, then I returned it to the shelf. To my mind, there was nothing extraordinary about it.

"I know you're not overly impressed," George said, bending protectively towards the shelf and realigning the brooch with the others, "but if you took some time . . . if you were to look carefully. And, of course, the best is gone."

Who, I wondered, would want to take it?

"Smashed," he continued. "It couldn't be helped."

I imagined an accident in transit. Poor George, I thought, picturing him opening a package from England filled with small shards.

He straightened up and smiled. "So, you'll look after this then, if I am killed?"

"Only if you die with your boots on," I joked.

For one short instant, irony existed in prewar Davenport. George laughed. "With my boots on," he said. "You can rely on that. And with my orphaned collection destined for a foster home, another shore." He turned towards the door. Again there was this sense of undefinable eagerness about him. He wanted to get back to the glorious day. As we scrambled down the stairs, he referred to the collection one last time. "It will be right here," he said brightly. "Just drop by and pick it up."

When war between Britain and Germany was declared in August, George's battalion was ready for departure within days. Like everyone else in Davenport, I went to the railway station to see "the boys" off. I, though a boy myself, felt alien, excluded; my American nationality, my lack of uniform making me appear to be almost like another genus and species. The Davenport Heavy Battery was to go to Valcartier in Quebec for training and from there to Salisbury Plain in England. I had never seen the normally subdued population of the lakeside town in such a state of celebratory excitement. Their Dominion Day festivities had a certain joviality to them, but they were nothing like this ecstasy connected to the idea of participation in a distant war. Perhaps the young country yearned for engagement of one form or another, wanted to leap into the chorus and onto the world stage. How many wars ago this was. How little any of us knew about the chorus, or the stage.

I had visited the China Hall the day before George left and had watched with genuine sadness as he packed away the few vases he had been painting and the small turntable on which he worked. His father would have to mind both shops, he told me, until he returned. I was having trouble imagining George in foreign landscapes, was only comfortable with the idea of him in the shop, or in the pavilion, or the Northumberland Hills. Despite my lack of respect for it, I knew that the china painting defined George somehow. He was the lake, it was the wind. I was sorry to see him have to part with it.

He placed his carefully cleaned brushes in a rectangular wooden box and stood looking down at them, absorbed, before closing the lid and fastening the brass clasp. In those few seconds, it was as if I weren't there at all, as if I had not opened the clanging door and was not leaning on the counter that he stood behind.

I was filled with the alertness, the energy of youth then. In spite of the bouts of solitude prescribed for me by my teacher, reflective thought did not come easily to me, and yet, standing there, watching my friend take leave of the tools he loved, I knew that I was witnessing an act of great intimacy. I was confused, embarrassed, and surprisingly moved by it.

Before I left the shop that day I bought a souvenir ink pot, painted by George. It had a view of Davenport's Victoria Hall on the front of it and the pavilion on the back. He had completed a number of items of this nature over the period of the previous winter — salt and pepper shakers, cream pitchers, sugar bowls — and they had sold so rapidly to the Americans who were in town for the summer that the ink pot was the last of the batch. At first he didn't want me to have it, it being "purely commercial" and, according to him, not a good example of his work. And then, when I insisted on having it, he didn't want me to pay for it. He accepted the money finally when I told him I wanted it as a gift for my father. I was lying, of course; I never intended to give anything to my father.

I have kept the little ink pot with me all these years. It has moved with me from desk to desk to desk, and I am dipping my pen into it, even now, as I write.

The boys were leaning from the coach window when I arrived at the station. The surrounding air was filled with laughter; any tears I saw were tears of joy glistening on radiant faces. There were, I remember, two bands playing opposing tunes at either end of the platform and a blur of white hands shaking small flags against an overcast sky. A few years later, when I was passing through Union Station in Toronto, I would see British Bull Dogs with Red Cross collection boxes strapped to their bodies and tired-looking, grief-stunned girls who, not knowing I was American, or perhaps not caring, would approach me with an accusatory white feather in their hands. But now there was only a rhapsodic fantasy concerning the Motherland; a migrant's battle hymn.

Davenport's Canadian National Railway station was at the northern limit of the town. Across the tracks, in the fields that stretched out towards the Northumberland Hills, there were small groupings of calm beige cattle and stooks of yellow barley. Directly in front of this pastoral scene, right on the edge of the tracks, were gathered three or four decrepit houses of an advanced age, which suggested that there might have been a village there before the larger town grew out to meet it. In the second storey of one of the homes, at the front of an odd-shaped dormer, was a tall Gothic window. Behind its dirty glass, a woman stood holding back a sheer curtain with one hand. I have no idea how old this woman was, being far enough away that she appeared to be nothing but a shadow. I could not tell if she was beautiful or plain, happy or sad. But the way she slowly turned first her face and then her whole body away from the scene, as if in indifference or disgust, the way the tattered curtain fell back into place, filled me with something approaching dread. I have never forgotten her.

I pushed my way towards the train, was finally close enough to George to be able to shout good luck and goodbye.

"Remember, if anything should happen, take care of my collection," he yelled. "Especially my treasured brooches."

"I'll do my best not to lose another to accident."

"No accident," he called over the hiss of the train. "She crushed it under her heel."

When the steam from the locomotive cleared, I could see George's beloved Northumberland Hills in the distance. He was gone before I was able to ask who had smashed the brooch.

I left the station and walked down Division Street towards the lake, my father's house, and my exercises in reclusiveness. A state of solitude was not going to be difficult to achieve. There were no women in Davenport who interested me, and, as for company of my own sex, I was the only young man left in town.

Sometime during August of 1935, the last month of the last summer that I spent at Silver Islet, Sara told me what it was like to wait. She said there were two kinds of waiting: the waiting that consumes the mind and that which occurs somewhere below the surface of awareness. The latter is more bearable, but also more dangerous because it manifests itself in ways that are not at first definable as such. She then told me that over the period of the last winter she had finally realized that everything that she did or said — every activity — was either a variant of, or a substitute for, waiting and therefore had no relevance of its own.

There were no telephones at Silver Islet — there still are none, as far as I know — and very erratic mail delivery. Telegrams were considered important enough to be pushed through, regardless of the weather, by boat in the summer or by dog team over the ice in the winter, but I always let Sara know the date of my arrival in June by dropping her a card early in the month. Over the course of the year I occasionally sent her a note to let her know I was fine, and now and then an announcement of one of my exhibitions. Winter was the time when I worked intensely in the studio on the large landscapes, figurative pieces, and interiors for which I had done oil, charcoal, and pencil sketches the previous summer. It was also a very social period. I went to parties and the art openings of friends. I performed duties attached to the various clubs and organizations to which I belonged. For me, winter was always a busy season, one I enjoyed immensely, especially as my reputation grew and my sales increased. Wealthy New Yorkers, it turned out, loved wilderness landscapes. They wanted rocks and water, twisted trees and muskeg on their smooth plastered walls. And some of them wanted Sara's fair skin and dark-blonde hair; some of them wanted that as well.

When I was in New York, Sara became a series of forms on a flat surface, her body a composition adapting to a rectangle, her skin and hair gradients of tone. She became my work, and then, when the work was finished, I lost sight of her completely, turned towards ambition. Very occasionally, even when we were together, it was like that — the bed a large white canvas and me manipulating the positive, the negative space, a finished, saleable picture dominant, fixed in my mind. But most often she would not allow it, would refuse to pose, or even to remain in the room if she sensed this other side of me surfacing. "There's someone in you," she once said, snatching her robe from a chair. "Someone I don't want looking at me."

She intuited, you see, the entrepreneur.

It had not been easy to get her to pose for me in the first place, this waitress, this miner's daughter whose only experiences had taken place on the sparsely populated shore of a northern Great Lake. It wasn't until after we'd been lovers for over a month that she agreed to do so, and even then she would ask me, before each session, if I were certain that I wanted to paint her. She couldn't understand why I would be interested enough in her to want to put her in a picture. Her knowledge of men was necessarily limited, so, at first, she was physically quite shy. There had been a boy during her late teenage years, a boy she had been fond of, but he left the settlement to find work.

"My father was sick by then," she told me. "Otherwise I'd likely have gone with him. He said he'd come back, but ... When your own father came and there was talk of the mine reopening, it crossed my mind that he might return then. You'll think I'm crazy, it was years later. He was the only one, you see, and I never knew what became of him." She smiled. "He was probably in some place like Timmins with a wife and four children."

As it turned out, there wouldn't have been work anyway. My father's speculations had been a complete bust.

"But," Sara said when I pointed this out to her, "your father brought you here." She looked at me, her expression clear and frank. "The mine closed," she said, "but you came back."

———◇———

Sara visited me in the city once, tracing the route that I so often took when I was leaving her, stepping on board *The Canadian* in Port Arthur, waking in Union Station in Toronto, then changing trains, continuing on to New York. What was in her mind, I wonder now, on that journey, and what long agony of conscious and unconscious waiting caused her to make the decision to take it? Port Arthur would have been all she knew of cities; she had never bought a railway ticket. Did she feel terror or joy, or excitement? Was she able to sleep while the train rocked through the night? And did she come carrying a message, a message I refused to receive?

She surprised me and I responded with my own crazy form of panic. I took her to a series of pointless parties and heartlessly ignored her, talked to everyone else in the room, especially women, while she sat tense in a corner, her spine straight, her hands folded in her lap, her forced smile gradually fading. When we were alone together in the studio, I made love to her over and over again, coldly, suggesting by my actions that I believed this was the reason she had come to me, that I was doing my duty. I didn't want her there and she knew it; I made certain that she knew it. She had no place, no relevance at all, in this part of my life. She belonged in a light-filled room in the north, a room with a view of landscapes I could frame and sell, her body frozen into poses I could also frame and sell. Her presence in my city life, my winter life, was unacceptable. I let it be known that I thought being seen with her was vaguely scandalous, as if one of us had a partner who might object.

She left quietly one cold, early winter morning, having groped for her clothes in the darkness while I pretended to sleep. I was angry at her decision to travel to see me and was glad at her departure. I didn't communicate with her again for four months, then I sent a note to tell her the date of my arrival in the north.

But, ultimately, it took much longer than four months to finally erase the pictures in my mind of Sara walking awkwardly beside me on city streets, struggling to keep up, or of her lying emotionally wounded on my rumpled bed while radiators banged and voices on the telephone announced invitations to more and more parties. Two decades later, after I withdrew to this house in the city of my birth, I completed five paintings entitled *Night Journey from the North*, *The Surprise Appearance*, *Five Parties*, *The Used Bed*, and *Departure at Dawn, or Winter Morning*. The series occupied me for the better part of two years.

What I was able to accomplish during those four months of silence between Sara and me back in the late 1920s or early 1930s, however, was to reconstruct the woman I knew waited for me on the northern edge of the largest of lakes, to separate her completely from the woman who had, against my wishes, visited me in the city.

But nothing successfully removed that episode from my mind. It bruised my memory in some way. I felt invaded by it. Sitting here, an old man, I can recall it graphically.

Between the artist and the model, you see, there must always be a distance.

By the third or fourth summer she had given me complete run of the house — total access. There were days when I wanted to work very early in the morning so that I could watch one of the downstairs rooms fill with quiet, liquid light. Often I remained in the kitchen during the dawn hours, but sometimes I would move into the front sitting room, which had an eastern window through which I could see the pink and yellow sky. I never painted the horizon, wanted only to capture the effect of it, the way it changed the appearance of the objects in the rooms. There is something pure, almost virginal, about rarely witnessed light; northern light that appears in what would be, in other seasons and latitudes, the middle of the night. Light that does not often waken sleepers. I felt covetous of it, wanted to share it only with my art.

I would let myself in with the key she had given me and sit quietly in the kitchen or the front room until a particular object was touched by this light. At the time, I believed that an intimate knowledge of the interior of Sara's house would enrich my paintings, not only with its spaces but also with the regions of her body, and so I would make pencil drawings of her handbag resting on a chair, or of her jacket hanging on a hook behind the door. This was a lesson in portraiture given to me by Robert Henri. In class he would often have us turn our backs on the posing model and tell us to draw instead her robe where she had left it on the floor beside the podium, the whole time keeping in mind what we had learned from our previous drawings of her. When I told Rockwell about this later, he remembered loathing such activities, and said that the discarded robe on the floor had no more resonance than a simple still life. "Never forget," he told me, "that the French call still life *nature morte*. There has to be a reason for that." But I was excited by the idea of keeping one picture fixed in my inner eye while allowing my outer eye to focus on something connected but physically separate. It seemed an exercise designed for me and my eidetic facility.

I was perfectly happy in these early-morning moments at Silver Islet and felt, in some ways, closer to the model – closer to Sara – than I did when she was naked and in my presence. I even began to develop certain theories of association. All of the objects in her house had, to my mind, the potential to be transformed by Sara's recent handling of them, so I looked specifically for those things she had touched or relocated since I'd last seen them.

Then, one morning, when I had been drawing a collection of pots Sara had left on the draining board to dry, I became so involved with their shapes, the geometric angles the handles made in relation to each other, that I let her face drift out of my mind. Most of the time, when my eidetic memory was functioning perfectly, this split vision had been easy for me to achieve; I never wanted to lose sight of the fact that it was *her* coffee cup, *her* crochet hook. I was insisting that the sketches should be theoretical exercises in intimacy, not anonymity. But that morning anonymity crept up on me before I recognized it. When I realized what had happened and tried to bring Sara's face back into my mind, I found I couldn't recall it. It wasn't that I had forgotten her hair or eyes, or even her strong mouth and the curve of her cheekbone, it was just that I could no longer picture these things with my inner eye, and this frightened me a little. But if I could picture them, I could only see the way I had painted them; the ice-white dot in the middle of the pupil, how this alone makes the eye live, various pale flesh tones, rose and beige, and the yellow ochre of her hair.

It had been a cold spring, Sara had told me that; though spring is always cold in that country. She had taken me out to see the patch of snow that remained at the bottom of the tall cliff at the end of the settlement track, as if its tenacity proved a point she had been trying to make. It was the middle of June then — I had just arrived — and we were still awkward with each other after my nine-month absence. For a few days I had painted both the cold and the awkwardness into her skin, her gleaming shoulders. Then, finally, I walked across the room and thrust my hands into the warmth of her hair.

Now, on an early morning in mid-July, I found I couldn't call up her face. I began to hone my pencil with her paring knife, wanting as always to make the instrument weapon-sharp. Then I left everything — the shavings, the pencil, the sketchbook, the knife — on the table and ascended the dark, enclosed staircase carefully, because I knew Sara would not rise for another hour and I didn't want to wake her. Her father's room was full of the kind of shimmering light that was always reflected at this hour from the lake. By nine o'clock a rippling, luminous stream would trickle down the hall to Sara's room, where it would cross her bed, climb her wall, pulsate on her ceiling. But now, in the early hours, her room was dark, then suddenly lighter, then dark again. As I came to her doorway, I could see that the breeze was pushing through the open window, lifting the shade she had drawn the night before, then slowly letting it drop before beginning the process again. She was lying on her back, her head turned slightly towards the window so that her face caught the light when it entered, then darkened again as it withdrew.

I stood in the doorway and watched Sara's face disclose itself and then return to shadow. It was not the face I remembered.

It was more transparent; a naked face. I had no desire to render it on paper, on canvas. Its privacy, I knew instinctively, was impenetrable.

Now, I think, if I had tried . . . perhaps with something loose and fluid, like watercolour. But how was I to get in the coming shadow? That was the question.

There was something disturbing, I suddenly thought, about the way the living lay their defences down in darkness and give themselves — surrender themselves — so completely to the awful vulnerability of sleep. Terrible harm could come to a creature in such periods of utter passivity. How badly equipped life seemed to be for survival, how much more opportunity was given to the certainty of death. I could hear Sara's slow, steady breathing, which seemed to be oddly connected to the lightening and darkening of the atmosphere. She had slept in this room every night of her life, she had been a child here.

I became embarrassed by my own voyeurism, stopped looking at her face, and began to examine the sheets in which she slept. They were gathered and twisted, contained the full narrative of one night's dreams, a history of sequential, unconscious gestures. I would draw this bed, I decided, but I would wait until Sara had risen from it.

I remembered what my teacher had said about drapery, how it was composed of rhythms, echoes, continuations. He hated the word "wrinkled" when it was applied to cloth but, strangely, didn't mind it when it was used in relation to human skin. It was as though he felt much more affinity for the inanimate than the animate. Once, after listening to him talk about drapery, I returned to my small Greenwich Village studio and spent a full afternoon dropping my handkerchief on the floor and drawing the unusual shapes that it made there.

In Sara's hallway, I passed through the trembling light that had begun to move towards her room, and I descended the narrow staircase, gathered my drawing materials together, and let myself out by the front door. Several crows were gliding in the air near the lake, the fringe on their wings like black fingers against the sky. Soon Sara would walk where I was walking. She would be dressed in her waitress's uniform, ready to serve breakfast to me and to the other guests at the hotel. When she poured coffee into my cup that morning, I felt for the first time ashamed, though of what I was not precisely sure. Ashamed and almost shy.

I could never bring myself to tell Sara that I had seen her naked face.

And it would be many years before I was able to understand that all through those long winters in New York, winters when I had convinced myself that I had no wish to see Sara, the truth of the matter must have been this: I did not want Sara to see the man I really was. I did not want Sara to see me.

2

NIGHT IN THE CHINA HALL

Many of my most recent paintings, paintings that make up the series now universally referred to as *The Erasures*, are based on vivid fragments, on ragged-edged episodes from my own life and the lives of the others. Often the making of them is painful to me. The underpainting is inadequate because although the scenes painted within it are powerful, the information contained there is scant. Slicing into the lives of others, I have walked away with only disparate pieces; walked away with both permanent and fugitive colours, with distinguishable and vague shapes. But it is simply not possible to fit everything together with any real accuracy, despite my overdeveloped powers of recollection. Sara always attempted to give me her autobiography – whole. But I tore it apart, silenced her, tossed the parts of her narrative I felt I couldn't use, like shredded paper, into the wind. I was constructing her, after all, in my paintings. I wanted no interference with the project.

Augusta Moffat was different. Although there was no attachment between us, I carry the whole of her life with me into every room I enter. I have not recomposed her. What I came to understand of her nature would simply not allow it. She was her own full canvas — we had no relationship. Almost everything I know about her I learned in the course of one long night in the winter of 1937. She unfurled her history in my presence not because she wanted to explain herself to me, or because she was trying to move me in any way, but simply because the story had to be told and there I was. I am certain she would have spilled her words into empty air had there been no one there to listen. When the need for disclosure is that fierce, one's motives cannot be anything but pure. Augusta's was the narrative that precedes a private gesture, a kind of review, I suppose, of everything that had led her to that moment.

It had to be spoken. And it has to be remembered. Entire.

That night while she talked I could see our dark bodies reflected in the large front window of the China Hall, each of us seated on either side of the counter. My own silhouette something I had come to know in other night windows; hers almost completely unfamiliar but gaining weight, substance, as the hours slid by.

Augusta was George's woman. They treated each other with tenderness. One long winter night in the China Hall she told me the story of her life. There is nothing to modify, to obscure.

She had been raised on a farm northeast of Davenport, the eldest child and only girl in a family made up of what appeared to be a never-ending series of baby boys. Her brothers broke her dolls, soiled her embroidered handkerchiefs, interrupted her studies with their fights, spilled her bottles of rose water, and ate all the chocolates her father invariably gave her for Christmas. As a young child she had had to throw rocks and sticks to keep them from surrounding her on the way to school. Later she had never dared bring a suitor home for fear of the taunts, their tricks and jeers.

They jumped up and down on her bed, breaking the springs. They left a small pet pig in her closet. They wrestled in the front yard, flattening her first attempt at a flower garden. They caused even the oldest and most subdued of the calm workhorses to run away with her if ever she tried to ride one of them. Once, in her teens, when she had been out later than she ought to have been and was stealing carefully through the dark parlour in an effort not to wake her father, she opened the door to the stair-well and was met with a sudden cacophony. Pots and pans that had been tied together with a string and wound at one end around the doorknob came tumbling down the stairs towards her. Her parents would not allow her out after supper for a month while, night after night, the boys who were old enough to do so swaggered across the kitchen and out the door.

There was a swift river of male children running enthusiastically through the house all winter long. The younger boys were so dedicated to activity that they literally had to be tied to chairs and pushed towards the long kitchen table in order to finish their homework, while the older brothers were isolated in various rooms so that they would not fight. As the tribe increased, the pantry was locked and the key kept in Augusta's mother's pocket, otherwise the cupboard would be bare. For many years Augusta never experienced a full night when her sleep was not interrupted by a baby's demanding cry.

And yet her love for her brothers was fierce, bright, and pure. She knew their bodies better than her own, had seen them saw and pitch stripped to the waist in the summer heat or slouch under coats into dark winter dawns towards barns and chores before school. She had sponged their hot skin when epidemics swept through their ranks, had bandaged knees and elbows, had combed lice from their hair. Because of them, before the age of puberty, she had experienced the full range of human emotions: grief, terror, loathing, loyalty, passion, and tenderness. If she had died before the age of twelve, it could have been said that her life had been almost full.

Although she could not imagine awakening in a house from which chaos was absent, the architecture of her own character in the face of all this was, not surprisingly, built around a desire for order and restraint. Privacy was an alien concept, but tidiness was not, and so the achievability of folded shirts and dusted shelves made her glad, frustratingly short-lived though these things were. Often the results of an entire Saturday of labour were undone in the half-hour before sundown, and she would be forced to watch, unhappy and powerless, as everything she had put together flew apart again.

Still, the truth was, this team of boys was the energy that drove her self into being, wrenching her out of sleep in the morning, keeping her alert all day, flinging her, exhausted, into bed at night. Unconsciously she attributed all change and each event to her brothers' existence in her world, believed that without them the crops wouldn't grow, the animals would not give birth, and that time would be suspended.

Among them, Fred was the only quiet boy. Two years younger than Augusta, he stayed close to her skirts, eager enough to be near her that he would stand on a stool and slowly, methodically dry the dishes that she had washed, or he would hold the dustpan when she swept up discarded flakes of cedar in the woodshed. Throughout her life she kept a picture of him in her mind; he was standing by her side on the long front porch that faced the gravel road. "That was the road," she told me, "that would lead us both — all of us, actually — away from the farm, towards brutality."

In the end, it seemed to her, that the road itself was a kind of weapon.

By the time she was ten, in 1905, Augusta's domestic abilities were better than those of a female three times her age. Her skills with a needle, for example, or with utensils in the kitchen, were breathtaking. I could imagine that each task she undertook was completed with the same earnest serenity, her small face calm, on occasion, radiant.

In early morning, while the boys were hollered at and often shaken from their beds by their father, Augusta would already be downstairs with her mother, her dark hair combed and pulled straight back from her forehead, her two braids tracing the curve of her back as she kneaded dough or bent over the oven to remove a loaf of bread. I imagine she would have loved the talcum texture of flour, how it would make her pale hands paler and cling to the seams of her fingers; this and the brightness and sharpness of needles entering, and emerging from, cloth.

Sometimes her mother, Kaziah Moffat, would allow Augusta to pull shirt after shirt from the perilous rollers of the wringer, while she herself cranked the handle round and round. Then Augusta would take the damp garments out to the platform her father had built beside the clothesline and pulley, pin the clothes to the rope, and run them out to dry in the wind. Occasionally one or two of her own cotton pinafores or dark calico dresses would appear among the more masculine laundry, and Augusta would like the look of this; her ghost family performing in the air, the landscape of her own farm as far as she could see.

Her father barely noticed her, she was so quiet, so predictable, and he so busy moulding his battalion of rowdy boys into dependable farm hands. Once in a while he would stop and look at her and his expression would be one of surprise, as if he had forgotten, or couldn't quite believe, that he had helped to bring something this feminine into the world. Then he would speak to her respectfully, as he might have spoken to a stranger whose good opinion he sought, asking her about her school work or about the Bible passages he insisted all his children memorize. He would sometimes praise her, but not lavishly for fear of encouraging vanity, and two or three times a year he would take her hand and press a dime into her cool, dry, curiously unchildlike palm.

She loved him, of course, though she would never come to really know him. When she was twelve she gave him a cross-stitch sampler she had made for Christmas. It was decorated with rigid flowers, a perfectly symmetrical house, the alphabet, the numbers one to ten, and a verse she thought he would approve of:

> "Fragrant the rose is but it swiftly fades in time.
> The violet sweet, but quickly past its prime.
> White lilies hang their heads and soon decay,
> And winter snow in minutes melts away.
> Such and so withering are our early joys,
> Which time and sickness speedily destroys."

On Christmas morning, Edward Moffat held the piece of unframed fabric in his large, calloused hands and read all the words of the verse, his mouth silently forming each syllable. Then he looked at his only daughter, glanced in the direction of her mother, who was pregnant with their seventh child, then stared at his daughter again. Augusta met his gaze with solemn expectancy. It had taken her two years to complete the picture and the words. There was not a tangled thread among the stitches. Her own name was at the bottom with her age and the date, Xmas 1907, and then the message, "To Father."

This was not an unusual gift, nor was the cross-stitch an unusual pastime for girls (though its popularity had waned somewhat with the advent of the present century), and thousands of these projects hung, proudly framed, on parlour walls all over Ontario. The verse was taken from a booklet entitled "Sayings Suitable for Samplers," which could be got, along with "The Women's Institute Cookbook," from the Methodist Church at any bake sale or bazaar. Yet when Augusta's father read it, then read it again, the fog of habit and toil was swept from his mind and it seemed in its bleakness to carry with it a vague, but nonetheless terrible, portent. Life's something miserable for girls and women, he thought, for the first time in his life.

To Augusta, at whom he was still staring, he said bluntly, "Thank you for this, you have done it well." Then he cleared his throat and announced, "You will go outdoors, for two hours a day, twice after school and once on Saturdays." He paused, then added two more words, though they probably sounded foolish, even in his own ears. "To play," he said.

"What shall I play at?" asked Augusta gravely.

"That," said her father, glaring at the boys who were noisily demanding equal privileges, "you must discover for yourself."

"I was not at all happy with this decision," Augusta said to me, "but my father prided himself on never changing his mind, and his word was law. It would have been pointless to argue and, besides, it would never have crossed any of our minds to be that impertinent."

She told me her father, Edward Moffat, was known as a taciturn man but was, nevertheless, much given to the telling of family legends during the evening meal and had often explained at his quiet table (the children were not permitted to speak unless spoken to) that no Moffat within living memory had ever changed his mind. The children knew that it was the Moffat men he referred to and that this statement included all of their uncles, their great-uncles, their grandfather, and their withered and aged great-grandfather, all of whom lived on the Moffat farms sprinkled liberally throughout Northumberland County. Because Augusta had told her mother that she had no wish to go out to play, and Kaziah Moffat had passed this information on to her husband, Edward Moffat felt compelled to remind his children about the Moffat men.

"They never change their minds," he said at the supper table a few days after New Year's. "Their word is law."

"What about great-uncle John?" asked Fred suddenly. He was ten years old and even more taciturn than his feared father, but he loved Augusta and wanted her inside with him. Augusta and the boys turned to look at him in amazement: he had spoken without being spoken to. An awful silence fell over the table. "Didn't he change his mind and come back from the Klondike?" continued the child weakly, his voice barely a whisper.

"Did I ask you a question?" Edward Moffat peered at the boy from under a severe ridge of thick dark eyebrows. "Did I speak to you?"

Fred stared at the mashed potatoes on his plate. Augusta reached for his hand under the table.

"Fred," said his father, "I'm speaking to you – I'm asking you a question now. I am asking you if I spoke to you."

"No, sir. I forgot, sir."

"Don't forget again."

"No, sir."

Edward Moffat picked up his knife and fork, and his relieved wife and family reached for their own utensils. He chewed thoughtfully and then laid his knife and fork back on the table.

His pregnant wife and silent children followed suit, all except for baby Cecil, who banged his spoon once or twice on his mug.

"Fred," said Edward Moffat, "do you remember what Uncle John said before he departed for the Klondike?"

"Yes, sir."

"Well, what did he say?"

"He said, 'I shall never return.'"

Edward Moffat had begun to eat again, as had the rest of the family. Except Fred, who was recovering from being spoken to.

"And Fred," his father continued, "do you remember what happened to Uncle John after he changed his mind and returned from the Klondike?"

"Yes, sir," he said. "A horse kicked him in the head."

"And then?"

"And then he walked slowly like, across the field, through the gate, up the walk, through the back door, through the woodshed, past the kitchen, into the parlour, where he lay on the sofa and died."

Their father had one more question for Augusta's favourite brother. "And what did he say before he died, Fred?"

"'I should never 'ov changed my mind. I should never 'ov left the Klondike.'"

Edward Moffat gazed meaningfully at each of his boys in turn, including baby Cecil. "Let that be a lesson to you," he said.

"And so," Augusta explained to me, "when school started again after Christmas, I was dispatched twice during the week out into the dark, cold winter late afternoons. On Saturdays I remember looking out the window with dread while I ate lunch, knowing that soon I'd have to be out there in all that snow, all that snow and nothing to do."

At first she would merely stand stunned, quite still, inside the confines of what her mother called "the yard." She did not weigh enough to break the crust on top of the snow so she was able to walk back and forth alongside pickets that had been as high as her waist in summer, pickets that now only reached her ankles. What drew her to the fence was that it was connected at each end to the house and so was soothing to her mind in that the territory inside it could be thought of as just another chilly room. Augusta spent much of her time remarking to herself that on Saturday afternoons her shadow on the snow was two times taller than she was, that after school it grew to ridiculous lengths as a result of the setting sun, and that on dark days or as supper approached, her shadow grew in the opposite direction, as she was lit from behind by the wonderful lamps in the warm house.

Once it became dark, Augusta was able to look with longing directly into this comfortable domestic world from which she had been banished. Fred sometimes waved to her from the kitchen window, where he kept watch, not wanting to let her out of his sight. The other boys made faces through the glass or scratched their initials in the upper panes where frost had formed. Sometimes they called her names when they were forced outside to shovel a path through the accumulating snow to the back door. Augusta eventually learned that it was necessary to keep moving, otherwise her hands and feet would become unbearably cold. Gradually, like a caged animal pacing in a pen, she beat a deep circular path around the edges of the yard.

Her father passed her on weekdays as he returned from the back acres where he carried on a small lumber business in the winter. He would walk right up the path one of the boys had shovelled and often not notice Augusta at all, such a shadow she was in the dusk. But, as the weeks went by and the days lengthened, she became, of course, more visible, and one day he actually stopped and stared at her with that odd combination of surprise and tenderness that visited his face whenever he looked at her. Then, as he remembered why she was outside, his expression changed and he asked her what she was playing.

Augusta looked at her brown boots on the white snow. She always told the truth. "I am playing at nothing, Father."

Her father turned to give directions to one of the boys who was to take the two draughthorses into the barn. Words concerning water and straw and harnesses were exchanged. Several minutes passed before Edward Moffat turned to his daughter again.

"You say you are playing at nothing?"

"Yes, Father." And then hopefully, "Do I have to play, Father? Do I have to stay out here?"

Edward Moffat considered Augusta's question for a few moments. Then he said firmly, "Yes, I have not changed my mind. I know what's good for you. You must learn to make your own play." He looked at the circular track in the snow. "Why, you have not even left the yard," he exclaimed. "Go to the edge of the woods or down in the meadow. You should go to the other side of the barn, near the creek, then the playing will be more natural-like. It will just come to you."

Augusta's heart sank.

"You will go where your mother can't see you from the house," he continued in a commanding tone. "And the playing will just come to you."

Two days later, with great reluctance, Augusta trudged out behind the barn and then followed the lane that ran beside the creek. She stopped just short of the woods into which her father so often disappeared on winter days, looked down the white path that bisected the two dark armies of fir trees, and thought about play.

Other girls had dolls; hers had all been broken by her brothers. Some of the children she knew at school spoke of game boards and dice and even, occasionally, of cards. These were all considered immoral by her Methodist father. There were books – schoolbooks, almanacs, *The World's Great Exposition of Civilization*, and *World of Strange Wonders* – but they were not to be removed from the house.

The early March snow, heavy now, dense and wet because of rising temperatures, was beginning to seep through her boots. Her socks were damp.

"I will not play," she said aloud, though no one heard her. "I won't do it."

She bent down, picked up a handful of snow, ate some of it, and threw the rest at the trunk of a cedar tree, where it stuck, making a white circle on brown bark.

"Anyone who plays is stupid," she whispered angrily.

She squatted, made another more solid ball of snow that she rolled across the ground, watching the way it grew as she pushed it in front of her. Soon she was standing beside a large white sphere almost as big as she was.

I have made something, she thought.

Half an hour later she had constructed seven of these globes and had positioned them side by side so that they made a kind of wall with open triangles at their tops and bottoms. She filled in these areas with more and more snow until her mittens were soaked and her hands were burning.

By the time she heard the dinner bell she had completed a second wall at a right angle to the first and was standing a few yards away admiring her white handiwork in the grey light.

She was hugely pleased with herself.

I will come back tomorrow, she thought, completely forgetting that tomorrow was Sunday and that she would be forbidden both work and play.

"We could make a snow sculpture tonight," I said to Augusta. Although the streetlights were still lit, because of the storm I could barely see Victoria Hall, which stood adjacent to the China Hall. A thin coating of snow was beginning to inch its way up the large front window. "God knows there's enough of it out there."

"Not one like mine," said Augusta. "We couldn't make one like mine."

In the end, it took Augusta four and a half sessions to finish her snow house. She had remembered to leave a space for the doorway and had entered and exited several times. It wasn't until she had completed the roof — which was made from scrap boards she had found behind the barn — that she realized she had no window. She crouched in the dim interior, on a floor of packed snow, and thought. If she returned to the woodshed to fetch a shovel, the boys would want to know what she was up to, follow her back to this spot, and gleefully smash her walls. This was her house; she was the only one who knew about it. It was hidden by a clump of cedar. No one could see it from the farmhouse. She imagined she was the only one who had ever thought to make something like this. She wanted it to remain unwitnessed, to have it all to herself.

Using a stick, she dug through a wall, first from the outside in, then from the inside out. This project took her the better part of an hour. The snow had settled in recent days, and hardened, and there were thick inexplicable pieces of ice here and there that made the going difficult.

When the light finally broke through, it was in the form of a single beam thrown from the intense orange sun. Augusta had thought to create a west-facing window. It was always going to be afternoon in her house so the light was always going to be perfect. She enlarged the window as much as possible with the stick, admired the view, squinting, her face taking on the colour of the sun, which was by now quite low. Then, in the last half-hour of perfect light, she rolled several large balls of snow through her door and constructed one white armchair, finishing it just as she heard the sound of the dinner bell travelling across the field to fetch her home.

Augusta returned to her snow house two days later after school. She had every intention of making a snow bed, a snow table, was, in fact, designing these pieces of furniture in her mind as she walked the path behind the barn. When the small structure came into view, Augusta noticed with pleasure that her roof of boards had disappeared under four or five inches of fresh snow, making the whole house white, as if it had always been that way. Though it was now late March, they were experiencing what her father called a cold snap, and the snow was not as manageable as it had been in recent weeks. There was a stiff wind that made white wavelike drifts in the meadow and that cut through Augusta's coat. She lowered her head so as not to hit it on the doorway and entered her snow house.

"There was a grey girl," Augusta said, looking directly at me to gauge my response. "A grey girl sitting in the white chair."

Concealing my bewilderment, I nodded. I wanted her to continue.

She must have blown in through the window, was Augusta's first thought. She was startled – how could she not be? – but she was not as startled as she should have been and this intrigued her. Augusta squatted near the window and studied this grey girl. She was quite beautiful and older, more grown up than

Augusta. Her hair was so fair it was almost white, the skin on her hands and face a little darker. Narrow drifts had settled in the folds of her blue-grey skirt, as if she had sat very still on the snow chair all day long. She had breasts under her grey-blue bodice, Augusta was certain of this.

The grey girl didn't seem at all surprised to see Augusta, and she didn't appear to be uncomfortable with the way Augusta was staring at her. She just sat, entirely still, in the white chair. It was a sunny day but, because of the wind, curtains of snow were entering through the window. Occasionally the grey girl's face was obscured, but it always came into focus again when the wind died down.

"I am quite comfortable here," said the grey girl at last. "And you are too."

Yes, thought Augusta, I am. "I like houses," she announced, then wondered why she had said this.

"Yes, you do," said the grey girl. "I myself live in this house," she continued, "but you may visit whenever you like."

"No," said Augusta, "only Saturday afternoons and Tuesdays and Thursdays after school. My father never changes his mind."

"No, he doesn't," agreed the grey girl.

Augusta could think of nothing else to say. She had decided that the girl might be eighteen years old, or even older. There were no mittens on her hands and only a dark-blue cape on her shoulders, but she didn't seem to be cold.

"I've been waiting," said the grey girl, "for a long, long time."

"All day long," said Augusta.

"Longer than that."

"For two whole days?"

"Longer than that," said the grey girl. "I've been waiting for twelve years. I may have to wait for ten more."

Augusta said nothing. The grey girl's voice seemed to be scolding her in some way. But when she looked into her eyes, which were more blue than grey, she saw they were filled with kindness, happiness.

The following week the snow softened and Augusta was able to construct some additional furniture for her house. The table, the bed, a second chair facing the first, which allowed for conversation, and one side table on which she placed a solid white vase. Sometimes the grey girl was there, sometimes she was not. Often she did not appear until Augusta had stopped working and had collapsed into her own chair.

"I've been here all along," the grey girl would say as she came into focus in front of Augusta's eyes.

One day when the snow was soft enough for Augusta to be able to make several bowls and even a sort of teapot for the grey girl, a robin perched on the outside of the window ledge and looked inside inquisitively. And then, the next Saturday as she approached the snow house, Augusta had to admit to herself that it had begun to lose its shape.

"Don't worry," said the grey girl as Augusta entered an interior filled with a kind of slow rain, "one or the other of us will be back. Maybe both."

The following week the snow house collapsed. Two weeks later there was not a trace of it left.

Augusta turned thirteen, just a few weeks later, in May of that year. On her birthday her father gave her a gold locket with the initial "A" engraved on it. After she had opened the gift, thanked him for it and gave him a formal kiss, he ordered her to remain inside from then on, to help her mother and to concentrate on her school work, housework, and needlework.

"In case you think I have changed my mind," Edward Moffat said to his daughter, "you are entirely mistaken. You are a young lady now and young ladies don't play. If you were still a child, you would go outside on Tuesdays, Thursdays, and Saturdays."

For just a moment Augusta envisaged her own thin reflection in the circular lake that had been left behind for several days after the snow house had melted. Clouds mirrored there had sometimes taken on the shape of the grey girl, but the image had dissolved as she looked at it.

"I didn't think you'd changed," she said, then paused. She was going to add the words "your mind" to the sentence, but in the end she let them go. "I didn't think you'd changed at all," said Augusta to her smiling father.

"Did you ever see the grey girl again?" I said to Augusta. I could hardly believe that I had asked the question without irony, but there it was.

She had moved down to the front of the China Hall while she was talking, was now searching the dark, empty street, looking, I thought, for some sign of George.

"Yes," she said, "but not until the war."

"Was she a ghost, was she someone who was haunting you?"

"Yes, no. . . . She was someone who was going to haunt me. For a time, though, she was very real."

By now I was genuinely astonished. "She was *going* to haunt you?"

"Look," said Augusta, walking back towards me and holding on to something near her throat. "Here is the locket. I have worn it every day since my father gave it to me. There is a picture of my father inside, if you'd like to see it." She slipped a thumbnail into the seam at the edge of the tiny golden heart.

He didn't look at all the way I'd imagined him from Augusta's story. His face was narrow. He looked thinner than I expected, less sure of himself.

"He was thinner and less sure," said Augusta when I remarked on this. "The photo was taken after the war."

I won't let Mrs. Boyle anywhere near the collection. She has been forbidden to set foot in the end of the room where it is kept, ever since the day I found her pawing through it, a large plastic garbage bag close at hand, disapproval written all over her face. "You're a grown man, for God's sake," she said to me. "What on earth do you want to be doing playing like a child with pieces of china?"

I told her it was absolutely none of her business how I spent my time.

"None of my business, is it?" she retorted. "And me the one that keeps you going day after day. You're such a strange one, you'd lose the power of speech if it weren't for me coming in here every morning. And praying for you. Oh, yes, don't look at me like that. You are exactly the kind of person I feel compelled to pray for."

I explained that I'd much prefer that she would do no such thing. "If there is a God," I said to her, "which I seriously doubt, then I'd much rather not be brought to his attention. And as for the china," I said, "I want you to leave it alone altogether."

"I'm the one," she said, "who cleans the room."

"And I'm the one," I replied, "who pays your salary. From now on you will clean only the end of the room where the china is not."

She looked hurt then, sniffed, and left. But she has stayed away from the shelves ever since.

Each day I try to spend an hour or so working on the collection, even though the colour and the clutter of it sometimes disturbs me more than I can say. Also I resent enormously having to spend time in shops searching for the correct kind of wire contraption for wall hanging, or for those balsam wood easels used for shelf display. To find these items I must visit the pathetic tableware sections of large department stores because, like so many other things, the China Halls of the past have all but disappeared from the planet. As I pick my way through the merchandise, the salesgirls eye me suspiciously and are only very occasionally able to supply the required object. Robert Henri would have wanted me to paint these young women, to abduct for the canvas their expressions of ennui in the face of materialism. But my own ennui now will not allow their faces to come into focus, and they are lost to me before I reach the escalator that leads to the ground floor and the street.

This afternoon I placed on the shelf a Tower Blue Willow plate — one only superficially like the common Blue Willow that George showed me all those years ago. As I looked at the tower in its improbable, cerulean landscape, I knew that the lovers had not fled those hills and streams, but rather that they had never been there in the first place. Only the tower — broken, decrepit, uninhabited — has a role to play in that scene. Stark in the daylight hours, its window grimly unlit night after night, it neither protects the territory around it nor sends messages to any other territory. Having no history, it is instead a comment on stasis. Nothing has ever happened to this tower, or because of it, except its own slow, sad decay; that, and the inching up of ivy.

And yet it is a beautiful piece, a prized addition to any collection. Josiah Spode had perfected this type of blue underglaze painting when the East China Company reduced its imports of dishes to England. George told me this, said that over the centuries thousands of ships had carried china around the world and that many of them had ended up on the bottom of the ocean. Some, he claimed, had been sunk by the storms of our own Great Lakes. As for the Blue Willow, George could draw from memory the design of each of its variations: Chinese Plants, the Lyre pattern, Ruins pattern, Old Peacock, Sunflower, Indian Sporting pattern, and so on. He told me that, at the porcelain museum in Sèvres during the war, he had seen a blue porcelain violin, about which the director of the museum had written a complete novel, a novel George had been trying to get someone, anyone, to translate for him.

I have never been much moved by music.

———◇———

Hills and Streams. Skies and lakes and distances. Each summer I removed myself from cities and travelled north in search of landscapes. Although I loved the look of the vague fog produced by long views and the use of aerial perspective, I nevertheless painted the horizon in a crisp, possessive way, as if, having chosen to render it, I felt I must bring it up close for inspection. That which was not in my line of vision at any one time did not interest me for the simple reason that I was not looking at it. My life was that compartmentalized.

I will admit now that it is impossible to master skills utterly foreign to one's character.

For years George and I would often make day trips along the shore, away from the sands that stretched in front of Davenport to beaches made of round stone. It was here that he found the best shards, their sharp edges dulled not only by water but also by being sifted through pebbles. He always claimed, when he took me to these places, that he wanted to paint seascapes, or the view of Davenport's lighthouse from a new vantage point. And once we settled ourselves down on a log or a boulder he would begin a couple of half-hearted sketches. But in no time at all he would remove his shoes and socks and begin to walk slowly along the water's edge, looking for lake-worn fragments of china. Once I tried to search as well, regarding the whole thing as a game, but I never saw anything but stones.

One early-summer afternoon George put an oval-shaped shard in the palm of my hand. It was well worn; only a bit of the glazing remained and under it two small figures.

"The lovers," he said. "They sank to the bottom of the lake."

Now that we were adults, I was uncomfortable when George spoke about things of a romantic nature, when his manner became earnest. Often I would try to lighten the atmosphere by making some clever, usually cynical remark. But that afternoon I gave the shard back to him without comment and he dropped it into one of his bulging pockets with the rest of his finds. We began to walk in an easterly direction down the shore, clambering over fallen, water-logged trees and crunching across sloping banks of stones. This was after the war – I would have been on my way to Silver Islet – after the war that George so rarely talked about. I'm quite certain it was the same day that George found the button from an officer's coat among some seaweed near a group of boulders.

"Poor bugger probably drowned himself," he said, laughing. Then he tossed the bright brass circle, like a coin, into the waves.

"Or threw his uniform into the lake as soon as he got back," I offered.

"If he had any arms left to throw with. Or any legs left to get him down to the shore." Then he paused. "But he was an officer, he probably drowned himself. From guilt." He smiled.

"That bad, eh? Real bastards?"

"No," said George, "not really. At least they were out there with us. And plenty of them are growing poppies now. My high-school English teacher, for example. Only five years out of the teachers' college and then off to France. Dead in two weeks."

"He should have stuck to books," I said. I had just found a fossil, a stone snail. I slipped it into my pocket.

"He had no choice," said George. "He wasn't married. He would have had to go."

Each piece of china I put on the shelf seems to bring me back to painting. I began to work on a canvas at seven this evening, working for four hours straight until I sat down to write this. Weeks will pass while I paint the stones, the water, the sky, the worn pieces of broken china whose delicate patterns are themselves being erased by the lake – the whole world of a summer afternoon.

And then, when it's all there, as bright and clear and clean as I can make it, I will take two weeks more to add the patina, the glazes, the semi-transparent layers.

The more that admiration is withheld, the more we desire it. And then when it comes, plentiful, unconditional applause, we turn from it in disgust, knowing ultimately that praise is the last thing we deserve. Oh, the fatal quest for the approval of the current authority!

We were really just children, those of us who began our careers in visual art during the teens of the century under the tutelage of Robert Henri. We were street urchins let loose to run with our crayons into bars and alleys and tenements, as if New York City were one large playground. And Robert H., the father of us all, lecturing about theory, arranging our exhibitions, encouraging our natural inclination to rebel (as long as he was leader, and controller, of the rebellions). There wasn't a young painter north of the Mason-Dixon line who didn't wish to be in some way associated with this man. We all wanted the touch of his hand on our shoulders, wanted to rise like butterflies to be collected in the net of his praise. Kent, Luks, Bellows, Sloan, Hopper had all preceded us as his students — we were the second generation — and we wanted our predecessors' notoriety. The attention, even the condemnation, of the press they received.

The patriarch, the prophet Robert Henri stood over us all. Theorizing, expounding — manipulating us. More than we knew. Or more than we wanted to admit that we knew.

There were times when the tension created by trying to please this much-respected master would break. If he left the studio for a few moments, for example, a kind of insurrection would often explode among us, as if we were primary-school children who all morning had been desperate for contact with each other and who, now that the teacher's gaze was averted, were going to make the most of the interlude. We would waltz with the model or with each other. From the broom closet someone would remove the skeleton used for anatomy lessons and set it on his lap, feigning a passionate embrace. One or two of us could tap-dance, and did so. Only the few women in the class kept on working after Robert H. had left the room, pausing now and then to give us looks of disapproval mixed with amusement.

I was one of the more active ones at these moments, bringing myself to the attention of the other young artists in the studio by acting the clown, making friendships that otherwise would have required the kind of intimate conversation that had always made me uncomfortable. I was quite agile, and had discovered that I could perform handsprings and cartwheels in a limited space without disturbing the clutter of the easels. For this performance I always received a round of applause.

So it must have been that while George was wading up to his hips in blood and mud and rotting flesh, I was engaged in buffoonery, using the studio as my own private gym. The war, which the Americans would not enter for a year anyway, simply slipped my mind. I never spoke of George to my art-school companions. In fact, I rarely thought of him. I was far too pre-occupied with painting, or our classroom antics, cartwheeling safely through rooms filled with marks on paper. No, I rarely thought of George, even when the master returned to the room and began to fill the sudden silence with words concerning the importance of emotion, the importance of life.

One afternoon I was chinning myself on a door frame of the studio, enjoying the laughter of my friends, when a man about thirty-five years old appeared in the doorway on the opposite side of the room and swung himself up to the lintel of the door facing me.

"Rockwell Kent," he said, introducing himself while bringing his chin up to his fists. "Whoever drops first buys the other a beer."

"But I've been at this for at least five minutes," I gasped. The laughter in the room had stopped. Everyone's attention had been diverted.

"Okay, after you stop I'll do six minutes more."

I disliked him immediately, this show-off, this braggart, this mirror of myself across the room. Every move he made was a parody of my own pathetic attempts to win the approval of the crowd. Then, as if to dispel any thoughts I might have entertained about mirrors, about equality, he chinned himself with one arm and performed a mock salute with the other.

"I won't drop," I panted.

Rockwell grinned at me from the door frame opposite, then crossed his eyes and allowed his tongue to loll out of the corner of his mouth. My entire audience had turned to watch him. "He's had it," he said to them.

"I'm younger," I managed to croak. This elicited a deep guffaw from my opponent, after which he began to sing a popular song. Some of the students were clapping in time to his movements.

Until that moment I had never experienced the desire for victory as a physical sensation. Sweat was running into my eyes, anger was ringing in my ears. "You'll drop first," I said through clenched teeth. I was damned if I was going to be humiliated like this.

Rockwell stuffed one hand into his back pocket while keeping a firm grip on the lintel with the other. He pulled out a large handkerchief and blew his nose loudly and aggressively without missing a beat. My fellow students cheered.

I had heard of him, of course, knew his painting, his reputation, all of which made this nonsensical contest more enraging. I was determined not to be defeated by him. I knew he could read the indignation on my face and I could see he was amused by it.

"Boo hoo," he said, bringing the cloth up to his eyes.

Besides my teacher and his colleagues, Rockwell Kent was the only real artist I'd ever laid eyes on. I had expected glamour and dignity to be a part of fame, yet here fame was, taunting me like a child in a schoolyard. I was furious with him for the insight his behaviour — and my own — momentarily brought to me. Too much energy was going to outrage. Exhausted, I dropped to the floor.

"You ass," I hissed, unsure whether this remark was directed at Rockwell or at myself.

"My sentiments exactly," said a voice behind me, followed by a barking laugh.

How long my teacher had been watching this farce I had no idea. Rockwell was still pumping away insolently on the other side of the room, effortlessly completing the extra time. "Take him out for a beer," the master whispered to me. "I could have told you in the beginning you would lose."

I would have preferred to fight Rockwell Kent, Robert H., and anyone else who happened to be in the room. Sweat was running from my hair, my heart was hammering, my fists were clenched.

Rockwell swung himself from the door frame and loped good-naturedly across the floor towards me. "C'mon kid," he said, throwing his arm across my shoulders. "Let's get drunk."

I felt myself soften in response to the warmth of this gesture. An hour later, like everyone he ever met, I was convinced I would be devoted to him for life.

A disapprover, a ranter, a man whose responses were often unprovoked and always unrehearsed, Rockwell Kent was an entirely different kind of pontificator from my teacher. I believe he often surprised even himself with his reactions; the only thing predictable about him being the intensity of his passion. That day and on into the night we staggered from bar to bar – arm in arm eventually – singing socialist songs. He was tremendously excited by the developing revolution in Russia. "Want one just like it!" he would shout at me, slamming his fist on the table. "Here –" *thump*, "now –" *thump*. But he could be socially withdrawn as well and would talk about the remote corners of the world with great affection.

"Am going north," he confided as we swayed into what must have been our fourth bar. "No ridiculous people there. Hardly any people there at all. Some good women is all I need."

We collapsed into chairs near a corner table. "But you're married," I said.

He looked at me in astonishment. "Jesus Christ!" he exclaimed. "How young *are* you?"

He had just been banished from Newfoundland for singing German lieder from the porch of his rented house, which was perched on a cliff above the town of Brigus.

"Hounded us out," he told me. "Wife and kids and everything. The authorities marched up to the house and asked me if I had forgotten the war. They didn't believe me when I told them that unfortunately I had not forgotten the war, that I was, however, choosing to ignore it. Being authorities and therefore unable to envision how anyone could show a lack of interest in the petty differences of the conflict, they concluded that my singing was an attempt to communicate with German submarines. So they gave us the boot. Bastard imperialists! You've got to go farther north than that to get away from the bastard imperialists."

"I've been to Canada, actually," I said with pride. "To the north shore of Lake Ontario."

"Lots of bastard imperialists there," he announced. "The Royal Imperialist Mounted Cops, the Royal Imperialist Royal Mail, the Royal Imperialist Parliament, His Majesty's Royal Imperialist Opposition. Lots of imperialists and lots of opposition. You've got to head north, into the woods. . . . No, on to the tundra. None of those Royal assholes can handle the tundra. Freeze their balls off."

I was having trouble enunciating. "I think I am a landscape painter," I said slowly, experiencing for the first time the odd sensation of each word working its way out of my mouth.

"You think you're what?"

"A landscape painter," I repeated, but with less certainty.

"Jesus Christ!" Rockwell responded. "I have to keep a closer eye on old Robert, make sure he's not filling you kids up with too much crap. Love the guy, and he loves me too because he could never push me around. I drop by the class every now and then, just to check up on the old man, make sure he's not dishing it out too liberally."

I was shocked by this irreverence. "But you were his student," I said.

"Sure was!" he said, enthusiastically pounding the table. "But you'll never catch me painting any cherub-faced children."

I had by now completely lost track of the number of pints of beer we had consumed, and was beginning to feel ill.

"Do you see any landscape around here?" Rockwell was asking me. "How in Sam Hill can you be a landscape painter when you spend all your time in bars or in Robert's classes, listening to his fancy theories and learning how to cross-hatch?"

I wanted to protest, to say that, in fact, I had spent very little time in bars, but I found I could only articulate the sentence I had been practising a few moments before. "I still think I am a landscape painter," I slurred.

"So's your old man," taunted Rockwell.

This was hilarious. I howled with laughter as the room spun away from me. "No, he's not," I gasped. "He's certainly not a landscape painter. He's a capitalist!"

Then I leaned over and vomited in the corner behind my chair.

"This is a terrible predicament," said Rockwell after we had been thrown out of the bar.

"I'm sorry," I managed to mumble. I seemed to be walking through water. I was surprised that I could still breathe.

"Oh hell, you can throw up on me any time." He plucked me out of the path of an oncoming taxi. "The terrible predicament is that you're too drunk to walk and I'm too drunk to go home and face the wife. If this were the Far North, we'd die of exposure."

I vaguely recall that he guided me towards a park bench in Washington Square, fumbled around in a trash bin for a while until he found enough newspapers to cover both of us, threw some over me, then collapsed on an adjacent bench himself. By the time the morning sun brought the pain in my head to my attention, Rockwell was gone. I looked down and saw that he had pinned a crudely lettered sign on my jacket. "Do not disturb me," it read. "I am a landscape painter and my father is a capitalist."

If I close my eyes now, I can see that drunken boy, stretched like the corpse of a clown on a battered park bench, the words pinned to his jacket making a fitting epitaph. I can see this as clearly as I would have had I been Rockwell and not myself on that October morning. As it was, though, nothing in me that should have died did die, and I was as immune to the experience of the world after I recovered from the hangover as I had been before I met the man and drank the pints that caused it to happen. Yes, I had a new friend. I was impressed and delighted by him, and flattered by the fact that he had spent some time in my company. But I was capable of allowing myself to travel only a short distance with him. I was a pedestrian, after all, and he was driven by the engines of emotion, of desire, towards destinations that I, clinging to safe, rectangular spaces, could scarcely imagine.

Well, what I wanted from life was just a good view, wasn't it? A paintable view, a perfectly composed view, and, now and then, a perfect figure in a perfect landscape. Decade after decade I spent summers standing on the north shores of huge bodies of water, gazing towards the south with my back turned to a whole country full of forests. Once or twice I allowed Sara to take me into the greenish dark of the woodlands that stood behind Silver Islet and stretched, I imagine, almost all the way to Hudson's Bay, but the effect on me was a growing sense of claustrophobia and a desire for open space and light, while she thrust her face into the needles of the pines and inhaled the perfume.

Rockwell himself crashed into the woods in every conceivable way, travelling farther and farther north until he emerged, radiant, beyond the timberline, where everything, he said, was white and clear by day and where stars broke through the black like a shower of diamonds at night.

When he wasn't in Greenland, or Alaska, or Tierra del Fuego, and while I was still a student, we got drunk regularly, twice a month. He would appear at the door of the studio, say a few words to Robert H., and while they talked I would clean my brushes, reach for my coat. Before we stepped onto the street Rockwell would be in full flight, as if I, some kid, had stumbled into a conversation – an argument really – he was having with himself. There were few certainties. Many of his sentences began with the words "on the other hand" or "let's play the devil's advocate" as he proceeded to take apart one of his own intricately constructed theories. He was Jacob. His mind was the angel. The dance that resulted from this contest formed his character. There were only three issues about which his views never wavered: the hideousness of the war, the immorality of capitalism, and the spiritual superiority of the north.

I loved him unconditionally, even when he ignored me, preferring the conversation of the bartender or the labourer at the next table, even when he humiliated me by telling the bartender and the labourer that my father was a capitalist. On several occasions he abandoned me early on in order to go home with a woman who had caught his attention. And once he insisted, against my protestations and growing panic, that I go home with a woman to whom he had slipped a five-dollar bill.

When it was over I found Rockwell waiting at the bottom of the stairs. "It's about time," he said. "Next time you pay your own way. Now, let's hit the Lower East Side."

Later that night, he offered the only piece of advice he ever gave me. "Pay attention to women," he said.

I couldn't imagine that this was going to be a problem. I thought about sex constantly and, now that I had experienced the real thing, I feared I was going to be thinking of nothing else.

"I don't mean sex," he said. "I mean pay attention to how they move, what they look at, what they think about, what they say." He lit a cigarette and twisted in his chair, signalling to the waiter who appears in my memory now like a white ghost in a black apron. "I'm perfectly serious," he continued. "*Faites attention.* They are far superior to us and beautiful besides."

Four years later, when I was taken to Silver Islet by my capitalist father, I believed that I was following Rockwell's instructions when I began to paint Sara, a miner's daughter in a northern setting. I remember thinking how pleased he would be by the fortuitous combination of landscape, class, and gender.

And yet it was my paintings of Sara that caused the final break between Rockwell and me, years later.

But, that night, I still loved him unconditionally, loved him and all his contradictions. "Women are like forests," he said. "You can't just enter them, you must let them enter you as well. You must let their fluidity form one-third of your character."

I idolized this man, yet I couldn't help but suspect that what he was telling me was sentimental nonsense. It wouldn't be the first night that one or the other of us had become maudlin.

"Hey," he said, reading my mind. "This is the only piece of advice I'm ever going to give you. It's a gift. Take it."

Gifts didn't really interest the thief in me. That night, however, I had not yet grown to know myself, and I was young enough and drunk enough to be moved by sincerity.

"I'll take it," I said. "Thanks."

After the financial disaster of my father's attempt to reopen Silver Islet Mine, he lost interest in Canada altogether, sold the summer house in Davenport, and turned his attentions to the stock market and rebuilding his fortune. I, however, having discovered the gorgeous north shore of Lake Superior, returned each summer, lured by landscape and by Sara.

During the 1920s, on my way to Silver Islet, I would often stop for a few days in Toronto, and sometimes George would drive seventy-five miles west on the King's Highway Number Two and meet me there. I would take him out for dinner at the Royal York Hotel on Front Street, and we would ask each other polite questions about the previous year while we ate roast beef and Yorkshire pudding and drank some of the worst wine I have tasted anywhere at any time. I remember that during these clipped, formal encounters George would sit with his back to the wall and his eye on the door — a habit learned from years of shopkeeping. I was aware that we both felt displaced and uncomfortable, and eventually I decided that I wanted Davenport, the

China Hall, and the memory of the prewar summers to be part of our visits, so I would take the train from Toronto along the shore to the lakeside town and stay with my friend for two nights. I liked the atmosphere of the store, George in his apron, customers coming and going. Because we knew that interruption was always a possibility our conversations remained comfortably casual, never developing beyond what I considered to be an acceptable level of intimacy. In retrospect I see that the China Hall was home to me in a way that nowhere else had ever been. I knew which of the two stools behind the counter was mine, and where the scotch was hidden. I always slept exceptionally well in the dark formal bedroom that had once belonged to George's mother and father.

It was in the China Hall, during one of my traditional two-day stopovers in Davenport, that George first brought up the subject of Augusta Moffat, a young nurse he had met at the Number One Canadian Hospital in Étaples and had rediscovered when he returned to Canada. We had been talking about his parents, who had been dead for some time now having succumbed to the 1917 influenza while George was in France. He said that when he was informed of their deaths he could barely process the information. Surrounded as he was by corpses and ghosts and a daily life that had all but obliterated his childhood, it seemed only natural to him that they should be gone.

"I suppose I never really mourned them," he confessed. "I found the idea of them dying unmaimed, and in clean sheets, to be almost soothing."

He noticed I was looking at him oddly.

"You don't understand," he continued. "Often when we thought about ordinary household objects – a pillow, or a sofa, or a bathtub – they would seem like the greatest of luxuries. That was at the beginning when some of us still spent our time talking about what we would most appreciate when we got back – those of us who still believed that we would get back. We'd say that we'd want warm fresh bread, a down-filled quilt – that sort of thing. But finally, anything at all beyond the basics of just staying alive seemed frivolous, almost intrusive. By the last year of the war some of the fellows didn't even bother to unwrap parcels from home. We began to resent the fact that human beings had wasted their time inventing things such as automobiles and furniture with which to pamper themselves." He laughed. "Even clean underwear annoyed us, the whole idea of laundry."

I couldn't imagine laundry being on the minds of soldiers, one way or the other, and said so.

"It wasn't, of course," George answered. "Unless we went to hospital in a condition that would allow us to notice. That was the only place that any of us saw even a trace of cloth that was clean. I remember one man, one of the walking wounded, totally refusing to get into a bed because it was so pristine. It was almost as if he were afraid of it. Finally they had to give him a shot of something to make him lie down."

At this point, a man George knew walked into the store and was quite surprised when I insisted on waiting on him. He wanted some trinket for his mother's birthday. Because in the past he had always given her teacups, we decided on a porcelain thimble. George stood by and watched the proceedings with some amusement. After I had got the money safely into the cash register and the man had departed with his tiny parcel, George picked up where he had left off.

"With me," he said, "my most memorable moment in the hospital was when I first heard a woman's voice singing. It wouldn't have occurred to me that a nurse would do this. And then later, when I got back from the war, I found the singer herself, this nurse, Augusta Moffat. I was amazed that she was here in Davenport. I remembered her because she had sung to me, well, to all of us in the ward. Some of us even ended up singing with her."

George had not been seriously injured, he told me — a flesh wound in the thigh — so spent only a few days at the hospital before returning to the front. "I remembered how she just started quite suddenly to sing. It seemed absolutely extraordinary, magical, at the time, though later she told me that nurses were expected to serenade the patients."

"And then when I returned, there she was. Up the hill. At the asylum." He jerked his thumb over his shoulder towards the south. "It began, you know, as a hospital for shell-shock victims." George was painting a delicate tangle of wisteria on a vase as he said this, and his voice was oddly cheerful, following the lilt and curve of the vines.

I had walked by the asylum several times on my way to and from the station. It was a large white-stucco building, each floor of which was fronted by screened porches so that it resembled a huge rabbit hutch. Sometimes, beyond the screens, I had seen dark shadows pacing. Behind a high wrought-iron fence was a lawn that always remained a sad yellow colour, whether the season was dry or damp, and on it one or two thin cedar trees swayed in the breeze. No, I hadn't liked what I had seen of the asylum.

"So your friend was nursing there," I said, encouraging George to tell me more. This was the first time since Vivian that I'd heard him mention a woman.

He spun the turntable on which the vase sat, then brought it to a stop with a gentle touch of his right hand. "She wasn't nursing there," he said, without looking at me. "She was a patient for a month or so. Some of them are still there, you know, from the war, though now it caters more to the secular insane."

"But what on earth was she — what was a woman doing there?"

The look that George gave me seemed to suggest that this might have been the most foolish question he had ever been called upon to answer. "She was suffering from shell shock," he said.

George continued to speak as he carefully removed the vase from the turntable, returned it to the shelf, and began to clean his brushes in a small sink he had installed behind the counter for this purpose. "A group of us went in at Christmastime, car-olling, just after the end of the war. She seemed to respond to the music, though it was hard to tell for certain, and it was then that I remembered her from the ward in Étaples. Some time later she told me that she had sung in the Mendelssohn Choir when she was in training at the Toronto General Hospital, before she went overseas." He paused. "I was as surprised then as you are now to find a woman there."

"I had no idea that women suffered from shell shock."

"Just her." George leaned against his stool, folded his arms, and smiled at me. "Just her and a hundred damaged men. The ones who couldn't cope. With the war. In their condition . . . well. She wouldn't have been bothered by them anyway. They knew she had been a nurse, that she had been overseas, and they would have respected that. And the odd thing was, she wasn't beautiful then. It was her awakening, her . . . recovery that made her beautiful. After that she just shone."

"Well, I'm glad she recovered."

"Oh," said George, "so am I."

Years later Augusta would tell me about the Davenport hospital, about coming to know George. She would tell me about the war. I imagine she was a very good nurse; George, in fact, told me that she was, but said he wished she were involved in a less hazardous occupation. I thought he was referring to the war, hazardous enough for her as I eventually discovered, but it was another danger altogether that he had been referring to.

Augusta later told me she had been a patient only twice: once in the Davenport Hospital for Shell Shock Victims — a period in her life she barely remembered — and once, a few years later, when persistent throat infections necessitated a tonsillectomy.

I have said that I have never successfully used the stories Augusta told me in a painting, and I did not lie. But there was something about her description of this simple children's operation, performed in peacetime in the safety of a Toronto hospital, and the strangeness of the dreams it triggered that made me want to explore the narrative. And so, at the beginning of last year, I completed a major canvas entitled *The Lost Jane Eyre*, and it is now hanging in my gallery in New York City. The critics assumed that the subject of the underpainting dealt with the heroine of the famous book, and much scholarly nonsense was written about the search for and subsequent elimination of the feminine in my own psyche. Some of them even suggested that the painting was a statement about the repression, the eradication, of all that is feminine in society, and about everything that has been lost as a result of this. The truth is that I spent nearly six months painting a series of images that related to what Augusta had told me about the aftermath of her surgery, carefully building up texture with layer after layer of thick paint, then adding glazes of increasingly paler hues. Sometimes I painted images directly on top of other images in order to create an hallucinatory effect. In the end, it took many more glazes than anticipated to obscure the subject because the colours I used in the underpainting had been so extraordinarily vivid.

But the results were not totally successful, despite the positive critical reception of the picture and the price attached to it. Augusta's character — what I was to know of it — would not permit obviation. All this is true. But my own character will not permit me to stop trying, and beyond this is the fact that the subject of her fantasies and nightmares, during her illness, fascinated me. It fascinated the visual bandit in me.

As she struggled back from the black pool of the anesthetic after the operation, Augusta maintained that she had begun to have dreams – delusions perhaps – about a real little girl called Jane Eyre who had been lost for a few days in the woods near Davenport during the first decade of the nineteenth century. The name, of course, is famous now, but at the time of the actual incident, twenty years still had to pass before the Victorian novelist would lift her pen to write the celebrated book. But in Augusta's post-operative, drugged mind, the small child George had told her about – the story was a Davenport legend – and the young woman in the novel she had read fused, became one lost female spirit. Voices called the name "Jane" in Augusta's brain while she dreamed about a weeping little girl floundering across a barren moorland setting or, sometimes, through the thick virgin forests that had existed at the back of Davenport in the early 1800s. It seemed as if the child were trying to elude her rescuers. She had Augusta's face, her will. She wanted the heath, the woods, the isolation, and her seekers were like hounds. She had no voice, it had been ripped from her throat. The followers, Augusta knew, would force the child to commit the act of speech, and then there would be the pain of crying out. George was among the searchers, beating the brush with a stick. "Augusta!" he called. "Jane!" Nothing in the child, or in Augusta, wanted to answer. Her voice had been torn out.

Later during that same night, Augusta believed she was back in the Number One Canadian Hospital in Étaples; that it was the spring of 1918 and that broken soldiers were calling out in agony from the surrounding beds. The guilt in her was so terrible that she could not rise from her own bed to administer to them. She wondered if it was her friend Maggie's shift and if she would be able to cope all alone. Then the calling voices were, again, those of the search party, the vigilantes, the brush beaters, and Augusta was again a child being trailed, the branches of the forest tearing at her clothes and hair.

The next morning the delirium abated and the territory of Augusta's bed once more had become starched white sheets. Beside her lay a kidney-shaped basin into which she vomited stale blood.

George made the trip in from Davenport and appeared with flowers, but she could not speak to him. He held her hand and bathed her forehead with a damp cloth.

Augusta's nursing colleagues came in now and then to visit. One of them brought a stuffed toy because, as she said, Augusta had had the children's operation.

Augusta smiled, but she couldn't shake the memory of the lost little girl weeping, her voice gone, and the world demanding she return. The sun cascading through the window, the white teeth in her friends' smiles, hurt her throat. She remembered that George had kissed her neck and she believed, as she slipped into sleep, that by doing so he had increased the pain there.

By the third day her temperature was 103° and the aching in her throat was like the voice she had lost, apart from her and howling. The infection had reached her ears and the pain rang there. She was assaulted by inner sound. Doctor Truscott wavered at the end of the bed, flipping through her chart, his face rippling with displeasure. The child in Augusta's mind crashed through the undergrowth, her hands covering her ears, which were ringing with the noise of the world searching for her.

When George materialized again, flowers in his hands, the bowler hat on his head made him look like a vaudevillian comic. The child ran from his voice. She had lost a shoe; the going was difficult. Her skirt was in tatters, her breath laboured, but she wanted to be rid of George, rid of him. His voice was a scalpel tearing her throat, knives in her ears.

The first injection of the morphia, as they called it then, brought the world back so brutally, with such violence, that she seemed to ricochet off it as if someone had thrown her at a wall. George sat by the bed, his arm outstretched so that his hand was on her shoulder. "Augusta," he said, "look at me." But the room was so full of stable colour – so full of static furniture – that his breathing, his moving flesh could not hold her attention. Then, in an instant, both he and the furniture were gone, and the head of the child in Augusta's mind bobbed against the chest of a true, familiar, and benign rescuer. Maggie's remembered gift. A needle full of balm. She was exhausted, overcome. The pain, however, was far away, a creature in another part of the forest.

The child had been without her bonnet, George had told Augusta, had been wearing a blue plaid cotton frock. People in Augusta's life wore hats and dresses. Girls most often ran about bare-headed, boys sometimes wore caps. The girl had been not quite six years old.

Augusta told me that when she was six years old her primary passion, apart from the love of an orderly house, had been Sunday-school cards, those coloured lithographic depictions of

Adam and Eve being expelled from the garden, Daniel braving
the lions, a procession of animals entering the ark, David facing
Goliath, his sling ready. She had kept them hidden in a white
cardboard box at the back of her closet, added one to the stack
each Sunday afternoon when she and her family returned from
church. Sometimes there were meaningful landscapes – a desert,
a mountain, a garden. When all other activities were forbidden
on the Sabbath, Augusta could enter these, walk around in them.
Her eagerness to attend Sunday school was admired by her
parents, even to some extent by her brothers, but, she admitted
to me, it was really the coloured card given to each child for
attendance and punctuality that she was after, rather than the
hymns, the moral lectures.

Eventually, like the unmoving furniture of the hospital
room in which she lay, the story of lost Jane Eyre took on a static
visual quality for Augusta, its episodes reminding her of the
Bible cards, or of the stories told by the stained-glass windows
in her church.

Little Jane had been without her bonnet. I painted the forgotten or abandoned object as it must have loomed in Augusta's
mind; huge, an ominous flower dark against a pale-blue wall, two
ribbons reaching up towards the nail from which it hung.
Another picture was superimposed over this one. In it, the child
stood with her back to a blueberry picnic, her face directed
towards the dusky forest that held all her future lostness, antici-
pation visible in every muscle of her miniature body. This, I
decided, was the moment when the small girl from the early nineteenth century and the woman in the hospital bed a hundred
years later would have joined, would have taken a position from

which they would never waver. They were going to be lost, missing, irreclaimable.

Augusta said that when she was feverish, or when, at the beginning of a four-hour period, the morphia was fresh in her bloodstream, the pale-green hospital walls broke into her concentration concerning the child. But after a day or two of this, she learned that by changing her position in the bed and closing her eyes she could fight her way back to the story.

She believed that at night the little girl would take shelter beneath a rocky overhang. Heather would spill in all directions away from this place where she crouched. But there was no heather in the forest. The child hugged a pine tree, pressed her cheek into rough bark. A curtain of rain fell over her – how lost she was, how dispossessed – her blue plaid frock darkened and clung.

There was a photograph somewhere of this Canadian Jane Eyre as an older woman. George had seen it. She was a distant relative of his, by marriage, and he told Augusta he believed he had met her once when he was very young, at a funeral, he thought, or some other occasion when fruitcake was being passed around. She was an old woman. Had she read the novel? Augusta wondered aloud. George thought not, they were not a novel-reading kind of family, though, oddly, in the photograph Jane had been holding a book. The Bible, more than likely. The others with her – probably her sisters – were holding china cups and saucers, and there was a teapot and a cream jug on the table they were gathered around. All of them would have been middle-aged women with names changed by marriage. The china appeared to be Limoges and George wondered what became of it. It was the china that made the picture remain in his memory.

"Was there a lost quality about the old woman?" Augusta had asked once, when the morphia had made her able to speak.

"Not in the photo," George had replied. "She looked very solid, matronly."

I painted the fields and then the dark edge where the fields stopped and the forest began. Even when Augusta was a child, each Ontario town and village was likely to be near a forest — a forest where it was possible for a child to get lost. In spring, before the leaves thickened, you could see trilliums glowing like stars deep in the woods. Boys often claimed to have spent long hours surrounded by trees. Girls would rarely bother with the forest.

What lured this child into the riot of disordered growth that the virgin forest must have been at that time? For most of her then-short life the trees would have been a black or green smear in the distance, an army that the men of the community were constantly pushing back. As the child drew nearer the woods, there might have been a dark and light pattern that attracted her. After all, inside a forest, as Sara showed me, light is more tangible, more distinct, a foreign element fighting for space. Perhaps Jane went into the forest to touch the light and found herself, ironically, surrounded by darkness. For Augusta, dreaming, drugged, this would have been an attractive, disturbing possibility. She would try to sort through the contradictions in this as the pain worsened. Augusta, turning on her side and looking out over the Toronto chimneys from the hospital window, would have thought about this, about her own snow house near the cedar bush of her own childhood. Often as the afternoon progressed, the pain in her throat returned and she longed for the four o'clock needle.

Once, years later, I found myself painting the four o'clock needle onto a canvas, but I scraped it off before it was finished, wanting not even the suggestion of its shape.

The first forested night, the child had seen a tree cracked open by lightning, or so she had said when she was rescued, and she had known then that this one blasted pine was all hers. She had slept near it on damp ground. She claimed that a large black dog had come and curled up at her back, keeping her warm until dawn. Augusta knew this black dog was exhaustion, followed by sleep, warm and panting. In the morning the animal had fled. The girl climbed the broken tree and saw women in white fanning out through a distant part of the forest. Searching for her. She tried to call, but her voice was gone. She remembered no words and even an attempt to remember caused the knife in her throat to twist.

On her second night in the woods, the child had slept in the fork the lightning had made in the tree. The dog leapt up beside her, she would later insist, appearing just as night fell. It was

June and everything was in full leaf so she would have had no awe-inspiring view of stars and sky. She had eaten nothing for thirty-six hours. Her hands and face were swollen with insect bites. Earlier in the day she had dipped her hands into a pool of stagnant water and, when she pulled them out, her wrists had been braceletted by leeches.

These would have merely caused small Jane Eyre some curiosity, though she would have been frightened by the blood that appeared when she pulled them from her skin.

Augusta confessed to me that she hadn't wanted to be a nurse, but it was preferable to being a teacher of unruly boys like her brothers, or a stenographer in a dull man's office — seemingly her only other alternatives. She said this in the China Hall decades after the war and years after her reintroduction, in a drab Toronto hospital, to the morphia. If she hadn't been a nurse, she would never have gone overseas. She would never have met George. She and Maggie would never have walked in their grey-blue uniforms across the sand dunes at Étaples. Maggie, her friend, had chosen the profession because of a love of healing, because of a belief that almost anything could be fixed. Each night in the Toronto hospital, Maggie walked into Augusta's dreams. "This will fix it," she would say, her voice soft, soothing, the needle sparkling at the end of her hand.

Augusta had tried to talk to George about all of this when he visited her late one afternoon. "That war," she had said weakly. "If that war hadn't happened, or if I'd decided to become a stenographer, we would never have met and I would never have met Maggie. I keep dreaming about her all the time." She was not aware that she was weeping.

George patted her hand sympathetically, but he appeared odd to her, almost like a dull businessman whose stenographer she might have been.

He looked at her with great fondness. "You are better today," he said.

"I'm better now. It was hell earlier." Augusta recalled the vividness of her fantasy concerning the lost girl, the wet branches of the forest.

"I'll have to be in the shop tomorrow," George said, "but I'll be back on the early train next Saturday. By then —"

"By then I may be dead."

"You're not going to die, Augusta."

"I'm a nurse," she snapped. "I know who is dying and who isn't."

"You're not dying. You've had a rough go of it, but you're not dying."

I remember how my contemporaries hated the narrative in visual art. It was, according to them, the primrose path towards either genre painting or illustration and should be avoided, utterly. No fresco cycle, no nineteenth-century history painting could convince them otherwise. They scoffed at Giotto, Géricault, David, Goya, Ingres. The knowledge that I spent months painting the tale of the lost Jane Eyre would have greatly perplexed them.

What would they have made then of the two or three weeks when I attempted to submerge its details, its form?

After George left the room that day, as evening approached and the drug was beginning to wear off, the static pictures returned to Augusta. The child with flies covering her face. The child with a necklace of leeches causing the pain in her throat. Then, after the evening injection, images broke into narrative. It was the third day and the little girl had suddenly become pure, clear. Her muddy blue frock was gone and replaced by a bluish-grey garment. Her skin began to resemble a beautiful white fog. The white women were fanning out, away from her. They appeared to be emerging from her own body, their skirts and white aprons rippling in the breeze. The child stood in the groin of the charred tree as if she were fireweed, as if she had grown there. In the distance were the whistles, the ringing bells of the search party, but closer, more intimate – more familiar now – was the bird song and the rustling of small animals in the trees.

Augusta became completely convinced that Maggie was the night nurse, convinced that Maggie took the needle from her own arm with great tenderness to share it with her best friend. Long dark trains filled with the wounded were on the way, she said. Without the drug they would not have the strength for the agonizing work of the next few days. They wouldn't have the strength or the courage to fix things, to make them better. Augusta and this girl – this best friend who stood by her bed, this lost child – they all wore the same blue-grey garments. They all entered the same forests, shared the comfort of the needle, understood each other.

In the underpainting, there were three lost grey children dissolving into the organic matter surrounding them. They were all clothed alike, though the greyness of their skirts varied at times from manganese violet to graphite. Three separate children — but as I worked on the subsequent layers of the picture, they began to cancel one another out.

Lying on her back Augusta would feel the morphia enter her bloodstream. She would close her eyes, spread her fingers fanlike on the starched sheet. The room would close down and the forest would open up all around her. Maggie would summon the white women to lure the seekers into another part of the woods so that there would never be a miraculous recovery.

Small Jane Eyre, you understand, could have followed any creek, any stream in the vicinity towards Lake Ontario, towards Davenport and safety. But some lost girls never attempt to return. The dark dog of sleep comes to lie beside them and they embrace him, keep him close to their hearts. Then, if any other kind of rescuer appears, the loyal animal bites the stranger's outstretched hand.

All day long I've been thinking about Sara's empty house, thinking about it as she undoubtedly knew that I would. I thought about it while I worked on the collection – I added a Staffordshire sheep today – I thought about it while I worked on the current painting, which is to be called *Sleeping in the Park*. I do not really dwell on the fact of the log structure's emptiness. Instead, I find I can't keep from visualizing the *countenance* of its emptiness.

This morning I was awakened by the sound of the garbage truck, the squealing of its brakes as it stopped to take away my meagre leavings: a few orange peels, an empty wine bottle, some bread crusts. Mrs. Boyle nags me constantly about the amount I eat; eats like a horse herself if I am to judge by her size. She is forever trying to push more groceries into my already over-stocked shelves and more food into my uninterested stomach. But what is the point of nourishment when of necessity it creates so much clutter? My questionable works of art, and the collection, both in their varying stages of completion, are disturbing enough when I face them each morning. Do I need the added complication of packages on shelves?

The log house, I'm certain, is still fully furnished with all the objects I know so well. Oh, how easy it is for all of it to manifest itself in my visual memory. I rendered every inch of the place, after all, with my well-sharpened graphite pencil. Now I can see the interior in the bright winter light, each item unwarmed by recent contact with skin. I can see the unlit windows of the house, dark enough to reflect stars at night. I can see the white blanket of the lake mirrored in these windows in the morning, and unwitnessed blocks of light moving through the rooms. Dust accumulating on abandoned furniture. Untouched clothing hanging from hooks. Water frozen in the kettle on the cold woodstove. Ashes in the grate.

This is what I have so effortlessly inherited; this cold, this dark, this emptiness. It is odd how vacancy becomes a kind of presence, how it becomes tangible, real.

It is what I live with now, this vacancy. I am full of emptiness.

There were things that Sara didn't tell me.

I was always startled by the discovery of this, not angered, really, but surprised because she had opened every drawer, every cupboard of her house to my dispassionate scrutiny, to the crazy inventory I was making in my sketchbooks. She often spoke of her small flower garden — something of a miracle in that terrain — and when I asked her how she managed it, she showed me her rakes and pruning sheers and spades and explained how she had placed used tea leaves all over the soil as a kind of fertilizer. Then she took me outside to observe while she staked tomato plants, as it was the time of year to do this. The garden had originally been her father's, and Sara said that it had been a great joy to him — this small, dense patch of colour — after the ebony dark of his workplace, on the one hand, and the relentless white of the winters there, on the other. I made a small drawing of Sara working in the garden, and another, a still life of spades and rakes and pots.

She never denied me anything, not one thing, ever. And God knows I took whatever was offered, and more. But there were certain things she didn't tell me.

I had begun to teach at The Art Students' League and my schedule one year — sometime in the late 1920s or early 1930s — did not allow me to leave New York until late June and would have, therefore, cut short the three full months I normally spent in the north. I have always been irritated by changes such as these, and so, to allow myself the usual amount of time for painting and because I hadn't intended to teach the following autumn, I decided to stay at Silver Islet until the end of September. Monsieur et Madame Bougereau, the couple who owned the hotel, were pleased with my decision. They rarely had guests who stayed for more than a week or two after the end of August and they were happy to extend the season. They were good people, had been particularly kind to Sara since her father's death, treating her not just as an employee but almost as a member of the family.

They must have been dead now for years.

I had tried to keep everything constant in my relations with Sara, tried to keep the emotional level calm and unfluctuating so that I could slip as smoothly as possible in and out of her life. I would not allow her, for instance, to come to the dock when I boarded the ferry at summer's end. Quiet appearance and disappearance were specialities of mine; I wanted no sentimental attention paid to either. For the most part I believed I had been successful, that each separation was without reverberations, that I had kept feeling behind the fence of my own selfish practicality. I cannot for the life of me think what it was that made me so certain that by controlling my own responses I could control Sara's as well. Her beautiful strength, perhaps, which I took entirely for granted and which, in my ignorance, I may have confused with a lack of vulnerability. Yes, that may have been it.

All those summers run together in my memory now, become one long summer. But because, one year, I stayed on into the autumn, because I altered the pattern, I recall the time with striking clarity, as if Sara were some other woman altogether and Silver Islet Landing some other place.

At the end of August, boatload after boatload of seasonal people departed, scarcely looking back at the summer shore, their faces turned towards the grain elevators of Port Arthur, towards schools and industries, brick houses and winter. This exodus was followed by several days of gale-force winds, rain, and crashing breakers. At one point the waves were so high and so energetic they hurled themselves over the lane I walked each day to Sara's house. I was unnerved by this, as unnerved as I had been by the brief, fierce storms of earlier in the summer that had swung in from the centre of the lake. But even they didn't have the insistency of this kind of equinoctial front that pounded the land and refused to pass on.

Still, it moved me, this wildness, and so I drew Sara standing by windows, looking out towards the frantic lake, the hectic sky. I drew her stillness in the face of torn clouds and rain — I wanted that contrast. Also, I was attracted by the muted light that comes into a room when the sun is buried under blankets of heavy clouds, the soft-blue tinge it lends to the skin. Two of my best canvases developed from my drawings of this period.

In the first, Sara's shoulders are draped with a light shawl and her face is turned away from the window, the furious lake. One hand reaches towards the opposite shoulder, and the other clutches the shawl over her breasts. In the second painting, she stands naked in the centre of the window that occupies the full canvas. Her arms are outstretched and her hands grasp the edges of the window frame. She is viewed from the back, her hair is twisted into a bun; each small knot of vertebra in her neck is visible. The backs of her knees shine, the muscles of her calves are clenched and firm so that she looks as if she were about to leap from the window into the angry lake.

It was not an easy pose for Sara — for anyone — to hold. She had to stand on her toes to make the muscles in her legs tighten and her arms were raised above the level of her heart, so we rested at twenty-minute intervals. The whole process, my drawing, the breaks in between, took us through the several days of the storm.

Sara brought food upstairs at noon on the second day, and we picnicked like gypsies on her father's iron cot. When we had finished I lifted the flannel nightgown she had hastily thrown over her and began to caress the legs, the body I had been so carefully rendering, pulling first one, then the other ankle towards me so that the limbs would straighten. I removed my own clothes and lay on top of her, stretching her arms out from her sides by grasping her wrists and finally, because my arms were longer, pushing the heels of my hands into her palms. After I had entered her, I clamped her legs shut with my knees, making sure every inch of her body was covered with my own, making sure she was immobile. I held her head still with the pressure of my mouth on hers, the weight of my torso making it impossible for her to arch her back. I couldn't see her at all. The only part of her body that was moving was her heart, hammering against her ribcage.

I had never before made love to her in September.

Later in the day she stood behind me and looked over my shoulder at the drawing I had been working on all afternoon. She pointed to the straight lines with which I had formed the intersecting mullions of the window and which were, at that stage, still visible through the body despite the tension of the pose.

"A cross," she murmured. "You've crucified me."

She wasn't touching me, yet I could feel the heat of her body on my back. I laughed out loud but did not turn to look at her. "That wasn't what I intended," I said. I wasn't even looking at the window by then. Instead, I was attempting to capture, as I might have with one of Mr. Eastman's Brownie cameras, the frenetic patterns of the water beyond the window as it was defined by the wind.

The next day the storm had finally worn itself out. The sky was a piercing shade of blue, and not a tree, not a leaf was moving. But the upheaval in the lake, the thunderous noise, was worse than ever; the water inkier, the whitecaps whiter. Spray shot up from the edges of offshore islands, including the one whose rumoured silver had brought my father and, indirectly, me to this spot. My rooms at the back of the hotel, rooms that faced the lake, were moist and uncomfortable. All night long the roar of the water and the dampness of my surroundings had me believe that the frame building might be cast adrift, and ship-wrecks had figured in my dreams.

In the middle of the morning – there was sunlight now, coaxing an impression of pastel colours from under her skin – Sara leaned her forehead against the glass of the window and said, "I can't do this. . . . I can't stand here any more."

I put my brush down on the ledge of the easel. "All right, we'll take a break then," I said, though nothing in me wanted to stop.

"No, it's not that. . . ." she said. "I can't look at the lake any more. I can't bear it."

I stared silently at her familiar back. I never thought about what Sara would be doing while she was posing. I was interested in anything that belonged to her in the immediate vicinity, felt that knowledge of the objects around her would enrich my drawings and paintings. But while I was working I believed that the gesture I had prescribed was absolute; her pose, my line, the contour of her shoulder working its way into the composition on the page. I believed that I was drawing – deliberately drawing – everything out of her, that this act of making art filled the space around me so completely there would be no other impressions possible beyond the impressions I controlled.

Three full days of staring at a seething lake, larger and wilder than some oceans, a man seated behind you concentrating on the seventh vertebra of your spine or the blue veins at the back of your knees, the dispassionate scratch of the pencil reproducing the creases in your flesh. What did I know of that? It would be years before I could admit that although I wanted every detail of her in my painting – her body, her ancestry, her landscape, her house – wanted the kind of intimacy that involved not just the rendering of her physical being but also the smell of her skin and hair, the way she moved around her kitchen, the sounds at the back of her throat when she made love, I would have preferred not to have been known by her at all.

But, at that stage, my motives were pure, uncomplicated. I was interested in anything that would enhance the quality of my work and oblivious to all manner of things that I felt didn't or couldn't.

"What is it about the lake you can't bear?" I asked her quite gently, careful not to let the irritation I felt at the disruption enter the tone of my voice. I needed at least two more hours.

"I've looked at it for too long," she said, still not turning towards me, still not turning away from the window. "I'm beginning to despise it."

I said nothing. I waited.

"I used to love it . . . but all these hours of looking at it. I've turned against it." Her forehead touched the glass again, the back of her neck gleamed. She had crossed her arms over her breasts. By concentrating on these things I was able to pass over the terrible sadness in her voice. "I think of you," she whispered, "looking at me, hour after hour, day after day, coming to despise me."

"No," I said.

"Coming to despise me more than you know."

"That's nonsense," I said.

"You are always on the other side of the room. There is always this gap between us."

The light had already begun to change. I squinted at the oil sketch in front of me. There might be enough there for me to work with in the studio once I returned to New York. But, perhaps not.

Sara's reaction to the lake might have interested me if she had not brought it directly to my attention, had I been able to discern it without her knowledge. Otherwise, it was simply an imposition. In my vanity, I wanted to choose my own subjects. I remember Robert H. had quoted Corot as saying that art was nature seen through a temperament. I believed him, I believed that. I had my own temperament. I didn't want it interfered with. I was at times interested in other views of the world, but only when they satisfied my own artistic curiosity.

"You need a rest," I announced. "We'll go for a walk."

She was dressing in a corner of the room. I walked over to the window and stared at the lake that had so disturbed her. I always turned my back whenever she dressed or undressed. I had been carefully taught, you see, to respect the model's privacy.

We walked that day away from the lake, taking paths Sara had known since childhood, into the woods of The Sleeping Giant, the man mountain, the Sibley Peninsula. We followed swift-moving shining streams that Sara referred to, poetically, as the veins of the slumbering Gargantua. She had read more books than I had. Her father had loved poetry: there were, and probably still are, old editions of Byron and Shelley in the log house. And then there was the public library in Port Arthur. Requested volumes could be sent over by steamer in the summer, dog team in the winter.

"There is more than one way to visit the body of a man," she said.

I thought the allusion was sexual, until she told me of the Ojibway legend that claimed that the whole twenty miles of the human-shaped peninsula was the warrior Nanibijou, whose body had been turned to stone after he revealed to the European acquisitors the location of the sacred silver.

She told me the names of the various trees, laying her hand flat against the bark as she spoke. She identified plants. She said that her Cornish father had taught her how to do this. Denied access to it for much of his life, because of his work in the mine, he had developed a passion for the surface of the earth and had taken his daughter walking far into the woods on Sundays, even when the snow was deep. Sara could not remember a time when she had not known how to walk through the woods on snow-shoes or how to glide over the frozen lake on skis.

The pines were straight and tall and thick. Sara wanted me to look up to admire their great height, but, captured by my own temperament, I barely raised my eyes. I preferred the visual to be a private experience.

I tramped along sullenly behind her. At one point she spun around and faced me on the path, real anger in her eyes. "Why don't you ever say anything?" she demanded. "Tell me what you're looking at, what you're listening to."

"It's not in my nature to say anything," I replied testily. A battalion of mosquitoes was circling my head. I wanted to be back inside the stillness of the room, shading the curve of her hip with my pencil.

"Is it in your nature to feel anything, I sometimes wonder?"

"What is this all about?" I asked. "Of course I can feel things. I get angry. I get hurt. I'm an artist, for Christ's sake, I feel things all the time, and I'm beginning to feel angry now."

"You feel things privately."

"Yes, privately. What's the matter with that? I'm not going to spend my life burdening other people with my emotions."

"I am talking about feelings . . . not some fit of anger, some temper tantrum."

"Anger is a feeling."

"You know very well there's a difference."

Yes, I knew very well there was a difference. Sara was searching the map of my character for the place where my heart was
hidden, but I was so busy guarding the site I failed to notice there
were no weapons in the hands of the woman who approached it.

We returned to the Landing in silence and then we parted at the
wharf. I stood facing the water for a full hour, watching the lake
gradually calm and playing my teacher's final statement on the
character of the artist over and over in my mind.

"The wise draughtsman brings forward only that which he
can use most effectively to present his case," Robert H. had said.
And isolates whatever he brings forward, I thought, as I turned
away from the view for just a moment to watch Sara's lone figure
move down the edge of the shore towards her house.

That night the temperature fell dramatically. The next day
the whole world had changed colour.

—◇—

The north-shore birch is a discreet tree in most seasons. In
winter, Sara told me, it practically disappears, having lost its
leaves and exposed its branches, which are almost as pale as the
surrounding snow. In summer its soft-green foliage blends easily
into the darker greens of the pines. But in the fall, as I discovered
that year, it dominates whatever region it occupies.

I awoke the morning after our walk in the forest to thousands
of bright golden leaves, a season quite unlike the multicoloured

autumns I was familiar with in upstate New York. It caught me off guard. I was not in any way prepared for it. There were several birches in the vicinity of Sara's house, and I wondered how this radical change of tone would affect the indoor light. Walking down the shore road the water was darker — almost vine black — the sky cerulean blue, the pines cobalt green in the face of this brilliance. Beside the log wall of Sara's house the red berries of a mountain ash looked exotic, tropical, out of place.

She was reading on the sofa near the open parlour window. At her feet lay an orange mass I couldn't at first identify. Then a small, intense face looked directly into mine for a fraction of a second before the animal leapt over the window sill and disappeared into the trees.

"A fox," I said, stunned.

She looked up from her book calmly. "Yes," she said.

"A fox in your house," I said stupidly. There was something shocking to me about the wild having come inside these walls, walls that I believed were meant to keep the wild out.

"He always comes," she said, "when the trees turn."

I kept looking out the window through which the fox had disappeared.

"Well, for the last five years or so," Sara continued. "He comes when the trees turn and after the summer people leave. You've never been here to see him before. He waits until the summer people are gone, then he comes in the morning for something to eat. Sometimes he stays all morning. Often we'll go for a walk."

"A walk. You and the fox go for a walk."

"Yes, like the one you and I took yesterday. He probably saw us, but he wouldn't have come near because of you. Sometimes in the winter he comes at night, particularly if there is a moon. Occasionally he sleeps at the end of my bed."

"You never told me." I had known this woman for years at this point, and yet I had not sensed in her the ability to tame something wild.

I realized I had never really pictured this place in the winter. I had never even thought about the lake, a birch tree, this log house, with ice and snow surrounding it, a fox in the moonlight trotting silently towards Sara's lit windows. "How is it possible that you tamed a fox?" I asked.

"He is not tame." Sara closed the book, placed it on the table beside the sofa. Then she sat up and regarded me with that steady, frank look that so often preceded something significant that she wanted to say. Something she wanted me to pay particular attention to. I did not meet her gaze for longer than a split second, looked instead at the table, the book she held on her lap. She was reading Anthony Trollope. "It is not necessary to tame a creature to love it," she said. "To have it love you."

I took Sara that morning to her father's room and posed her near the east window, where both the yellow birch trees and the scarlet berries of the mountain ash were visible through the glass. There was no noise at all from the lake now. Golden light shone through the quivering leaves, entered the room, warmed her skin.

She watched as I mixed together some cadmium orange and cadmium yellow, two of the most intense colours on earth. I was working on a small canvas. Watercolour would never have been able to mirror the heat of those colours, the gold of her skin.

"Don't put the fox in the painting," she said.

"I've never painted animals. You know that."

"He doesn't belong to you." She shifted in the chair, changing the pose slightly. "You never would have seen him at all if you hadn't stayed."

Unlike Rockwell, who was always trying to shed the city – in spite of his love for it – always trying to shed it so that he could disappear into weather and open country, Robert Henri spoke infrequently about landscape.

But when he did, he talked about its "motive," how it arranged itself in the visual imagination of the artist. He wanted everything on the picture plane to be expression or idea: the impenetrability of rock, the flexibility of wood and leaf. He told us never to paint informationally, as if we were saying, "There is a hill; here is a sunset." He wanted to get past the hill, the sky, to be rid of them, to leave an atmosphere or an idea, or both, in the scene's place, wanted all the freight carried in the mind of the artist exposed.

In the end, we painted ourselves over and over.

How we loved him, loved the way he led us to believe in the brilliance of our own singular eye, as if we were the models and the subject were painting us. He was honestly convinced, I think, that the whole purpose of daylight was to reveal a world capable of calling forth an acceptable response from his pupils. This relationship, this sense that the artist owns, controls, and is therefore free to manipulate any subject — animate or inanimate — any subject that has, however casually, caught his attention, was the centrepiece of his philosophy.

And yet he demanded an utterly detailed knowledge of the subject. He said he loathed the fact that landscape lent itself so easily to the sentimental, the picturesque, but, essentially, it was too large for the cold intimacy he required. "I would rather see a wonderful little child than the Grand Canyon," he would often announce. The truth is — it has taken me all these years to see it — the truth is that neither Robert nor any of the rest of us could manipulate the Grand Canyon. It refused to become intimate with us, to mirror our souls, to encourage our vanity.

And what became of us all, the children that he fathered? Eventually, we staggered out of his New York studios, away from his models and still lifes. Some went to paint the streets, the tenements and factories, some migrated upstate to paint grim houses and cold fields, and a few, like myself, were drawn to the northern wilderness, despite our teacher's warnings about landscape, wanting in our egocentricity to test our powers on the least responsive subject of all.

There was a great fashion among artists in the early decades of the century for groups and organizations — the New York Eight, the Whitney Club, The Art Students' League, the Canadian Group of Seven, and the like — so it was not unusual for three or four or even more men to go off together to the sea or the forest to paint in the summer. But I was never comfortable in a collective, having allowed the eye/I of Robert H.'s teaching to establish itself in my head and heart. I wanted no interference from the confusing vision of others. Jealously hoarding my own experiences, the intimacy I courted became an invasion, almost a form of rape. I absorbed everything I could, used it in my art, but gave nothing of myself in return.

But I never lost sight of the notion that an artist must never let technique move beyond the edges of his peripheral vision, regardless of whatever else might concern him at the time. Like viewing one's own fortified village from a valley during the Middle Ages, the gorgeous green of the grass, the deep, engrossing colour of the flowers, clouds throwing shadows on the opposite hillside, the possibility of unicorns: all this should attract and delight. But one must keep the village, the walls, and gates — the structure, the method — all of the protection and shelter in view, otherwise one will not get back before dark, before the invading armies appear on the horizon. One may venture out into the valleys, out into colour and texture, but the truth is, the fortified village is where one really lives.

Nowadays it is fashionable to refer to what a painting is "about." Although I dislike the term, and firmly believe I am no follower of fashion, I would have to say that the paintings I have produced over the period of the last decade or so are "about" both revelation and obscuration. This has presented me with some problems. I need to have made a realistic rendering of the details of the subject, otherwise the whole process would be fraudulent for the simple reason that in order to be obscured these images need to have existed in the first place. And not just in my own mind. My own memory. I wanted to concretize the images, turn them into the kind of physical realities that occupy space and suggest depth – however illusory. Then I wanted the physical reality veiled.

This was not a simple task. It wasn't long before I discovered that the underpainting – the original scene – was going to be at least as crucial as the overpainting, not only intellectually but also visually since I had decided that carefully chosen parts of its line, form, and composition were to be faintly visible in the completed painting. I was plagued for months, however, by premonitions of pentimenti: those ghosts of formerly rendered shapes that the artist had intended to paint out forever. In the future, I feared, they would rise to the surfaces of my pictures like drowned corpses, bloated and obscene, regardless of glazes or the number of layers of zinc white, titanium white, and lead white I applied to the canvases.

This nagged me while I was finishing the underpainting, made me wary of intensity; even though I was convinced that certain scenes demanded to be painted in bright pigments. Also there were several night views that I wanted to include that would have necessitated the use of lamp black, charcoal black, umbers and ochres, all reliable permanent colours and therefore difficult to cover up. The more fugitive colours, ultramarines and cadmiums, brought with them their own set of problems: chemical changes, fading, darkening – all potentially capable of affecting the surface above.

When I was a boy there was only one painting in our house. It had been done by a great-aunt on my father's side and depicted two dogs lying near a hill on which a rosebush flourished. My mother allowed it, I think, because it was so primitively drawn that it resembled very little the fixed images of the photographs of which she was so suspicious. I, on the other hand, was quite afraid of it, being able to discern a third dog — a dark ghost — emerging from the hill. I knew the dog wasn't meant to be there, that he was a mistake, and that I shouldn't be able to see him at all. I knew that the woman who had painted this ominous beast had been dead for a long, long time, and it seemed to me that her dead hand was attempting to change the painting before my very eyes. I wasn't certain whether other people could see the third dog, and was afraid to ask them if they could, didn't want to confirm my suspicion that this evidence of an ill-considered action from the past was meant for my instruction alone. What I dreaded more than anything was the possibility that one day I might awaken to find the concealed dog utterly visible on the canvas, his fur sleek, his eyes shining.

A few years ago, I finally put my fears concerning pentimenti almost to rest by devising a technique that I hope will be fool-proof. Once the underpainting has been completed in great detail, and is fully dry, I make what I call a "colour diary" of the work on a long piece of paper. This comprises a series of small squares beginning with the colour of the most intensity and ending with the colour of the least intensity. Then I pin this on the wall beside the painting and apply a thin glaze of the most intense colour to the entire canvas. When that layer is perfectly dry, I repeat the process with the colour of next greatest inten-sity, allow it to dry, and begin again, over and over, until I have reached the colour of least intensity. All of this takes a great deal of time, which explains why I can complete only four or five of these pieces in any given year.

During the long stretches when the various layers are drying, I add china objects to the collection and then catalogue them in the notebooks I keep for this purpose. I like to include a drawing of the piece as well as a few paragraphs concerning what I have learned about its manufacturer, the particular china painter (where applicable), the period, date, and so on. I enjoy drawing the designs on the pieces, then filling them in with watercolour. It makes me feel like a child.

Sometimes in the evening, when I am too tired to work, the grief, the remorse comes so close to me that I feel I could reach out and touch it with my hand, and then it's almost more than I can bear. But mostly I am kept quite busy, what with cataloguing, underpainting, the collection, and my walks. Every so often my dealer calls from New York to tell me that a critic from some art magazine or another wants to interview me about my work. I always decline, using my advanced age, my feebleness as an excuse. The truth is, however, with the exception of stiffness and ill temper, I'm in perfectly good health, despite the fact that all this tidying up, this assembling and cataloguing, this burying under layers of paint seems like a preparation for my own death.

It was a critic who came up with the term "erasure" when I first exhibited the series. There is nothing, you understand, like an obscured subject to give the critics something to talk about. Even those who had been either indifferent or hostile to my work in the past wrote long, reflective essays about the hidden subject matter that, under the circumstances, they were forced mostly to imagine. This led to some interesting fantasies. Some of the others ignored titles such as *The Sawhorse* or *The Lost Jane Eyre* or *Night in the China Hall* and refused to speculate about what was underneath the various layers. They wrote, instead, about the "act" of erasure; about absence, vacancy, abandonment. One or two of the men wrote about annihilation, about my decision to eliminate the object in my paintings, how this, in their opinion, would eventually lead to discarding the "art object" altogether and how my intentions had been "active" rather than "passive." Not one of them, however, not one, had a word to say about the casting off of despair, about catharsis, anesthetic.

I was as amazed by this as I was by the fact that anyone had paid attention at all, though, after all these years in the art world, absolutely nothing should surprise me. But I was surprised by this, then doubly amazed when collectors opened their cheque-books. Couldn't they see? Didn't they know they were carrying home a rectangle of sorrow? Couldn't they understand that grief itself would now be proudly displayed, hanging on their otherwise smooth living-room walls?

━━━━◦◦◦◦━━━━

I added a particular prize — a piece of great rarity and beauty — to the collection this morning. From where I sit at this desk I can see it shining on the shelf across the room, and were I to turn to look at the window behind me, I would likely see it shining there as well. So bright it is, so rich in colour. It is a Sèvres dessert plate from the Services des Petits Métiers, which was painted in the middle of the last century by a man called

Suchet, a pupil of the great Develly. Earlier, Develly himself had painted a dessert service of more than one hundred pieces representing each of the industrial arts and crafts of France. George had told me about these with great enthusiasm, having seen the drawings for them when he visited Sèvres while on leave during the war.

The few times he was able to visit the Manufacture de Porcelaine, George had looked at pattern book after pattern book full of the kind of watercolours I attempt to make when I want to feel like a child. He was always delighted by the quality of the seventeenth- and eighteenth-century paper and by the permanence of the colour of the paint. He loved these small coloured drawings, he said, because they were so pristine and so fresh that he could almost see the hand that had held the brush centuries before. And once, he maintained that, sensing a presence near his left shoulder, he had involuntarily swung around, believing for a split second that the long-dead painter of china was standing behind him in the room.

I remember the pleasure he took in speaking to me one morning in the China Hall about the idea of the Develly series; how it had celebrated the most minor of the arts, the most minor craftsmen. Wallpaper painters, artificial-flower makers, jewellers, hatters, and all the skilled workers who produced the great porcelain at Sèvres. He told me that it seemed to him that Develly loved his own life, and the life that moved around him, so passionately that each piece became a hymn of praise concerning the sanctity of labour. No task, no worker was so small that they were not cherished by him, given his full attention, painstakingly and lovingly rendered.

The plate I added today has the workshops of lock and key makers painted on it; men in aprons bent over miniature forges, or preparing moulds, or studying the inner mechanisms of a lock. A frieze of keys surrounds the scene and the outer edge is ringed with gold leaf. George said once that he thought he might have worked with gold leaf, might have been a gilder in a previous life, at Sèvres or at one of the workshops in Germany. He told me this shortly after the end of the war. I was slightly shocked by this fond reference to what he must have felt was enemy terrain.

He looked surprised when I remarked on this. "I have no quarrel with the Germans," he said, echoing the statements Rockwell had made when America finally entered the war. "It was curious," he explained, "but as time passed I couldn't dispel the idea that we were all in it together, that we were just vandals, really, bent on destroying western culture. Finally it seemed to me that Europe was one vast museum whose treasures were being smashed by hired thugs. We weren't making history, we were destroying it . . . eliminating it. Churches that had been lovingly maintained for seven hundred years were being obliterated in an afternoon. Simple men — farm boys who could trace their families back to the time of the Saxons and the Gauls or the Hun — were dying at eighteen and leaving no heirs. There will be nothing left, I kept thinking, when this is over, nothing at all."

When he spoke to me about the war years, George made only fleeting references to battles and bloodshed. I would have to wait for Augusta to tell me about all that in detail. Being in the business of cleaning up afterwards, she had been forced to view the war in terms of the unceasing cargo of ruined flesh delivered to

her ward. She was so steeped in blood resulting from combat that
eventually she was unable to remember a military uniform unsul-
lied by mud and gore, a boy's body unblemished by wounds. All
this despite the perfect billows of the dunes around the hospital
at Étaples, the fresh wind from the sea. She confessed to me that
George's body had shocked her at first because of its wholeness.
This was the only reference she ever made to the fact that they
were lovers.

The Kearns family had been supplying the town of
Davenport with china for over sixty years when war was declared
and so had had correspondence with various employees of
Sèvres and Haviland and Limoges. Before he left for France,
George had carefully printed four or five names on the back page
of the 1914 Baedeker his father had given him as a going-away
gift. Old Mr. Kearns fancied himself a sort of francophile and
had purchased the travel guide each year since the turn of the
century, optimistically believing that he would book a passage at
some time or another. To his mind there was no irony connected
to this German guide to Paris. In the beginning he viewed the
war as a wonderful travel opportunity for his son. And in some
ways he was right, or so George would have had me believe.

Later, in the China Hall, George would describe the streets
of Paris to me with such enthusiasm that had I not known better
I might have been able to conclude that he had been "on leave"
for the duration of the war. I myself have been there twice —
both visits in peacetime — and I must say I found the place,
beyond the wonders of its museums, confusing, exhausting, and
expensive. But, oddly, George asserted that the minute he arrived
he felt that he was returning to a life he had always known.

On his very first visit he left behind his companions who wanted to pursue the life of the cabarets and cafés and journeyed out to Sèvres to admire Develly's work and to look for a certain Mr. Monier, who his father had said was a fine painter of china. The porcelain factory itself had ceased to function as such and was now employed in fabricating earthenware receptacles for the transport of nitroglycerine to the front. George spent several ecstatic hours in the Musée de Porcelaine, adjacent, where the director told him that Monier was working in a district of Paris known as the Marais. Then he scribbled an address on a piece of paper along with a rough, hand-drawn map of the streets leading to the spot, and George retraced his steps back into the centre of Paris.

It was at this point in his story that George became almost incoherent with excitement, began pacing up and down the China Hall, circling one hand in the air as if making an invisible drawing. "There were two worlds of art," he declared. "One up there," he pointed to the ceiling, "and one down here," he gestured towards the ground.

When I asked him what on earth he meant, he explained that the nobles' houses in the Marais district, abandoned since the revolution, had gradually been colonized by the *petits métiers* — artisans, craftsmen — during the nineteenth century.

"There were escutcheons over every doorway," he said. "Marvellous, huge classical statues on many of the façades and, inside, beautiful crumbling plasterwork on the cornices. That sort of thing. And the walls, the walls were covered with carved panels and inset mirrors . . . all filthy, neglected, ignored, really. I saw chandeliers covered with so many spiderwebs that, at first, in the dull light, I couldn't make out what they were. Great crowds of gods and goddesses were painted on the ceilings. All the figures in the heights of these rooms were so large, so monumental, they looked like they had been made by a race of giants. And then, down below, the world was being reproduced in miniature."

Monier, as it turned out, was working in the atelier of an artisan on the Rue du Portfoin, employed – since the war had made him redundant at Sèvres – in painting the china faces of small mechanized figures – automatons. When George found him, he was putting the finishing touches on the eyes of a little Alsatian girl in traditional dress, who, when set in motion, bent down, grasped, and then lifted and waved each of the Allies' flags in succession.

George was enchanted. "Such delicate work," he said to me, "there in the Hôtel de Chantebrion under a looming Neptune and gigantic plaster seashells."

"They were making dolls then, in an old hotel?" I was having trouble visualizing the place he was describing.

"No, no," he said impatiently, "not dolls. An automaton is not a toy. The place was crowded with the most skilled workers – milliners, seamstresses, jewellers, clock makers, metal workers, and so on. China painters. *Hôtel* is the French word for a large house . . . almost a palace, really. When I looked through the windows and across the courtyard, I could see Apollo's horses carved above the stable door. In one corner of the room three people – two men and one woman – were working on the small Alsatian landscape where the little girl would wave her flags."

I watched George turn inward as he revisioned the room he was describing. "Such delicate work," he repeated.

Monier introduced George to "le Maître," an old man called Lambert who had occupied the premises for fifty years, his father having opened the shop thirty years before that. It was he who explained the term *petit métier* to George and told him that just twenty years before, the Marais had been crowded with men and women dedicated to making the most beautiful and the most frivolous objects. He had specialized in Fantaisies à Musique, not just music boxes but an astonishing variety of objects: cigar boxes, decanters, inkwells, even folding chairs into which a musical movement had been incorporated so that they burst into melody the moment they were manipulated. His father's *spécialité de maison* had been *paysages mécaniques* and *tableaux animés*, small idyllic worlds where animals frolicked, waterfalls tumbled, and lovers kissed before all became motionless once again. When George was shown examples of these, he felt his heart open, and then he was overcome by a tremendous sorrow when old Monsieur Lambert placed these treasures back on the shelf and said quietly, "There is not so much call for my things as there was before. Perhaps, after the war . . ."

"In fact," George said to me, "the war finished them off altogether. Nothing beautiful and fragile could survive it." He paused at this point and looked out towards the street, towards Victoria Hall with its Palladian portico and Greek revival pillars, its utterly imported architectural style. "As the fighting went on," he said quietly, "I knew that everything, absolutely everything, was dead or dying, was being pulled down or obliterated. A Belgian I met told me that he had tried to return to his village and had been completely unable to find it. Not a brick left.

Nothing. He thought he had lost his way or gone mad until, sticking out of the mud, he saw the metal head of a rooster that had been part of a weathervane on the church tower. He hauled it out of his knapsack and showed it to me. Not even the whole rooster, just the head. All that was left of his home town. It was about that time that Paris stopped being a comfort to me. I would visit Lambert's studio and know I was visiting a ghost ship. Everything was dying. I would see men sandbagging and wrapping the statues in the Tuileries and I would want to shout at them to tell them they were wasting their time. Everything was disappearing. Both worlds of art . . . gone, and the rest of the world with it."

Just then a customer walked into the China Hall. She was looking for a teapot, she said, having broken hers that morning while washing up after breakfast. I was thinking that it was just as well that George's "beautiful, fragile" objects were no longer being made, believing that, had I seen them I would have found them to be in questionable taste. I had looked at George's radiant face when he described them, but, as always, I had been suspicious of the light.

George had told me, but only when I asked him, about his visits to the museums I cared about in Paris, how he had been overwhelmed and exhausted by the quantity and the size of the pictures in the Louvre – the Delacroixs, the Géricaults – how he recalled the violent subject matter of the larger paintings, but couldn't say specifically what form the violence had taken. Everything in them, he said, seemed to be in conflict with everything else. And yet his visual memories of the Musée des Arts

Décoratifs, which was still bravely mounting temporary exhibitions as well as keeping open their permanent collection, were surprisingly vivid.

There was, he said, a heartbreaking exhibition relating to the Cathedral of Rheims right after that building was bombed, which included medieval drawings, plans for sculptural friezes, baptismal fonts, capitals, and the like. He was very moved by the fact that most of the artists who had worked on these were unknown, and that many of them had not lived to see the cathedral in its finished state.

At the time, I blamed his lack of regard for the great paintings I was familiar with on his inadequate formal education.

When George finished with the customer and turned to me again, I saw that all of the light had gone from his face. "I'll never forget the moment in Lambert's atelier," he said, "when I realized there were two worlds of art. One up there," he pointed towards the ceiling again, "and one down here, a little closer to earth."

I said nothing. I waited.

"It made me very happy," he added, "to be able to understand this." Some crates had arrived earlier in the day and George sighed and began to unpack them. I thought the design on the dinnerware was quite striking and I told him so. The pattern was geometric, with triangular shapes painted in bold colours. It caught the eye, made a quick, forceful statement.

"Mass-produced," he said to me. "It's all anyone wants any more."

I was preparing to leave. It was June and I was, as usual, on my way to Silver Islet Landing. George reached behind the counter and handed me my overnight bag.

"There is only one world of art now," he said. "The war finished the other one off." He was walking me to the door. "Only one world of art," he repeated. "Yours."

We shook hands and said goodbye. I left the shop and walked up Division Street towards the train that would take me to Toronto and from there to Port Arthur. As always, I passed that sad asylum on my route. It was a warm day; some of the inmates were seated in canvas chairs here and there on the lawn. They were in stark sunlight and threw odd shadows. I wondered about George's friend Augusta, whom I had not yet met, wondered how a girl afflicted with shell shock would behave. There were both men and women on the lawn, far back from the fence I was walking along. They were sitting so still they might have been monuments. I kept on walking, past the brick façades of tidy houses towards the station.

I didn't think much about what George had said to me just before I left the China Hall. It would be years before I would interpret his last statement as anything other than a compliment.

When I had known her for about a decade, Sara told me that profound sadness affected her physically in an unusual way. It caused her wrists to ache. "I didn't understand it," she said, "until I realized that the wrists are connected to the heart. The wrists are where the echo of the heart lives."

Her wrists had ached for months after her father had died; the largest loss she had ever had to contend with. She didn't remember her mother at all. Apart from what her father had told her about his young Scandinavian bride whose own father had worked alongside him in the mine, she didn't know much about her. He had been much older than she was, had almost given up hope of marrying altogether, had been stunned when this girl accepted his proposal. There was one small, stiff photo of her mother, which rested on Sara's bureau. A blonde, delicate-looking woman with Sara's frank expression.

"She died having me," Sara confided. "I always wondered when I was a child whether God intended me to be her replacement, and if that meant that I would die in childbirth too."

There was an uncomfortable silence after she said this. We both knew that Sara was, even then, almost too old to have children.

"Tell me about your mother," Sara said. She was lying on her father's bed with her arm flat against her forehead, her face in profile; she was not looking at me. It was late in the afternoon on a calm day. I was, as usual, behind the easel.

"Well?" she said when I didn't answer.

"What is there to tell?" I said. "She died when I was quite young."

"But you do remember her?"

"Yes, I remember her."

"Tell me something about her. Anything at all."

Silence.

"What colour were her eyes?"

"I don't know."

"How could you not know what colour your mother's eyes were?" If Sara had been able to break the pose, she would have turned to me then with her doubting look. "I wish I had seen my mother's eyes — my father said they were blue — but I wish I could remember them."

"Blue," I said, though I realized that I had never thought about this, and could not really say for sure. "They must have been blue. My father's were as well."

"He must have been terribly distraught when your mother died."

I remembered him shuddering with grief near the music box. I had no wish to re-create that moment, its tenseness. "I don't know," I said. I was working now on Sara's hair, which was spread out like a banner on the pillow.

"You do know," she said.

"Excuse me?" It had been a moment of botched tenderness on the part of my father. I wanted to forget all about it.

"But you must have known whether or not he was shaken. You just don't want to tell me."

I said nothing. One is kept so busy with oil paint. Mixing colour, adding oil, cleaning brushes.

"And what about now, do you see your father often?"

"Now and then, not often." I had not, in fact, seen him for over a year. He was waiting, I knew, for me to grow up, to give up this nonsense with paints and brushes. What he really objected to was my subject matter. I was unprepared for this prudish side of him. Still, he was somewhat mollified by the fact that I was beginning to make some money. It angered me and I had told him so. I had convinced myself that I was protecting Sara by not telling her this, by not discussing my father at all.

"I suppose that he is embarrassed about you painting nudes," she said.

I rummaged around in a shallow wooden box, looking for a sepia-coloured pencil.

"Why is it that you're always asking me about *my* father?" she asked. "You'd rather talk about him than your own."

"What is this?" I asked. "Psychoanalysis?"

Sara sighed then, most likely with impatience. I saw her ribcage rise and fall.

"He's more interesting," I said. "Your father is more interesting."

"But you never knew him."

I never knew my own father either, but did not see any point in telling Sara that.

Later, while we were swimming, Sara told me about the Cousin Jacks, a group of miners from Cornwall who would stop at the Miners' Hotel in Cobalt when they had emigrated from the Old Country, how they would board there for a few weeks before fanning out to the various mines in northern Ontario, or how they would sometimes settle in for a longer period of time if they found employment in or near the town. Her father had maintained that those guests at the hotel who were not miners — tourists and other visitors — would be thrown out in the middle of the night if authentic miners appeared and there was no room in the inn.

This charmed me, both for its clear policy relating to the brotherhood of miners and for the proprietor's simple loyalty to his chosen clientele. I could imagine weary salesmen and speculators (in my imagination they all looked suspiciously like my father) in striped pyjamas floundering about in the snow under a wintry moon while men in lit hats and overalls slipped into their warm, recently abandoned beds. I knew this wasn't quite the way the scenario would unfold, but the idea made me laugh, and I resolved to tell Rockwell about it when next we met, though it would be unlikely that I would credit Sara with this story. We had not yet spoken about her. But I had already told him that Cobalt had been the town that had made my capitalist father's surprise fortune. I knew he would be interested in that.

"Do you know if your father would have stopped at the Miners' Hotel?" I asked. Sara thought so, but couldn't say for certain, as it would have been before she was born.

"We'll meet there," I told her, "at the beginning of next summer . . . see if we're thrown out for not being miners."

She smiled and dove away from me, swam quite a distance in the direction of Burnt Island. I could tell that she didn't believe me. I was serious about going there.

The following afternoon I walked over to a wall in the upstairs room and wrote "Meet Austin, June 6th, 1933 at the Miners'" in large charcoal letters on the cracked plaster surface. Then I pulled out my wallet and gave Sara ten Canadian dollars for the train fare.

She looked at the money in her hand. "I've never been to Cobalt," she said, "though I think I heard the hotel owner has died."

"The hotel is still there?"

"I suppose so."

"Let's meet then," I said. "I want to see this legendary place. Maybe we'll encounter some Cousin Jacks."

"There aren't so many now. And it's two hundred miles from here."

"Ever since you taught me that song I've wanted to go there." I picked up a brush, pretended to conduct an imaginary choir, and sang, "Oh, we'll sing a little song about Cobalt. If you've never lived there it's your fault."

Sara did not laugh. I could tell by the expression on her face that she thought I was toying with her.

"Wasn't it you who told me that at the bottom of every hole in the world you could find a Cornishman?"

"My father used to say that."

"Let's meet there," I said.

The following June I appeared at the Miners' Hotel, having spent my customary two days with George in Davenport before heading north. Even as the train approached the grim little mining town, I was filled with ambivalence and waited to pull my luggage from the rack until the conductor had shouted the word "Cobalt" three times and the station came into view beyond the windows of the coach. I left my bags, my canvas and art supplies, at the small wine-coloured station, jumped down from the platform, stepped across the rails, and walked towards the unpainted frame hotel on the opposite side of the tracks. Some of its windows were lit. In one of them I could see a woman walking away from the view. It took me a moment or two to realize that it was Sara, that while I was storing my baggage she had been watching the passengers emerge from the train, and that, unable to see me, she had concluded that I was not among them.

When Sara opened the door of the hotel room she smiled, but there was still anxiety in her eyes. I stepped over the threshold, did not embrace her, but walked instead over to the window and looked out into the darkening sky. When I turned around she was sitting on the edge of the bed.

"I didn't know how long to wait," she said. "I've been here for two days."

It was only then that I remembered that I had promised to arrive at the hotel two days earlier.

"You and the miners."

"Me and the miners." She ran her hand through her hair, a gesture I was familiar with. "I saw some of them at supper in the dining room."

I remember now in detail the simple metal bed, the sink in the corner, the dirty window propped open to let some of the night air into the room, the overwhelming sound of a passing train interrupting whatever it was Sara was trying to say, the tension we both felt while the racket dominated the atmosphere.

"I thought you weren't coming," she said when the noise had abated somewhat. "Or that I had missed you somehow." She moved across the room to me and placed her cheek against my chest. "I was afraid to leave in case you came and found me gone."

"I have been working like crazy in the past few weeks," I said. "I actually lost track of the days of the week." I did not tell her about Davenport, about visiting George. "And then, of course, there was getting ready to leave, getting everything I needed to come here."

Silence.

"To come to Silver Islet, that is."

In that room Sara's clothes looked shabby and worn, her hair dull, her face strained. It pains me now to remember this, but for just a moment I thought her foolish for arriving early or on time, for taking me at my word. As the previous year had unfolded, the idea of this excursion had seemed more and more like a silly whim, the few times that I thought about it at all. What I felt standing in that room, forty-eight hours late for our appointment, was not shame but rather a vague irritation at the stirrings of guilt. I had passed an eventful winter. By the time I left New York I almost didn't care whether Sara would meet me in Cobalt. I had lost, as I did each winter, my connection to her world, her father's world, my interest in this faded hotel. By the end of May, as I organized my art supplies, I would have convinced myself that what was luring me to the north was the knowledge that it was there, and only there, that I was able to begin another year's worth of art.

Through the walls that night I could hear the snores of the miners, their coughs, and the bedsprings shifting under their weight. Sara said that in the dining room in the evenings, the hotel keeper walked through the room handing men letters from home, and that on both nights she thought there might have been a message from me.

"I was the only woman in the room," she said. "None of the men dared look in my direction. I think they pitied me."

Did I say I experienced the stirrings of guilt? I'm not certain that is an accurate description of my initial reaction. It was only later that I understood, or perhaps hoped, that the irritation I felt was in all likelihood brought on by the beginnings of conscience. Whatever the case, as Sara talked about her two nights in the dining room, my mild anger began to be replaced by something else, something I can only describe as a kind of prurience. Shortly before I left New York I had stood one afternoon looking at a finished picture of Sara, naked in her kitchen, and I had sensed suddenly that what the painting needed, what all my paintings of Sara needed, was a darker edge. I'm speaking about emotion here. There was an absence in these paintings, the nature of which I couldn't identify: the effect was muted, calm, almost sentimental. Then, quite spontaneously, I decided it was her calm, the model's calm, that needed to be shattered. She was, in the pictures and in actuality, like an animal at rest in a perfect habitat, a deer in an unthreatening forest. None of the energy caused by, say, entrapment, was present in her face, her body. I did not want my paintings to be mere reproductions of states of grace.

I listened to her speak in her understated way about her pain and shame in the face of these decent working men. Their curiosity, their pity for her. They would have known — anyone would have known — that she was waiting for a man, a man who had not yet and might never appear. And although she had told the hotel keeper otherwise, he and all his guests would have known that the man she waited for was not her husband. The humiliation of this was still with her when I undressed her and lay with her on the creaking bed.

Why did I not take Sara to the dining room for breakfast the next morning? Couldn't I have allowed her the comfort of showing the men in the hotel that the lover she had waited for had finally arrived? We went instead to a soda fountain up the hill, where we ate bacon sandwiches. As if I had planned this endurance test — and perhaps in some ways I had — I did not grant her respite from shame. I wanted to draw it in her face and body when we got back to Silver Islet. I wanted it to persist. I wanted to break her calm, add pain to the composition. The dark edge I was so certain I desired had entered the expression of her face.

She would not trust me again for a long, long time. I believed her attachment to me would be stronger as a result of her uncertainty. I became convinced that all of this would make the paintings better. But it was not Sara who caused the hollowness in my work.

How long did she remain in the memories of the miners, I wonder, this blonde woman, plainly dressed, alone at a table? Was there one among them who held on to a picture of her face, her downcast eyes. Or is it only I who retain the image of unease? She would have come down to eat in the dining room because she wouldn't have known what else to do. Sitting in a room full of men reading letters from home, a room full of received messages, messages for everyone but her, food growing cold on the plate, shame making it difficult to swallow, she would listen to the trains pass the hotel, watch the coal smoke descend through the evening light. Then, when she could bear it no longer, she would wipe her mouth with her napkin, rise, cross the dining room with all eyes upon her, and climb the stairs to the empty room.

What, I ask you, is more intimate than this: total recollection of a scene I had never witnessed, but one over which I nonetheless had perfect control?

When I was again alone with Sara in the upstairs room of her log house, I painted her with her head in profile and her back to the south wall. The charcoal reminder I had written the year before remained, smudged but readable, on the plaster.

I painted the wall and the words into the picture. I wanted the dark calligraphy of the appointment I had broken to look like an accusation emerging from Sara's mouth.

One of my stopovers in Davenport coincided with a weekend, but, according to George, his friend the nurse would not be in town as she didn't have the time off. We were spending a quiet Saturday afternoon in the China Hall. It had been raining and few customers had made their way to the shop. George was working on one of his vases at the end of the counter; I was writing a letter to Rockwell at a small table on the other side of the shop. I must have been chuckling to myself because, quite abruptly, George placed his brush on the counter and asked me why I was laughing.

"I've just written something terribly funny," I said.

George looked at me expectantly.

"It's about New York," I said. "Just something about an art dealer in New York."

George picked up his brush again. I had noticed, since the war, there was sometimes a slight tremor in his right hand. At this moment it seemed more pronounced. He was painting a delicate motif that involved stems and thorns and trellises, and I could see he was having trouble with it.

"Well," he said, "I guess I wouldn't know anything about all that."

"You wouldn't want to know," I said. "Art politics."

George placed the brush on the counter again, massaged his right wrist, then resumed painting. He leaned closer to the vase. He had begun to wear glasses now when he worked, and I saw he was squinting through the lenses. Without removing his gaze from the painting, he reached towards a pot with the brush, his hand now shaking quite visibly. He missed his mark, tipped over the pot, and enamel paint spilled across the counter. A small lavender stream trickled to the floor.

He made no move to clean up after the accident. Instead, he closed his eyes and was quiet for several moments. Then he dropped the brush, opened his eyes, rested his elbows on the counter, and looked at his hands, which he held, fingers splayed, about a foot from his face. Both of his forearms were trembling now. "God," he said. "Jesus."

He just sat there and stared at his hands twitching uncontrollably in front of him, the colour draining from his face. The white cloth of one shirt sleeve had turned lavender around the elbow. The paint made a ticking sound as it fell, drop by drop to the floor.

"I can't . . ." George said. "I can't . . ."

I could not interpret what was happening to him. "What the . . ." I began, unable even to form an appropriate question. Every cell in my body was moving towards panic.

George's torso began to shake, but not with the same intensity as his hands, the fingers of which had begun to twitch spasmodically.

"I can't," he kept saying. "I can't." Certain objects on the counter were beginning to rattle. He had pushed his stool against the wall behind him where cups and saucers on shelves were now making slight clinking noises.

"What is it? What's the matter?" My heart was hammering my ribcage. I registered a feeling of nausea, but I did not look away. I could see that George's teeth were chattering. It was as if he were experiencing his own private earthquake.

Suddenly I found myself across the room, holding both of his hands in my own. Anyone looking in would have thought we were involved in an absurd form of arm wrestling. "Stop!" I was shouting. His face was so close to mine I could see his pores.

"I can't," he whispered. But the shaking was diminishing.

"Stop," I said in a quieter tone, my own heartbeat beginning to slow.

"Just keep holding my hands," George was saying. "Keep holding my hands."

Later, when he had regained control, he thanked me, as if my actions had been ones of intentional kindness. "It's the war," he said, by way of an explanation, though I had not asked one question. "This happens sometimes."

I had been thinking epilepsy, stroke. The war had been over for at least ten years.

Not wanting to dwell on what had taken place I returned to my letter and began to reread what I had been writing. I saw then that the tone of it was mean-spirited, cynical. There was nothing amusing about it at all.

After this began a period of about a year during which George wrote me several long letters about his friend Augusta. It was as if he were trying to explain his attachment, not so much to me but to himself. He loved the notion that she had grown up not ten miles away from him, that she had lived on a farm, was reared in a world of fields and villages. He wrote that he wanted to restore in her everything that had been brought to flower in that life. Those things around her that had been all but obliterated by the war. Would he have succeeded, I wonder, even for a moment? In her love for him, would she let him believe that he was succeeding when, in fact, the opposite was true? After all, they were in so many ways each other's reminder of the war, having both seen the results of battles, having shared – if only briefly – the ward at Étaples. Still, they may have believed that restoration was possible, in George's unchanging China Hall and during her visits from the city. They would sometimes drive on the dusty country roads, passing small brick churches and schoolhouses. Now and then they visited Augusta's village for weddings or funerals, and quite frequently they took a Sunday meal with Augusta's now solitary mother.

Years later, Augusta told me that her most vivid memories of the farm concerned the infrequent days of complete silence in her house. "When we were older," she said, "my brothers and I were able to miss the first weeks of class because of the harvest. We considered this a great treat, though we worked harder than we ever did at school."

Early September was often the hottest time of the year; the autumn sun burning into the earth; creeks and rivers shrinking in size. The boys would be out in the fields from dawn until dusk, and her mother would be busy with the large market garden directly across the lane, so Augusta, the daughter of the house, would be left indoors alone to clean the kitchen and bedrooms.

The four oldest boys slept in what the family referred to as the "north room" at the top of the stairs. Situated over the kitchen and the parlour, it was the largest space in the house, incorporating four windows and a snakelike stovepipe, which thrust itself up from the kitchen woodstove and entered the room through the floor, travelled across the ceiling, pierced the wall overtop the door frame, and continued down the hall. This leviathan distributed a surprising amount of warmth in the winter, but would seem cold, useless, awkward in a season of heat.

Each morning during the harvest, Augusta would pull a child's wagon laden with stoneware water jugs out to the fields, which had become golden and lush with mature grain or which had transformed themselves into forests of tall corn. As they filled their cups, her brothers would sometimes talk to her about whether the work was going well, and this would please her. After this she would walk back, past the place where her almost forgotten snow house had been, return to the house, and climb the stairs to sweep the floor, to remove the cobwebs that would have formed on the stovepipe overnight, and to make the beds in the north room.

Even though it was not yet ten o'clock in the morning, the heat was often terrific, the room stained yellow by the sun beating against drawn blinds. Evidence of activity was everywhere, making the absence and the stillness more profound. Flies, drunk with sunlight, buzzed now and then in the corners of windows, but apart from this, Augusta told me, the silence was almost palpable.

The room was like a memorial to animation. Each bed that Augusta straightened seemed to have been the site of a skirmish, each garment that she lifted from the floor was like something that, moments before, had been filled with energy and motion; something recently killed. A pleasant languor would start to envelope her as she moved slowly across the floor, stooping, smoothing, stretching sometimes, to hang discarded overalls from a hook or a nail on the wall. Flies continued to buzz drowsily in the heat. The smell of sweat — hers, her brothers' — was always present. Occasionally Augusta would find herself standing perfectly still with a pillowslip, or a shirt clutched in a ball near her stomach. She could never remember what it was she had been thinking about.

This was the time of the year when the boys became particularly glorious. Their skin was darkened, their hair bleached by sun. Augusta said they looked to her like the apostles, or the muscular male angels she remembered from her Sunday-school cards. Calmed by labour, they were gentle, quiet, grateful at suppertime. Augusta could never understand how she, a girl with such dark hair, could be a sister to boys so blond. But the blood they all shared was the central river of her life. She adored them.

During the early autumn evenings of 1913, while George and I were dancing at the pavilion ten miles away, some of the boys would go into town while Augusta and Fred sat near the open kitchen window to catch the night breeze. Augusta would sew while Fred carefully buttered their mother's flat oatmeal cookies, and, between bites, read passages from *The World's Great Exposition of Civilization*. When he came across something he knew would make Augusta laugh, he would read it aloud to her. "Psychological Discoveries in Vegetables" was a popular section ("Plants Can Think!"), as was the chapter on the great subway tunnel under New York City or the illustrations and instructions for spying by kite. Fred was interested in the "Careers at Home" section, interested in raising silkworms or frogs. Of all the boys he was the most shy, too timid to go into town in the evenings to look for girls.

"The few girls he would get to know," Augusta told me, "would have to come to him and practically force themselves upon his attention."

While she was speaking to me about harvest time on her girlhood farm, two pictures of Augusta as a very young woman repeatedly appeared in my mind. In one, she was pulling a wagon full of stoneware jugs towards an empty field; in the other, she was shaking dust cloths and braided rugs from the windows of a north room. In both she seemed to be participating in a strange ritual of farewell.

"I never saw the end of the harvest of 1913," Augusta informed me, "and I was never home for harvest time again."

Sometime during the previous winter her father had announced that now that she was finished with her schooling, there were four possibilities open to her. "Four possibilities," he had said, holding up the fingers of his left hand, "marriage, teaching, nursing, and, as these are modern times, stenography."

Because some of her brothers had been having trouble at school, Augusta spent the remainder of the winter testing her pedagogical skills by forcing some of the younger boys to concentrate, after dinner, on a series of spellers and readers that she remembered as being far from interesting. The theme of most of the poems the boys were given to read at school, and all of the poems they were required to memorize, was fidelity to the Mother country. Years later, Augusta would dream about this night kitchen, the snow falling outside the window, and the boys, their eyes glazed with boredom, reciting:

> "'England, England, England,
> Wherever a true heart beats,
> Wherever the rivers of commerce flow,
> Wherever the bugles of conquest blow,
> Wherever the glories of liberty grow,
> 'T'is the name that the world repeats.'"

In the dream she would try to warn her brothers, but they behaved as if she weren't there, as if her voice weren't reaching them. She always awoke weeping.

But while she was attempting to teach them, she felt only the boredom, hers and theirs, and knew she could not devote her life to the passing on of memory work. In the early autumn of 1913 she enrolled in the Toronto General Hospital School of Nursing.

As George had, I have come to love Augusta's past. I like to think of her as a child, a child of perhaps eleven or twelve years, just before her brief bout of play was followed by mandatory adulthood. I like to think of her sitting in her village graveyard, surrounded by children, villagers, and farmers on Decoration Day. George wrote to me about this yearly event once, after he had attended the ceremony with Augusta, who had put flowers on her father's grave and placed a wreath at the war memorial. The church service was held in the cemetery on a Sunday in June, when the blossoms were out and the leaves were fresh. Several wagons were employed to bring the organ from the church, chairs from the parish hall, and benches from the Sunday school. And then all of this indoor furniture was arranged among the tombstones, on the grass.

The graveyard itself, as I see it, would be full of modest white stones, would be surrounded by a white fence, and there would be neither deep ravines nor mausoleums nor vicious weather. There would be enough shade for comfort, but not so much as to darken the atmosphere. The women would be wearing colourful dresses and there would be hats on everyone's heads, white shoes on everyone's feet. A breeze in the pines, fresh flowers on the grass, an uplifting hymn on the organ. Song. I like to think of Augusta there on Decoration Day, a warm day in June, the graves of her ancestors suitably decorated, her Sunday-school cards in a little crocheted purse, ribbons in her hair, and the war not yet even a rumour. I like to think of a day like that: George's beloved Northumberland Hills rolling off in all directions, the dark trees of the bush pressing down from the north, towards this gorgeous cultivation, this decency.

"I was never home for harvest time again," Augusta said. "I enrolled in the Toronto General Hospital School of Nursing and then, a few years later, I volunteered to go overseas."

Beyond the windows of the China Hall an ocean of snow churned in the streetlight.

"What about the boys?" I asked.

Augusta was silent for a long, long time. I began to think she wasn't going to answer. Perhaps she was never going to tell me what happened to her brothers.

"Some of them," she finally said, "were too young to go to war."

I know now that I could have talked to George. I might have told him almost anything. I should have, for instance, told him about Sara. But I didn't. I recall that when he revealed his relationship with Augusta to me I believed I had nothing similar to confide, despite the fact that I had been painting Sara then for five summers. Also, having years before taken Robert Henri's admonition concerning privacy to heart, I remained stubbornly fixed in the listening and gathering period of my life, keeping my activities so brilliantly compartmentalized I was called upon to disclose very little of myself to anyone, little beyond a superficial litany of my own questionable achievements. The deeper currents of the world, when I was lucky enough to stumble upon them, existed, I believed at the time, to be examined by me, then used in my art for my own advancement.

After what occurred on a winter night in 1937, controlling things, ordering them, became untenable. I removed my dangerous self from the innocent traffic of humanity, began to look inward.

I have taken nothing from the world since.

Now that I am old, and there is neither the opportunity nor the desire to change the pattern of my life, I am forced to admit to myself how much of my experience has been second-hand. I think constantly about the others: those I knew who entered wars and love affairs, those who, unlike me, let passion break them. George, Rockwell, Augusta. Sara. I cannot forget how they crept near and, like merchants unfurling silk scarves on table-tops, placed narrative after colourful narrative in front of me. I cannot forget how they pulled their knowledge of the world back into their own hearts and slipped out of my line of vision, more interested suddenly in death or fame or the Arctic. All except for Sara, who would have stayed, I think. But who can ever know these things? And perhaps I'm being unfair. God knows I was frequently more interested in my own fame and my own interior Arctic. Unable until now to muster the concentration necessary to report my memories verbally to anyone, all my energies have gone into the past, to exorcising ghosts, to obliterating conscience.

They say that in old age the long-term memory becomes vivid, punches its fist through the skin of the present, insists on being heard and seen and felt. George and Augusta bring their inner landscapes with them into these white rooms of mine, and I feel their sorrows and tendernesses, their resentments and anxieties, in a way that I have never experienced my own emotions. But how crowded and unfocused this looking back is; all these foreign fields, the battles, this china collection. Views of rocks and trees, hills and streams. I scarcely know which images are mine and which have been taken by me, fully developed, from the others, or whether there is, in the final analysis, any difference.

This is the uncertainty I have been left with. This is the true inheritance.

Mrs. Boyle is very impressed with the carefully rendered scenes and landscapes of my underpainting, told me so just this morning when I discovered her standing, hands on hips, staring at the most recent work-in-progress.

"This side is just lovely," she said, pointing a feather duster towards the least finished area of the painting. "I feel like if I touched that water I'd get my fingers wet, it's that real."

"You would get your fingers wet," I told her. "The paint is not dry yet."

"You know very well what I mean," she said. "But what have you gone and done with those wonderful stones over here that you spent all last month exhausting yourself by painting, one by one, at any hour of the day or night, that's what I want to know?

You've gone and smudged them up so that you can't tell any more what they are at all."

"Mrs. Boyle," I said, feigning both gratitude and surprise, "I didn't know you cared. You're becoming a real art critic."

"Oh, I'm no art critic," she said, "but I know when you're having trouble. You start smudging everything up when you're having trouble, then you call up some truck to come and take the paintings away."

"That truck, Mrs. Boyle, comes from the art gallery in New York."

She looked at me with great scepticism. "You can't fool me," she said. Then she told me something very odd. "I'm very fond of places," she said. "Which is why I like your paintings so much before you smudge them up. I always pray for my three most special places — Cappangrown and Mastergeeha in Ireland, and the small house on David Street."

"I wonder what you hope to accomplish by praying for a place?" I was really quite taken aback by this.

"The farm in Kerry where I grew up, the farm we had to leave to come here, and the little house we have now. I pray for them every night."

"Well, I suppose you should pray for this house then, rather than the owner of it."

Mrs. Boyle looked around her uneasily. "Who'd pray for a great cold barn of a place like this?" she said. "Begging your pardon," she added, as if my feelings might have been bruised by her statement. Then she offered me this advice: "If you'd just leave those places you've painted alone when they're all filled up with those lovely trees and water and people and houses, then everything would be fine. You always come back and muck around afterwards and ruin them. If you'd just let them alone, they'd be the most wonderful paintings in the world."

I rarely completed pictures while I was at Silver Islet Landing; my time was mostly given over to drawing and oil sketches. But each summer I began three or four large figurative canvases, which I shipped to New York a few days before the end of the summer. I cannot now recall where those paintings might have gone after they were finished, exhibited, and sold. Collectors. Galleries. If I knew, and had I the courage, I might make the journey to look at one or another of them, to look at Sara. It seems fantastically odd to me now that I spent all those winters apart from her, meticulously colouring her flesh, and never once wanted to know what she might have been doing at any given hour, as if during those cold months she had ceased to exist, except on canvas, had become merely a composition. And what had I become to her? A ghost, perhaps, a shadowy figure. Why did she allow me entrance summer after summer, her face welcoming, exposed? I think now of the life she chose, the isolation, the huge lake pounding mere steps from her door, the world she had known in childhood diminishing and then gone for good with her father's death. I think of her living through the harshness, the loneliness of those winters, living on her summer wages. I once asked her how she managed, thinking I could contribute something if she was in need. She looked at me with that frank gaze of hers and said that she stockpiled what she got in summer, preparing for the inevitable return of winter. I was aware that she was referring to more than money, but I let it pass without comment.

"You and the fox," I said.

"Me and the fox," she replied.

Nothing in her voice suggested that she had ever felt sorry for herself; she was too proud for that. There was a kind of dignity, a stateliness to the rhythms of her life, and I think in some deep way she was aware of that. She insisted that she was never really unhappy in the winter. "I chose this," she would say. "I could go somewhere else if I wanted to, but I chose this. Hasn't that ever occurred to you?"

It hadn't. I was so involved in trying to direct my own life, my own work, I took it for granted that others must necessarily be victims of circumstance.

I had learned that if we removed ourselves from the subject, if we used a combination of sketches and memory when we were working on a painting, we would be more likely to put our true feelings into the work. I removed myself each year from the subject, there is no question about that. But did I ever put my own true feelings into the work? Might I see some evidence of them now if I were to look at one of the pictures of Sara? Would I recognize my emotions if they were there? What the hell do they look like?

And how did I appear to Sara? Who did she see when she looked at me?

A man in love with the stifling order he had imposed upon his own life.

"May you get what you wish for," Mrs. Boyle always says to me when she is finished for the day and preparing to leave the house. "May you get what you wish for and may it be what you meant."

The problem as I began to see it towards the end of my attachment to realism was that I had lost sight of the necessary interval on the picture plane, the visual pause that had happened quite naturally when I still worked with landscape, still worked with the spatial interrelation of rendered form. There was always a break in detail of rocks, say, or foliage, an unencumbered space that pushed forward from distance, something large and unmeasurable, like sky or water.

When I painted Sara now, she filled the picture plane, her body spilling forward as if she were about to separate from the surface of the painting and enter an embrace. She would be trailing behind her the light of northern summer afternoons. Her face would be welcoming, disclosed, as if she were about to tell you that there is a source of light out there where you stand, that there is a world beyond this painting. But even so, the brilliance poured from her body, her self, into the viewer's life. It was relentless. There was no dark pause, no negative space at all.

I thought this was a mistake. I believed in distance, believed in stepping back from the canvas in order to see it better. I believed that no one should ever feel ambushed by the subject of a painting.

Here is something Augusta told me, that night in the China Hall, about the war.

There was always a fresh wind from the sea around Number One Canadian Hospital in Étaples, she said. A fresh wind from the sea, even in the fog, so that she couldn't understand why the greyness persisted, why it didn't just blow away. On clear days the dunes changed constantly under the moving sun. Once when she was sitting on the back steps of one of the wards she watched a red tide climb a distant sand hill — poppies coming into first flower under the touch of daylight. It was dawn, after a long night during which she had anesthetized five soldiers for amputations. Two had died. The poppies were like a stain on the hillside, she said, like blood.

Behind the hill there was a huge half-circle of sand with an acre of flat space at its foot that stubbornly held its shape despite the inconstancy of the surrounding dunes. The French called it the amphitheatre and maintained it had been there since Roman times. Here the staff played baseball and soccer and held Dominion Day celebrations on July 1, performing skits and singing songs about a country Augusta could barely remember, the world of the hospital having become the only nation she felt any allegiance to. It was here, later in the war, that she would come to know Maggie.

Nothing was fixed or permanent in that geography, Augusta said. The wind moved in from the sea and changed the shape of the acres of dunes that surrounded the hospital and base camps. Soldiers departed for the trenches and returned, ruined, on long hospital trains that unloaded their freight into the wards. The men were treated. Some died, some were moved to England or Canada, depending on their wounds. Many were patched and sent back to the front. The medical staff too was often being posted to new locations: a manor house in England, a large hotel on an empty beach, something unimaginable in Italy or Greece. Encounters were brief; brutal or tender, gone like dreams in the morning. The King visited the hospital wards once and was forgotten the next day, another face in an ever-changing sea of male faces. Aviators dropped messages from planes for nurses who had left Étaples months before. "God and the Hun willing," one of the letters read, "we'll meet again someday."

Augusta had been in the Number One Canadian Hospital longer than most, for a full year by the time she met Maggie. Before that there had been Salonica, then Kent, then Boulogne. She kept odd memories from each posting, memories that mostly concerned her own person, as if her body were the provider of the only reliable information. She had combed lice from her hair in Salonica, had recovered from diphtheria in Boulogne, and it was here, in Étaples, that she had pierced her own arm with a needle in order to fight the fatigue. Only once, she whispered to herself, only once or twice, she said, recalling the flood of calm, of comfort, which followed the injection.

In late November of 1917, Augusta began to visit the buried amphitheatre in the dunes as often as she could manage it. There were few hours of daylight in that season and the rain was almost unceasing, but none of that mattered to her. Weather would not stop her, work sometimes did, though even when the casualties were pouring in from the front she was frequently able to steal a half-hour — sometimes in the middle of the night — to climb the sand hills behind the hospital and to settle herself down for a few moments beside the scrub pines that clung to the edge of the circular ridge. The amphitheatre was definitely there, she decided, sleeping under the sand. It would always be there; it had to be. She had no desire to unearth it, no desire for proof. The shape it described in the sand that protected the territory of the arena below, her own conviction, provided more certitude than she had witnessed anywhere in recent times. Its constancy brought comfort to her.

Fred had been reported missing at Passchendaele. Even in death there was no certainty, though God knows Augusta had seen it close the faces of enough young people to believe in its finality. She would awaken in the nurses quarters each day and whisper over and over, "Fred is dead, no, Fred is not dead."

She hadn't seen her brother for three years. When she tried to remember the shape of his eyes, his hands, they became confused with the hands and eyes of the thousands of men over whose beds she had bent under the billowing ceilings of tents or beside the cold wooden walls of huts. Early in the war, when she had been told that her brother Charlie had died of meningitis at the training camp on Salisbury Plain, she had dreamed of him each night for months and had awakened sobbing each morning. But she could not call up Fred's face, hear his quiet laugh. Because her dreams now all took place in the wards, they were filled instead with grey blankets and soiled linen. Her mind seemed incapable of playing with other images. Fred was dead. Fred was not dead. The amphitheatre would be there, she decided, under the sand. Forever.

She walked to this spot each day she could, through sand-storms, through thunderstorms, through snowstorms. By February of 1918, the weather was uncharacteristically bright and calm; the hospital itself, when she turned to look back at it, appearing in this clarity almost permanent, huts having by now replaced almost all of the original tents. It was as if, Augusta mused, a tribe of nomadic hunters and gatherers had progressed to a fixed agrarian society — except for the fact that nothing would grow on these dunes, and the population was constantly changing, and civilization still slept in its stone solidity beneath the surface, tens of feet down.

March was the time of the most disorienting fogs, fogs so thick they obliterated the views from the windows of the wards. But by then Augusta could have walked to the amphitheatre in her sleep, she had made the trek so often. She liked the indeter-minate quality of these grey days, enjoyed the sound of trains she wasn't able to see rattling on the bridge that crossed the

River Canche and the odd voice reaching her from the hospital below, or, by contrast, no noise at all except that of the wind from the sea, which should have blown away the fog.

It was in early March, in the midst of a particularly dense fog and after she had been sitting on the sloping sand for twenty minutes or so, that Augusta became aware of unfamiliar sounds – scratching, and a slight fluttering – somewhere quite near her at the amphitheatre. She straightened her spine and listened more carefully. Then she relaxed again.

"Birds," she said. She told me she often spoke aloud when she was alone at the amphitheatre, liking the reassuring sound of her own voice when it was meant for no one but herself. "Birds," she repeated. "Birds in the fog."

The girl's voice surprised her. "Hello," it said. "Hello, are you there?"

Augusta did not reply right away. She was a little shocked by what she felt to be an invasion of an exclusive territory. Having never met anyone out on the dunes before, except at planned events, she wasn't quite sure whether the voice was intended for her. "Here," she eventually said. "I'm over here beside the pines."

"I can't see you," the voice said. "So keep speaking until I find you."

A command. Augusta swallowed, then paused. "What shall I say?" she asked.

"Sing the 'Marseillaise.'"

A hoot of laughter.

"'The Maple Leaf Forever' then."

"No," said Augusta. "I can't bear that. No maple leaf is ever forever."

"'The thistle, shamrock, rose entwined . . . the maple leaf forever.'" The girl's voice was strong and clear now.

"I can't bear songs with dauntless heroes in them," said Augusta. She thought for a moment. "'In days of yore, from Britain's shore, Wolfe the dauntless hero came,'" she sang, remembering how she and her twenty classmates had sung the patriotic Canadian song at the village school whenever there were pageants or Christmas plays. How many of these children were dead now, or wounded? "'And planted firm Britannia's flag on Canada's fair domain,'" she continued, recalling the now suddenly old-fashioned colonial words. "What tosh!" she added, though she was speaking mostly to herself.

"*Britannia est magna insula*," said the voice. An interval, then, "But it isn't really, is it? Such a small place for so much trouble."

"Trouble," said Augusta bitterly. "Yes."

"I can almost see you." The girl emerged from the fog. "There, now I can see you." She smiled. Radiantly.

The girl was thin, with extremely fair hair, and was, Augusta decided, quite beautiful in a fragile way. She had taken off her nursing veil, probably once she began to walk out on the dunes, and now, because of the wind, it looked like a large white bird fluttering at the end of her hand. She stood looking down at Augusta and wrapping the white cloth around and around her wrist like a bandage. Then, abruptly, she sat down on the sand. "I'm Maggie Pierce."

Augusta was thinking, I know her. "Augusta Moffat," she said. And then, "Have I seen you before?"

"Maybe, probably not. I've only been here for two days . . . transferred from Boulogne. But I saw you, from a distance. You were on your way out here when I first arrived. I thought, Wherever she's going . . . away from the hospital . . . it will be the perfect place to write my letters." She placed her hand on some bright-blue notepaper folded and tucked inside her belt. "I like to write them outside."

What Augusta had presumed to be birds was merely the sound of a girl attempting to write a letter, outside, in a strong wind.

"I haven't finished this one," the girl said, touching the paper again with her long white fingers. "It's hard to find the time to finish them. Sometimes I write in the dark after lights out. Have you ever tried to write without looking? You'd be surprised; the writing is as neat and as straight as ever."

At that moment it occurred to Augusta that she hadn't written a proper letter in years. Nothing except postcards to her mother with a series of similar messages: I am fine. We are working hard. It is cold and rainy. "Who are you writing to?" she asked.

"To Peter," the girl said. "A very exasperating boy. I'm mostly very angry with him. Sometimes I'm writing to tell him why. Other times I tell him what has happened to me during the day. I've already described this place to him . . . the river and the sea and the dunes. He would be interested in the river. He used to like to go fishing, but he would never let me go along. That made me angry too."

Augusta remembered that Fred had liked to fish. All her brothers had, but Fred liked it especially because of the quiet. She tried to picture him, entering the kitchen with three or four brook trout. She could see the fish, the kitchen, but she couldn't

see Fred's face. The fog had lifted a little, giving her a better view
of Maggie, though she still seemed exaggeratedly soft and pale.
Augusta was a bit embarrassed that she had asked her new companion such a personal question.

"I never know where he is posted," Maggie continued, "and
he refuses to tell me." She touched the blue paper at her waist
again, as if to assure herself that it had not blown away, then
wrapped the veil, which had unfurled in the wind, once more
around her wrist. "I keep asking him where he is and he won't
tell me. He never was much of a talker, but this is ridiculous."

"But he can't tell you where his company is," Augusta said.
"It would be censored anyway, even if he did tell you."

Maggie looked directly out into the fog. "We've known each
other since we were children," she said, determination in her
voice. "I'll keep writing until he tells me. Sometimes I stay up all
night writing."

Augusta sighed. "You should get your sleep instead. God
knows there is little enough time for it."

Maggie slowly unwrapped her veil from her arm, lifted it to
her face, and burst into tears. "I'm quite mad," she said, her voice
choked with sobs. "I can't seem to stop writing to him, even
though I'm not sure he ever really liked me. Since we were children I was certain I was going to marry him."

Augusta touched Maggie's shoulder, tears coming into her
own eyes. This pain was such an ordinary pain, she was suddenly
filled with nostalgia. In peacetime two young women might have
been having this conversation and one of them might be crying.
Here in the fog, this girl with her white hair, her white apron and
veil, her pale-blue uniform greyed by mist, looked almost like a

photographic negative, as if she were already a memory. "At least you write to each other," Augusta said sympathetically. "That's something."

"But he doesn't answer . . . not since the Somme. I don't think I know where he is. He hasn't answered for two years." Maggie had stopped crying now and was attempting to pin her veil back into place. She removed her cap from the bib of her apron. "He is impossible, you see." She turned and smiled at Augusta. "I like it that you come out here," she said. "I think we are going to be friends. I saw you walking out over the dunes all alone and I thought, That one will be my friend."

Augusta's hand was on the girl's back, between her shoulder blades. She did not remove it. "Maggie," she said, closing her eyes, "are you saying that Peter was at the Somme?" The Allied casualties there had been unlike anything experienced so far in the history of warfare. "Maggie," she repeated, shaking the girl's shoulder gently when she didn't respond. "Was he wounded?"

"No," Maggie said, looking at her cap, which she was turning around and around in her hands. "No, not that, I won't let that happen."

"Did something happen to him at the Somme?"

A silence, followed by, "I'm quite mad, you know."

Fred was killed at Passchendaele, thought Augusta. Fred was not killed at Passchendaele. What is madness?

Maggie stood and Augusta looked up at her, so grey and ephemeral in the fog. Maggie crossed her arms. "I know I am off kilter, but there is nothing you can say to make me stop writing the letters. I came out here to meet you but also because I like to write the letters outside if I can, either that or in the dark."

"We should be getting back," said Augusta. "Matron here is fierce."

As they walked over the dunes towards the hospital, Augusta told Maggie about the amphitheatre, how it had been there for centuries under the sand. The fog thickened again, but Augusta was able to orient herself by identifying certain groups of scrub pine that now and then erupted unexpectedly into her view. "How did you find your way out there?" she asked Maggie when they were on the path that led to the wards.

"I knew the direction and after a while I followed the sound of your voice."

"I was saying things — out loud?"

"Enough for me to get near to where you were."

They walked in silence for a few moments, their feet digging into the sand. "What did you hear me say?" Augusta eventually asked.

"You were saying something like 'Fred is dead, Fred is not gone,' then you said that thing about the birds."

"The grey girl," I said to Augusta, while snow blew through the metallic illumination created by the streetlights outside the China Hall.

"Yes," she replied, "but I hadn't thought of that yet."

I was quite stunned by the audacity of what I had presumed, that and my sudden unquestioning belief in such a phenomenon. I remembered my mother telling me about the Rochester Rappings, but I knew this was different from all that.

"Nothing was certain in that world." Augusta stood now, placed her hands on the small of her back, stretching her spine. "Each reality was perpetually being exchanged for another reality. And it was the spring of 1918. Stationary hospitals nearer the front were being transformed day by day, becoming casualty clearing stations, then advanced dressing stations, then preparing to evacuate altogether – the shelling was that bad, beyond all description. We received thousands and thousands of casualties. There were no more shifts, everyone just worked until they collapsed, then rose to their feet three hours later and began again. Maggie and I became quite close, almost immediately; there was never time in the war for developing a friendship gradually. We pushed her bed down the length of our quarters until it was near mine. But we were so busy we were hardly ever in the nurses' quarters at the same time and, when we were, there was nothing, absolutely nothing, that could keep us awake for very long. I was administering anesthetic by then – they had to train some of the more experienced nurses as anesthetists – there just wasn't enough staff.

"Sometimes Maggie and I went to the amphitheatre rather than to bed, just to remove ourselves for an hour from all the frantic activity. We never had any idea what time it was. Sometimes it was dark, sometimes it wasn't. In the dark while we sat on the dunes Maggie and I could see battle fire in the distance. I remember her face flickering in that strange orange light. It was in the middle of all this, when we had stolen half an hour to go out to the amphitheatre, that she turned to me and said, 'I am quite comfortable here, and you are too.'

"It was then that I recalled the little snow house and the grey girl and how she had said the same thing. I thought about how Maggie's pale-blue uniform had appeared grey the morning that I met her in the fog. I didn't question any of this. It seemed as valid to me as any other kind of reality. Besides, we understood each other, had become close friends. I thought the fact that I had hallucinated her, or imagined her, as a child spoke of a kind of predestiny. I didn't tell her though. I wish now I had told her."

"Did you ever tell George?"

"No, I never told George."

After they had pushed their beds together at the far end of the nurses' quarters, Augusta often heard the sound of Maggie's pencil scribbling in the dark. Sometimes in the operating theatre while she was anesthetizing some poor broken boy, Augusta would see Maggie at the other side of the room where she was sterilizing instruments. Occasionally the blonde girl would stop for a few moments, pull the folded blue paper from her belt, and quickly jot down a few lines. No one else appeared to notice. Within a month of her arrival she was one of the most respected nurses in the hospital; her efficiency in the wake of the increasing chaos, a marvel to behold. The surgeons, even the matron, had nothing but praise for her.

But it was not this efficiency that caused Augusta to love Maggie Pierce. It was the way she refused to relinquish her own personal obsession, the letters she insisted on writing to her dead lover, and the way she posted them, by casually dropping them into the River Canche or by releasing them, like pigeons, out on the dunes in a wind that would carry them either into the line of battle or out to sea.

Anesthetic was beautiful to Augusta. It was only during its administration that she felt completely satisfied by what she was doing. Men howling in agony could be brought under her hands to a state of rest, calm entering their features so completely that she was able to recognize in their serene expressions the children they had been. Some boys were so desperate for unconsciousness that they tore the mask from her hands. "Please, Sister," they would gasp, shout, or whisper, "put me to sleep, put me to sleep." And behind them, stretching down the hall, a long line of the groaning wounded. It was a wonderful moment, she maintained, when a body in the clutch of pain finally relaxed — a warm tide of balm moving over the table.

By the last week in March of that year, the level of casualties was so high and so persistent that the surgeons and nurses were practically delusional from lack of sleep. Often everyone around the table wept — when an operation was successful and a life had been saved, or when it was unsuccessful and the boy died. From the corner where she was sterilizing instruments Maggie often sang "The Maple Leaf Forever," moving into the more obscure verses, with lines such as "Then swell the song both loud and long, till rocks and forests quiver." All this to make Augusta smile. Sometimes giddiness reigned at the most inappropriate times, when the surgeons found one of His Majesty's buttons pushed by a bullet into a liver, or when after a successful four-hour operation to remove shrapnel from a brain, they discovered a deadly, malignant, and inoperable tumour just before they were about to close the skull. The boy died three days later, though whether from injuries or the tumour no one could really say. Sometimes when it was very quiet Augusta could hear Maggie scribbling in the corner, describing the previous operation and its results to her vanished lover.

In April, the number of wounded abated somewhat and, after long bouts of sleep, the fatigue began to lift. Maggie and Augusta were able to talk. Augusta told her friend all the things she told me, about her farm and her brothers, about her strict father and the snow house — leaving out the part about the grey girl — about her sampler, her Sunday-school cards. Very occasionally the girls shared a needle, but only when they were very tired and convinced that without it they would not have been able to carry out whatever task they had been called upon to complete. A different kind of exhaustion had them in its clutches now that they had slept off all the adrenalin brought about by the crisis. They walked on the dunes and visited the amphitheatre. Maggie continued to write the letters. Augusta continued to think about solid stone arches and benches, fluted columns and curved halls, stable and unchanging, tens of feet down. They promised each other they would be friends forever.

On a clear night in May, Augusta walked alone over the dunes to the amphitheatre. The moon was round and cold in the sky.

There had been a dance a few days before in the nurses' quarters to celebrate the fourth anniversary of the Number One Canadian Hospital, and both she and Maggie had been able to ignore the irony of a celebration long enough to have a good time. They had spent hours dancing with patients; some on crutches, some in wheelchairs, others who were unable to hold their partners because they had no arms. The atmosphere everywhere since then had been light and warm, the weather echoing this. Maggie had written to her dead lover about the feeling of camaraderie that surrounded her, and had shown Augusta the letter. "I feel I belong here now," she had written, "and that you belong there, wherever you are." Then she had wept a little, but not for long. She had made a special friend among the wounded soldiers.

As Augusta walked alone under the clear night sky, her inner voice chanted, "Fred is dead. Fred is not dead," but it had become more like a melody one couldn't shake from one's mind than a painful announcement.

She knew the night was beautiful, and was sorry that Maggie was not with her, had chosen sleep instead, having begun her shift at four the previous morning.

A train clattered over the bridge on the River Canche. Its fire box was open and for a few moments the dunes turned an unearthly shade of orange because of this light, reminding Augusta, strangely, of a painting in her grandmother's house that showed the first Canadian Houses of Parliament the night they burned to the ground. Then the dunes turned silver again in the moonlight, and Augusta settled herself down near the buried and permanent stone of the amphitheatre. Below her, the lights of the hospital complex were like the lights of a fashion-able resort. Beneath the sand the memory of a constant, ordered world slept on.

She heard the planes before she knew what they were, assuming, until she saw most of the lights below her extinguish, that the noise was that of another hospital train arriving with wounded from the front. Then she heard the shrill song of the bombs. This disembodied noise seemed to go on for a long, long time, and reminded her of the whistle from the nearby canning factory where children were occasionally permitted to pull the cord that caused its high voice. Augusta had time to remember her brothers arguing over who would get first crack at it, time to wonder what on earth they had all been doing in the canning factory in the first place. Then she saw the only world she had come to understand shatter. At first she could not move, sat on the sand as if entranced. When the fires started they looked almost benign, tranquil, as if they had been lit on a beach for recreational purposes. The engines of the planes droned calmly into the distance.

———◦———

Augusta worked that night in the miraculously undamaged operating theatre by the light of five candles, everyone having agreed that any more illumination would guarantee further attacks. Her shoes filled with sand as she ran towards the disas-ter. Every step had been a struggle, a treadmill nightmare, the dunes giving way under her feet. Her thighs still ached from the effort.

One by one the men were brought to the operating table, soldiers who had been torn apart in battle, sliced open just days ago by the surgeons, and who were now torn apart again. Among them were staff members from the hospital: orderlies, doctors, cooks, caretakers, ambulance drivers. Sometime during the night the moon moved into the window near where Augusta stood holding the black rubber mask over the face of a patient, making her hands look blue and cold. Just then the planes returned, and the bombing resumed, though this time the target was the base camps closer to town. Still, the force of this shook the hut and knocked over two of the candles, setting fire to a supply of bandages. Eight medical personnel rushed forward to extinguish the inconsequential blaze, as if by mastering this one problem they could somehow control the devastation around them.

It was far into the night when Maggie was brought into the room and lifted gently from a stretcher. Her beautiful fine hair was matted with blood, her legs and arms bent in ridiculous directions. One of her hands was missing. The surgeon began pacing up and down beside the table. "I don't know where to start," he was saying. "I don't know where to start."

Augusta heard herself shout, "Who is this? I want to know who this is?" And she was surprised by the sound of her own voice asking this question because she knew. She knew.

There was no sign of the girl's left eye and her nose had been pushed sideways so that it lay against her cheek. Her faded blue-grey uniform was covered with blood.

"Re-tourniquet that arm!" the surgeon commanded.

"Don't touch her!" Augusta heard herself yell.

"I'll start with the head, then look for internal injuries," said the surgeon. But the man did not move. He looked oddly at some kind of instrument in his hand. Candlelight quivered on the blade. "I haven't operated on a woman since before the war," he said to Augusta. And then, "My God, is she really alive?"

A medic touched Maggie's wrist. "She's alive," he said.

The tune stopped playing in Augusta's mind. Fred was dead.

The surgeon looked directly at Augusta. "Anesthetize her," he ordered, anger in his voice.

"This can't be Maggie," she whimpered. "I don't want to touch her face."

The nurse on the other side of the table was crying, her sodden mask hanging heavy around her neck.

The doctor shook Augusta's shoulder. "Anesthetize her!" he commanded.

Wincing, she brought the mask down over the broken face. For a fraction of a second she was back on the dunes at the moment when Maggie first emerged from the fog. That odd combination of greyness and radiance. Then she heard the sound of the saw. When the skull had been opened for some time, she touched the surgeon's sleeve. "Doctor?" she said.

"I'm trying to save her," he responded testily. "Though God knows why."

The moon had gone down by now and the room was filled with the golden light of candles. A banquet hall. A basilica. Maggie's blood made a sucking sound beneath Augusta's sand-filled shoes.

Doctor? she had asked. *God knows why,* he had replied.

No one noticed when Augusta turned up the dial, causing the amount of diethyl ether to rise well above the level of safety. But by then, Augusta had redefined safety.

After that it seemed to Augusta that she was a child again standing in the slow rain of the interior of her snow house waiting for the grey girl to appear. The world she had so carefully constructed was dissolving around her and no golden light poured through the window. Shrinking before her very eyes, the white armchair remained cold and empty. The ice walls were streaming with moisture and the snow was soiled by mud.

I couldn't even remember what she looked like," she told me. "I had lost both the premonition and the memory of her physical presence, as if she had never existed, as if I had imagined her completely. This terrified me even more than the fact that she was dead. Everything about her was lost, utterly."

Augusta had anesthetized two more boys and then, just as the dawn broke, the surgeon had made her leave the operating theatre.

"I'm sorry your friend died," the doctor had said to her as she was untying her mask, "but there was nothing anyone could do."

"No," Augusta had agreed, "there wasn't anything that anyone could do."

During that same spring of 1918, I was attending Robert Henri's classes intermittently – he himself was often not there – and I was working on a more or less permanent part-time basis at the advertising firm of Carter and Fielding, making drawings of carpet sweepers, kitchen ranges, wringer washers, and the smiling, improbably glamorous women who stood beside them. I had a decent flat in Greenwich Village and was able to set up a reasonable studio there. Despite the fact that my father regularly supplemented my income, I believed myself to be, in what I called my "real" work, an authentic painter of the people – as was the fashion then – and so I spent a great deal of time under the bridges, down on the docks, and in the bars near the waterfront. Sometimes I visited brothels, having convinced myself that it was necessary to do so in order to better understand certain aspects of my subject matter. The girls loved to pose, and as I was often able to be there in the afternoon, I wasn't keeping them from their more lucrative nighttime activities.

He who had introduced me to this particular side of life had set up housekeeping with his wife and family on Staten Island. This, of course, meant that there was a convenient stretch of water between his responsibilities at home and his questionable though more interesting conduct in Manhattan. This is not to suggest that Rockwell did not love Kathleen and the children; he loved them deeply, wanted nothing more than their happiness. Years after he and Kathleen had separated forever, he would speak of her with such tenderness it was possible to believe that she had stepped out of the room, out of his embrace, just minutes before. In his exuberance, his enthusiasm for everything that existed in the world – at least everything he considered to be innocent – the focus of his affection would shift and change, was capable of being multidirectional. Sometimes it even attached itself to the inanimate.

Once, when we were walking behind a tenement on the Lower East Side, Rockwell spotted an abandoned sawhorse in a heap of trash. He stopped in his tracks and shook his head sadly. "The poor darling," he said. "A fate like this after selflessly committing his body to a lifetime of helping carpenters."

He was not joking; his eyes were filled with tears. "We must take him away from here," he insisted. "We must take him to a better home."

After we dug the sawhorse out of the trash pile, Rockwell caressed it, wept over it, praised humanity in the light of it. While he expounded on its service record, its long, patient hours in the company of labour, he ran his fingers gently over the hundreds of saw marks on its battered surface. He was quite sober at that moment, but was determined that we should take the sawhorse with us on our tour of the bars, where he would use it as a point of departure for various lectures of a socialist nature. How vividly I remember the last glimpse that I caught of him that night. He was standing on the deck of the Staten Island ferry, singing "Solidarity Forever" and waving goodbye, with the sawhorse — now called Dobbin — tucked protectively under one arm.

Much later I would paint the dark water with bright-blue lights reflecting on it, and I would use the same shade of ultramarine blue to illuminate the life buoys on the ferry and Rockwell's kind face. I would paint the angular form of the sawhorse in lamp black, and, for the first time, I would put myself into the underpainting, almost a silhouette, shown from the rear.

Oddly enough it was this dark figure, this witness to departure, that was the most difficult to transform, that bled through the subsequent layers of paint, and finally had to be scraped off with a knife.

One afternoon, sometime during the previous winter of 1918, I had returned from class to find a note from Rockwell pinned on my door. "Be at Sloan's Bar, 5 P.M.," it read. "There's someone from upstate I want you to meet."

I opened the door, tossed my portfolio inside, and clattered back down the narrow stairwell that led to the street. It was already after five. Rockwell's energy made him a restless man with a tensile attention span. He might not still be there.

But he was, and in the company of an older man, wonderfully dishevelled; a man who gave the impression that, although sitting reasonably still, he was nevertheless being buffeted by invisible forces. He was sweating profusely and kept mopping his wet brow with a large, stained pink handkerchief.

"Austin," said Rockwell, "meet Abbott Thayer. He hates this bar."

Rockwell had called the establishment Sloan's Bar ever since the painter John Sloan had made a picture of the place. It was, in actuality, named McSorely's Ale House, as was the work of art.

"I do not hate this ale house," said Thayer. "I hate no place on earth. But it is far too warm and there are no angels here."

I looked at Rockwell. He was listening attentively to what the older man had to say. "You hate Sloan's painting," he said to him.

"The painter has depicted only that which is here, not what might be here, not what should be here. Why, why," demanded Thayer, "why would he want to do that?"

"He has painted the dignity of the common man, Abbott." Rockwell motioned in the direction of one of the bartenders. "Look at him, Abbott. There he stands in his long white apron. He probably is an angel, and if not now, he will probably become an angel."

"There are no animals here either," said Thayer, ignoring altogether Rockwell's fantasies about the bartender. "There aren't even any concealed animals here."

"Thayer here," explained Rockwell, "has written a most scholarly volume entitled *Concealing Coloration in the Animal Kingdom*. Tell Austin about the blue jay, Abbott."

"I don't want to talk about the blue jay," said Thayer. He looked around the room suspiciously. "The enemy might be listening. One can never be too careful." He rose to his feet, approached the potential angel, and ordered another glass of water.

"Thayer is in town," Rockwell told me, "because he is trying to encourage various and sundry worthies to take his theories to the War Department. He's had a hell of an ongoing row with Teddy Roosevelt about birds, concealing colouration and all that."

"Teddy Roosevelt?" I choked on my beer. "Are you serious?"

"Absolutely. They've been battling it out for over a year." Thayer returned to the table and slumped dejectedly in his chair. "How many letters has Roosevelt written to you, about the blue jay?" Rockwell asked him.

Thayer drew his chair closer to mine and whispered, "The blue jay is invisible in snow. He is coloured blue and white precisely so that he will blend with the snow. I have made a painting entitled *Blue Jay in Snow* in which the bird is entirely invisible, can't see him at all." He loosened the dirty, faded cravat at his throat. "Mr. T. Roosevelt refuses to accept my incontestable proof of this, to the great peril of the war effort. What was the point of us entering this godforsaken war if concealing colouration is not used to our advantage?" He thumped his forehead with his handkerchief, attempting to capture various beads of sweat.

"I helped this man do a painting once of a snake moving through leaves," said Rockwell. "And when we were finished, the snake had completely disappeared from the canvas."

"Why did the *Titanic* meet with disaster?" Thayer demanded of me, as if I were a schoolboy and he the master.

"Because it hit an iceberg."

"And what colour was the iceberg?"

"White."

"Well, there you have it."

"Thayer says," Rockwell clarified, "that a white object floating on a dark sea at night is invisible. And since Roosevelt himself has had white ships under his command, Thayer believed he might have been a kindred spirit."

"What does this have to do with the blue jay?" I asked with as much gravity as I could muster.

"Nothing," said Rockwell.

"Everything!" thundered Thayer, the possible presence of the enemy evidently forgotten. "The blue jay is blue and white in order to make itself invisible in shadowed snow, whether Mr. T. Roosevelt believes it or not! That means that anything may appear to disappear!" He had attracted considerable attention in the bar. He pulled out his handkerchief again and mopped his brow. "Forgive me," he said to the dozen or so curious faces turned in his direction. "I have a nervous disposition."

"Henri always says that brilliancy is moving towards colour, not towards white," I told Thayer, who immediately became even more agitated.

"You should have a beer," said Rockwell.

"I have never touched alcohol."

"I'll bet there is beer in heaven," said Rockwell. "I'll bet the angels drink beer. I've never seen even a hint of a nervous disposition in your angels, Abbott." He turned to me. "Thayer paints angels as well," he said.

"In 1912," Thayer said to me, once again ignoring Rockwell's remarks, "well before the outbreak of the war, I invited Mr. T. Roosevelt to witness the disappearance of the blue jay in the shadowed snow of Central Park. Three or four of the birds had concealed themselves beautifully there in full view of the fifty witnesses who had accompanied me to the spot the week before. The blue feathers are for the shadows, and the white feathers are, of course, for the snow. The smaller, darker markings are there precisely so that you will confuse them with twigs – the markings, of course, not the jay – though there *are* birds that look exactly like twigs all over and that conceal themselves in dead bushes and the like. Do you know what he wrote to me?"

I did not.

"He wrote to me that my experiments with the blue jay and snow have as little relation to real life as would such experiments with 'a blue-rump baboon by the Mediterranean.' The audacity! The pomposity! Oh, I am certain he has spoken to the War Department and that is why they ignore my theories of concealing colouration! Why, why are we in this war?"

"My sentiments exactly," said Rockwell.

It had only been three years since Rockwell, his wife and children, had been turfed out of the British colony of Newfoundland. Rockwell could never understand why his singing of German lieder from a cliff edge at dawn, and at the top of his lungs, should have so upset the authorities. He offered lessons in music appreciation, and when those were refused, he painted a large, fierce German eagle on the outside door of the little building he used as a studio, partly as revenge and partly as a sign of respect for the northern Europeans whose culture he so loved. This was the final straw. He was given notice to leave immediately, though permitted to delay his departure by two weeks when he explained that his children had the measles. He had loved Newfoundland. This war meant that he couldn't be himself and remain there. He was disgusted when America entered the fray.

"I'll tell you why we are in this war," Rockwell was saying now. "We are in this war so that fat capitalists, like the father of Austin here, so that fat capitalists can get fatter."

"Your father is a capitalist, sir?" Thayer looked at me for the first time with genuine interest.

I felt my face grow red, but said nothing.

Rockwell assured him that such was the case. "One of the worst," he said. "Exploits miners, ruins pristine northern land-scapes, slaughters virgin forests."

Thayer smiled at me. "I have never," he said, "approved of Kent's socialist politics."

"I'll say!" said Rockwell. "He threw me right out of his house! Never let me back in the door! Now he only sees me in New York."

"A terrible influence on the children," Thayer confided. "Couldn't have him spouting all that nonsense in front of the children, and other winged beings."

"Look at that bartender," Rockwell said. "Look at the small dark wings of his bow tie. In his own simple dignity, his minis-trations to the tired, decent, honest, working men who visit his establishment, is he not also an angel?"

Thayer snorted, glared at Rockwell, and once again turned to me with a smile. "I paint winged beings," he said. "The larger ones are angels, the middle-sized ones are portraits of my children, who are angels but whose wings are cleverly disguised by concealing colouration, and the smaller ones are of birds . . . some concealed, and some, though it grieves me to say it, hopelessly exposed. Might your father be interested in any of these?"

"I'm afraid he is no collector," I replied.

"Might he then," Thayer persisted, "know anyone at the War Department? Would my theories of concealing colouration interest your father, do you think?"

"No, they wouldn't," interjected Rockwell. "Capitalists have no imagination, Abbott."

"Neither do dogmatists," retaliated Thayer. "There is nothing winged about them. Dogmatists never hang large, expensive angels in their homes. They will not admit that a zebra's stripes were made by God to conceal the beast in long, thin weeds."

"Hold it," said Rockwell. "I helped you paint that invisible snake, remember?"

"That is true, Kent," said Thayer. "I really wasn't referring to you . . . yet. And, as you may gather, I am unwell. I am torn to pieces," he lamented. "I am tied in knots. Why, why am I in this overheated bar? Why, why am I in this city?" He rose to his feet. "I must conceal myself in the country in the company of my winged creatures." He placed his bowler hat upon his head. "Goodbye, gentlemen."

"I love you, Abbott," said Rockwell, leaping from his chair and embracing the older man.

"I love you too, Kent," said Thayer, "but you are never again to visit my home."

"I suppose it must be so," said Rockwell.

"Yes, it must," agreed Thayer. And then, after shaking my hand, he left McSorely's Ale House, and not too many hours later I assume he left the city of New York.

"Well, aren't you the fortunate one," said Rockwell after the door had closed behind Abbott Thayer.

"How so?" I asked. I handed Rockwell a cigarette, lit one myself, then passed the lighter to my friend.

"God, I really do love that man. He introduced me to the Nordic sagas and God knows I love the north. But it was one of the happiest days of my life when I was banished from Thayer's house. To be a bona fide member of the Thayer school, you realize, it is mandatory to visit his house . . . often. Now I am a man who loves the snow, the cold. Can you think of anyone who loves it more?"

I could not.

"Well, I can," continued Rockwell. "Thayer loves it even more than me. Aren't you the lucky one that he didn't invite you."

I wasn't so sure of this. I had been drawn to the eccentricities of the man. "What's the problem with the house?" I asked.

"The problem is, it is completely unheated. Thayer doesn't believe in any form of artificial heat. Thinks it's unhealthy." Rockwell laughed. "I was there once in winter and almost died of pneumonia! Each morning when I woke, my chin was frozen to the blanket, my shoes frozen to the floor. The family sleeps outdoors year-round under makeshift lean-tos. Guests are permitted to bed down indoors. Not that it makes much difference;

all the windows are left open. For ventilation! Thayer says that if
the men and women of the sagas could live without artificial
heat, then so should we. He also says that angels waste away in
artificial heat, and Thayer believes that all of his children are
angels; though few of them are children any more."

Rockwell described his first indoor blizzard. He had been
sitting in a wooden armchair — Thayer did not approve of
upholstery — talking with the man, when a sudden hard wind
from the east had brought driving snow and sleet directly into
the room. "Feel it!" Thayer had enthused. "Experience it!
Thoreau should have known such indoor weather. He should be
here with us." They had been discussing Walden at the time.

Rockwell walked up to the bar and ordered another beer.

"So, I suppose he is insane," I said to him when he returned.

He looked at me with astonishment. "Insane? Absolutely
not. He is himself . . . relentlessly himself. Not a man to change
either his art or his character as a result of, for example, a show
of contemporary European cubism."

His reference to the Armory Show, which had taken place
the year before I came to New York, was not lost on me. I
myself, influenced by those who had been influenced by it, had
attempted one or two cubist nudes.

I never met Thayer again and, in the early 1920s, I heard that he
had died. I wonder what he would have thought of this cold
white barn of a house I now live in. He would have approved,
undoubtedly, of the lake-effect blizzards that regularly visit
this city, but would he have approved of the effect that his brief

appearance in my life was to have upon my work? For when the idea of *The Erasures* began to take shape in my mind I remembered that afternoon in McSorely's Ale House; the beads of sweat on Thayer's forehead, the bartender appearing more like a ghost than an angel behind Rockwell's left shoulder, the tobacco-stain atmosphere of the bar, as if it were mirroring the varnished image Sloan had made of it. I allowed my memory of that afternoon to slide past my friend Rockwell Kent. I did not revisualize the beautiful, assured gestures his hands made as he talked, gestures that would appear in his drawings of men lashed to the masts of ebony-coloured boats. I had laughed at Thayer, but what I had taken into myself on that winter day near the end of the first Great War was not his commendable qualities of energy and uniqueness but rather the idea of concealment.

Yes, when I began to think about *The Erasures*, it was to Thayer's *Concealing Coloration in the Animal Kingdom* that I turned for instruction, haunting book dealers until I finally found a copy. I did not know, in the beginning, that mere camouflage would not satisfy me. I had no intention of using Thayer's theories to protect innocent winged beings. No, even by then I had developed sufficient detachment from innocence to want to protect only one being in the world. Me. Thayer's peacocks screened by emerald forests and blue jays blending with snow were not enough for me. I wanted total disguise. I was moving towards white.

I met Sara at the beginning of the summer of 1920 and left her at the end of the summer of 1935.

"Fifteen years," she said.

"Fifteen summers," I corrected.

During the time we were together I was moving away from landscape towards the figure. Occasionally the landscape eased its way into the corner of my figurative work, but the opposite was never true. But then what do all these descriptive labels mean anyway? They are nothing but words. Robert Henri had taught me early on that it was the expression, not the subject, that brought beauty into a work of art. And, oh, how I valued my own expression. Perhaps my creative activity at the time was nothing more than a recital by rote of appropriate learned responses.

Still, sometimes standing in Sara's kitchen when she was not there, drawing the discarded work gloves she had used for gardening, or her father's oiler hanging on a hook on the back of a door, tears would inexplicably enter my eyes. There was something touching, I suppose, about the way she wore her father's clothing for protection, as if she were placing her soft body, on purpose, inside a layer of his skin. But the truth was that the smallest thing connected to her could move me in the strangest way, cause me to experience something like sorrow.

Each autumn in New York, as towards the end of the year darkness folded itself around light, I could feel the bright northern summer begin to evaporate, the candles the sun had lit on Superior's dark waters being put out one by one by my winter life. Finally, by January or February, I would not, despite the intensity of my visual memory, call that shore to mind at all. By then I would be involved in what, in retrospect, I can only call the promotion of my own career, in submitting my works to juried exhibitions, encouraging my dealer — when I finally had a dealer — to mount one-man shows of my work. As time passed, these activities altered only by virtue of the distribution of power among the players involved. After a decade or so I would find myself sitting on the jury rather than being judged, and my dealer would be urging me to bring together a collection of my paintings, my paintings of Sara.

I had publicly shown my work for the first time just a few years before I met Sara, before I began to spend my summers at Silver Islet. In 1917, I was coaxed by Rockwell to hang two of my New York scenes — one of which looked suspiciously like Sloan's *Ale House* — in the Independent Exhibition he was administrating, which was to take place in the Central Grand Palace. I was tremendously flattered by his insistence that my pictures should be included, until, when scanning the list of exhibitors and their works on the day of the opening, I noticed an entry that read, "Kent, Rockwell, Junior, *Nice Animals, Newfoundland.*" Then I realized that, true to his principles of socialist democracy and equal opportunity, Rockwell Senior had insisted that absolutely everyone should be included. He had observed, as was his nature, the exhibitions credo "No Juries! No Prizes!" down to the smallest and most subtle interpretations of that phrase.

In the course of the years following this inauspicious début, Rockwell cartwheeled in and out of my winter life in the city. After being thrown out of Newfoundland and coming back to New York, he went to Alaska and came back to New York. He went to the Straits of Magellan and returned to New York. He bought a boat, sailed the icy waters of the North Atlantic, was shipwrecked on the coast of Greenland, had great adventures there, and returned to New York. Unannounced, penniless, bursting with enthusiasm, and laden down with canvases, he would reappear in the offices of Chappel and Ewing and, inevitably, George Chappel would give him a job, or the Folio Society would commission illustrations, or his old friend George Putnam would arrange to publish the tales he had written about his most recent travels. At the end of the 1920s, he bought a farm in the Adirondacks and determined to stay there for life, painting views of forested hills. He became sought-after on the lecture circuit. He went to Greenland again. He returned to New York. He withdrew to the Adirondacks. He returned to New York.

Some people walk up a flight of stairs, others trot. Rockwell, a slave to his own boundless energy, galloped, creating such a singular racket that I always knew it was him. I heard the commotion of his approach for the last time in the winter of 1934.

I was no longer the kid that Rockwell had hauled out of Robert H.'s class at The Art Students' League. I had, in fact, developed enough of a reputation that I'd been able to survive the worst of the Depression years on the sale of my work. That night I had been preparing for a spring exhibition and had, as a result, about twenty paintings – landscapes and nudes – leaning against the walls of my studio. I liked to leave them like this for the month or so preceding a show so that I could add highlights or finishing touches in a casual way as the days went by.

Quite late at night I opened my door to an uncharacteristically overdressed Rockwell. He said he had been delivering a lecture entitled "In Defense of True Art" to the Whitney Club and had decided once the evening wrapped up to drop by and see what I was up to.

"They were delightful," he told me, referring to the crowd of people at the club. "Believe it, Austin, there is a lover of art at the centre of each bright human spirit. The problem is that most have been made to feel inadequate, ashamed of their own preferences. Why shouldn't art serve mankind?"

"You'd better be careful, Rockwell," I teased. "There must have been a great number of capitalists in that group."

He waved aside my comment, hung his coat on the door-knob, and crossed the room. "Even the rich can be educated," he said. "I'm just doing my bit."

I raised my eyebrows. "Whatever you say."

He was leaning on one of the window sills in the studio. Two tall, narrow paintings I had done of Sara were reflected in the glass on either side of him, and beyond him I could see the dark shapes of several rooftop water towers silhouetted against a vaguely yellow night sky. I walked across the floor to the old cupboard where I kept the liquor, removed a bottle of scotch, and placed it on a table in the centre of the room. I noticed that the electric light was shining on the top of Rockwell's head. I realized that in the time that I had known him he had become almost bald, and yet somehow he looked no older than he had in the beginning. I, on the other hand, though a decade and a half younger, was starting to notice of late that there was grey in my hair and that the tired look around my eyes did not disappear after a good night's sleep.

I went into the kitchen to collect glasses, and when I returned Rockwell was strolling around the studio examining the pictures.

"I should go there," he said, looking at one of the views of the north shore of Lake Superior. "I've always wanted to go there."

"Scotch?" I asked.

"Absolutely."

I poured three fingers in the glass, handed it to Rockwell, and poured another three fingers for myself.

"Why are you so well ordered?" he was asking. "Don't you just sometimes want to get up and go somewhere else? I mean, just recklessly chuck it all in an inappropriate season . . . just go?"

"I'm not like you, Rockwell," I said. "Few people are."

"I'm not asking you to be like me," he said, pausing in front of a full-sized nude of Sara. He walked away from it and approached a smaller painting: one of Sara's house huddled under the rock cliff. "I like Canada," he said. "I like it up there. 'With glowing hearts we see thee rise, the true north strong and free,'" he sang.

"Obviously that tune didn't make it big on Broadway."

"It's a Canadian song. Who is this model of yours anyway?"

"A woman I know. She lives there. Her father was a miner . . . from Cornwall."

"He worked for your father then?"

"He was dead before my father tried to reopen the mine. What a disaster that was! But short-lived, thank God. You'll be happy to hear, Rockwell, that my father lost a barrel of money on that one. We went up there together that first summer . . . but he never went back again."

"What happened to the mine?"

"The same thing that happened when it closed in '84. The lake flooded it, then the lake took apart the superstructure. There's not much left at all now on the islet. Mind you, there wasn't much there in the first place. The mine — the tunnels — are under the lake."

"All flooded now."

I nodded, took a generous swallow from the glass. "I sometimes think about that, those tunnels down there filled with water."

"Any silver left?" Rockwell's glass was almost empty.

"So some people say." I laughed. "Thinking of investing?"

"Usury!" he announced. He was looking at a small land-scape I had made of the bay from Thunder Cape, the only one I had completed, the climb up there being so bug-filled and exhausting. "Some good painters in Canada," he said. "Ever seen any of Harris's work, or Varley's?"

I hadn't. "Don't think so," I said. Rockwell handed me his glass and I walked over to the table and poured him another drink.

"Your father would have lost all his money anyway, in the crash."

"He was dead by then." I lit a cigarette, offered one to Rockwell.

"Oh. Sorry," he said, as he bent towards my lighter.

It seemed to me that Rockwell was unusually solemn. Despite his spirited ascent of the stairs, there was something studied and measured about the conversation we were having, and I was beginning to feel tense. He was frowning at a picture I had made, a picture of Sara leaning against a rough plaster wall, her arms crossed in front of her chest, the veins on her hands visible. It occurred to me that the drinks we were now sharing were perhaps not the first my friend had tasted this evening. He had seen my work before – landscapes, figures – but had never commented on it. I had always assumed his silence sprang from his dislike of qualitative opinion when it referred to artistic expression, himself being a man who disapproved of competition in the arts. But tonight there was something Rockwell wanted to say, and I knew it. I swallowed the remaining scotch in my glass. "Well?" I said as lightly as I could manage. "What do you think?"

He was pacing up and down in front of the nudes. "They are quite good, Austin," he said, rolling the scotch around in his glass. "Quite good." He pulled a chair away from the wall and straddled it, his arms resting on the back. He was still looking at the pictures. The glass shone in his hand.

I thought he was patronizing me, was annoyed by his tone. "Come on," I said. "I haven't been a student for fifteen years. Tell me what you think."

"Are you in love with her?" he asked abruptly.

I said nothing. I had no answer for this. Multiple images of Sara all over the room.

We both remained silent for several moments.

Finally, Rockwell shook his head, then looked directly into my face. "Are you going to answer my question, or what?" he demanded.

"Excuse me." I placed the glass on the window sill, stood up straight as if to leave the room.

"She's the same one," he continued, "isn't she, that we see exhibition after exhibition?"

I felt my face redden and I turned towards the night view so that Rockwell wouldn't notice.

"This has nothing to do with you," I said quietly, but I was beginning to become genuinely angry. He had no right, I believed, to inquire into my personal life, particularly if one took into consideration his own, which was certainly no shining example. I turned away from the view of water towers and faced him. We were both reflected in the window and Sara was every-where in the room. "I think we should talk about the painting," I said, "not about some woman."

"Some woman," he repeated. In the silence that followed, the radiator banged four times, like a gavel requesting order in a court of law.

"Let's talk about the paintings," I repeated. By now, I'm certain, my expression was grim, my voice hard.

Silence.

"Well?" I wasn't going to give it up.

Rockwell looked at the floor for a few moments, then, avoiding my eyes, he shifted his glance to the radiator, which had begun to emit a combined clatter and cough. "I was talking about the paintings," he said calmly, almost sadly. And then he added, "They're as cold as ice."

There is something peculiar about night and electricity in spaces such as artists' studios, spaces chosen for the quality of the natural light that enters them during the day. The easels, the tables, the jars of brushes and tubes of paint, even the walls and floorboards look awkward and tawdry under the overhead glare. Unless I am working furiously in a night studio, I have always felt vaguely disoriented and terribly, terribly alone, almost as if I were an intruder about to burgle another's workshop. Only unquestionably finished paintings do not alter in this unflattering light, paintings that cannot be changed regardless of what the artist does to them. Looking at my own work now in this harsh atmosphere, I knew that no final touch, no highlight was going to alter them. They were completed. And they were flawed.

"Cold . . . as . . . hell," Rockwell was saying, each word like a knife slipped between the ribs.

"Get out," I said, keeping my voice as steady as possible.

"I am doing you a favour by telling you this."

"Get out!" I yelled, the anger finally verbalized. "Get out and don't come back!"

"It's your choice," Rockwell said. Then he emptied his glass, put on his coat, and left.

This great white house, in which it appears I shall live out the remainder of my days, was designed to welcome natural light. During the day any one of its cavernous, echoing rooms would make a perfect studio, though I have chosen to work at the rear of the building as I cannot bear the idea of being observed by passersby on the street. At night, electricity has the same effect on my surroundings as it had on my old studio in Greenwich Village, and the same effect upon my soul. No arching lamps or muted shades can change the horror that I feel towards walls, floors, objects, furniture, my shoes, the sleeve of my jacket, the liver spots on my hands when they are exposed by artificial light. Normally I arrange to be asleep rather than witness this monstrosity of illumination and its attendant combination of darkness and images mirrored in my walls of glass. But today, after working on the collection all morning, I fell asleep in my chair in the afternoon. So now I find myself here in the electric light, painfully alert, remembering my break with Rockwell.

Get out. Get out and don't come back.

What was it that caused the anger to burst out of me that night? Why did I feel I had to reject the criticism — the man himself — so forcefully? Did I have any idea what I was doing? Friends had criticized my paintings before, sometimes publicly, in print, and while the experience was never pleasant, the accompanying feeling of ill will disappeared in a week or two. But Rockwell's comments stuck. I took them with me to the opening of the exhibition, where I could hardly bear to glance at my paintings on the wall and where I considered the patrons dupes for their purchases. Even months later, in the summer, I took them with me to Silver Islet, where the entire landscape looked used and cheap to me, as if it were suffering from the effects of the same artificial light that swims around me here now. I couldn't forgive Rockwell — perhaps because I believed him — though I never would have admitted that then. I couldn't forgive him, and I lost him, completely. He had caused me, you understand, to see my work as flawed. I believed I would look at my painting forever through the lens of his disapproval, and, though I refused utterly to examine the possible source of his disapproval, I hated him for it. In my vanity, I could not blame myself. For a while I tried to blame Rockwell, but he, after all, had not painted the pictures, so, despite my rage, I had to abandon that convenient option. But I could not indict myself, my own cherished expression. So I blamed the subject matter. I blamed Sara.

I looked at her standing, stricken, on the other side of the room. It was the end of summer and I was preparing to leave. For good. "This is an aesthetic decision," I told her. "I'm not talking about character."

"Fifteen years," she said, turning her face partially away from me.

"Fifteen summers," I corrected.

I was wrong. I had been talking about character. My character. It was not in my nature at that time to commemorate the past, just as it was not in my nature to be able to forget it. I never forgave Rockwell and I never forgave Sara. And those you never forgive you find impossible to forget. It would be years before I relaxed, paused long enough to wonder if they ever forgave me.

I was a creature of habit. Winter demanded that I remain in the city, but summer was for landscape. Once I decided to never return to Silver Islet, I was out of sorts when the heat came to New York. I made a couple of brief trips to the coast of Maine but was able to produce very little. So the next summer, on a whim, I drove to Rochester, left my car, and took the ferry to Davenport, where I visited George for a week or two. During this time I often met his dark-haired friend Augusta, who was on holiday from the Toronto General Hospital. I was admittedly grateful for the comfort of their company, these two unassuming Canadians, and a bit startled by the tenderness between them.

Early one evening, I remember, after I had returned from a walk on the beach at twilight, I removed my wet shoes and entered through the open back door. As I made my way down the hall to the stairs I passed by the dining room, where George and Augusta were still at the table. Augusta sat with her hands folded on her lap, her thin torso perfectly erect, her head lowered. George, who was diagonally across from her, had extended his arm over the width of the table so that his hand was resting on her shoulder. Neither of them was moving at all; they had not heard me enter. "Don't," George whispered, looking intently into Augusta's downcast face. "Don't." There was an air of sadness about the tableau they formed, which was so profound it was almost suffocating, as well as a sense that nothing, no one, could move into the private region they had entered. "Don't," George whispered. Still, she did not look up. He shook her shoulder gently. "Don't," he said again. I turned away then, moved with extreme caution towards the stairs.

On another occasion, I met George in the dark hallway on my way to the bathroom in the middle of the night. He had a glass of water in his hand for Augusta, who he explained had awakened from a nightmare. But most often it was George's nightmares I was aware of, his shouting in the night, followed by Augusta's soft murmuring, and then silence. They were able, you see, to give each other the gift of sleep.

Halfway through my visit, Augusta returned to her job in Toronto. After she'd gone, George handed me an apron and encouraged me to stand with him behind the counter in the shop. I laughed at myself in this uniform, fervently hoped no stray tourist from New York would recognize me, but the truth is I enjoyed the trade, the gossip, the tidy rows of numbers in the account book. The following summer, I insisted that I would accompany George to the China Hall the first morning after I arrived. Earning my keep, I said, as an excuse. In fact, I was eager to see the new patterns, and, by the end of a week, I was almost as excited as George when a small crate containing the latest addition to his collection arrived in the shop all the way from France.

During the first few winters after Silver Islet, those first few winters after Sara, I worked on a series of ostensibly mystical cubist paintings that have now, mercifully, all but disappeared from the face of the earth, my dealer having been instructed to purchase them for me if ever they appeared at auction, and I, in turn, having instructed myself to subsequently dispose of them as quickly as possible.

I began to frequent the theatre during this period, partly, I imagine now, so as to liberate myself from the stifling boredom of painting one revealing shaft of light after another shining on one stylized mountain after another. Sometimes a wealthy patron would give me a ticket and I would attend a concert or play that I might not otherwise have considered worthy of my attention. And so it was that in January of 1937 I found myself watching the final New York performance of Vi Desjardins's first North American tour, about which there had been so much talk during the preceding weeks.

The seat was excellent, far too expensive for the piece of silly frippery I was forced to view at such close range. The star was beautiful, I suppose, but wearing a tawdry costume and heavily made-up. The tunes she sang — and sang quite well — were ordinary in the extreme; one wondered how she, her orchestra and chorus, remembered the melody and the words, one was so like another. Still, there was something about her, a face beneath the painted face, that held my attention and wouldn't let go. It wasn't until the ballroom scene, however, that I knew. It was the way she moved her arms when dancing with a partner, the line of her neck, the way she threw her head back when she laughed. I swear I could almost hear waves from twenty years before bubbling across the shore at Davenport beach. Jesus, I thought, that's what happened to her. All those years. She hadn't disappeared at all. She had become someone else.

When I presented myself at her dressing-room door, having used my reputation and that of the purchaser of my ticket to get past her battery of slaves and protectors, she looked at me quizzically for some thirty seconds. Breaking the silence, I told her who I was and she began to laugh, an infuriating, taunting sound that made me feel threatened, awkward, in ways I hadn't since my teenage years. And then, in reaction, I felt determined. To seduce her.

It wasn't a difficult task. Within minutes she had dismissed her entourage and was demanding that I take her to the rooftop lounge of her hotel so that we could drink Manhattans.

"We are, after all, in Manhattan," she said. "And we can dance . . . just like old times."

George's younger face, its passionate, angry expression, flickered for just a moment in my mind, but I ignored it. "Five cents a dance, Vivian," I said, leaning in a self-consciously casual way in her door frame.

Neither of us spoke about George that night. We were too busy
assessing each other, circling each other like animals on the edge
of aggression. We were both showing off, performing: our
younger selves demanded this. What, after all, is the point of
reputation if it can't be flaunted in the face of the anonymity of
the past?

Vivian was a remarkably fine dancer, but, by then, so was I.
Others on the floor pulled back and watched us, and the room
buzzed. She was famous, a household word. It was, she told me,
what she had always wanted.

"Even then?" I asked her.

"Especially then," she replied.

She owned a house in St. John's Wood in London, and
another somewhere in the south of France. Men appeared and
disappeared at her command. She really didn't have time for
them, she claimed. Only now and then did one of them become
difficult.

She eyed me closely as she told me this.

I decided to postpone rising to the bait. In all truthfulness I
did not really desire her, but some angry sliver of my personality
made it essential that I sleep with her. As if this single act, once
accomplished, would prove my sophistication, my cleverness, my
superiority.

Had I been able to suppress my lust we might have become
passably good companions. She actually had the most marvellous sense of humour: abrupt, controlled, carefully balanced on
the cusp of cynicism. A kind of frantic gaiety drove us forward.
And then there was her beauty. Her beauty was violent and

shining, almost unbearably so, especially when she laughed. Our repartee was stunning, sharp and quick — blade-bright. Everything around us spun and glittered.

Eventually I asked, "Shall *I* appear then?" knowing full well that I could just as easily disappear any time she or I desired it. I added that, if it made any difference, I was far from difficult.

"Why not?" she said, sweeping her dark hair away from her forehead with one perfectly manicured hand.

Suddenly nothing I looked at, neither the lights that shone in the room nor the lights I could see in the streets below me, nothing I recalled from the studio, neither the twisted tubes of paint nor the brushes arranged by size in glass jars, none of it seemed to have anything at all to do with me. It was as though I were suffering from a peculiar brain disorder that caused me to perceive what was going on around me, and to remember something as simple as my own living quarters, as if these perceptions and memories belonged to someone else. I knew then what was wrong with my current paintings; those explosions of questionably spiritual light carried nothing across the canvas that really belonged to me. I had never felt so distant from the creative as I did during that brief bubble of time in a rooftop bar overlooking the city. This disorientation was temporary, however, gone almost before it had fully caught my attention.

I smiled at the woman seated across from me and then I downed what was left of my fourth cocktail. "Let's get out of here," I said.

Vivian was the only woman I have ever known who laughed when she made love. At the beginning I was somewhat disconcerted by this, but quite quickly I came to understand that for her this was an expression of appreciation, of pleasure. Unlike the mirth that had accompanied her witty conversation, this sound had no sharp edge, no ironic reference, and addressed itself only to the present. Memory, you see, was not a part of who Vivian was. She slipped easily in and out of roles, in and out of men's arms. Her enjoyment was so honestly connected to the moment that it carried with it an odd kind of innocence.

We made love together in a large bed in her hotel suite. Apart from her musical laughter I remember very little else about our lovemaking except that it took place and that she wanted the lights left off. The next morning while she slept, however, I saw the young girl she had been in the past in her relaxed face, the curve of her mouth.

When she opened her eyes, her expression revealed no surprise at my presence by her side. She sat up and reached for my watch, which was lying on the bedside table, squinted at it, then buckled the strap around my wrist. "I suppose you drive," she said.

"Yes, I have a car." My new Packard was one of the few things about which I had been able to develop a genuine enthusiasm in recent months.

She lay down again and drew my arm close to her body. "Then take me to Canada," she said. "I have four days before I sail. I want to see Davenport again, and George."

I pulled back from her and looked into her face to see if she was serious. "Now?" I asked.

"Yes, now."

My studio, my daily life was miles and miles away, had nothing to do with me. "Why not," I said.

We spent the night in an almost empty hotel somewhere in the Adirondacks. At the last moment Vivian decided that she wanted her own room.

"You don't mind, do you, darling?" she said. "I have to get my beauty sleep, you know."

I assured her I did not. I was tired, recovering from a hang-over, and beginning to be annoyed by the fact that I had agreed so quickly to make what was turning out to be a long journey over icy roads at the worst possible time of the year. There was no ferry, of course, in the winter, so we would have to drive along the St. Lawrence River and cross over to Canada at Ogdensburg. It was going to take us most of the next day to drive the north shore of the river and then along the edge of the Great Lake until we reached Davenport.

"I wonder if George will remember you," I said, half seri-ously, the next day in the car.

"Of course he will. . . . How could he not?"

I laughed at her vanity. "Vivian," I said, "it's been more than twenty years. I don't think he knows who you are. I mean, that you are *who* you are."

"He knows who I am."

"He hasn't said anything. . . . Nothing at all since the end of the war, nothing for twenty years."

"He knows," she repeated. She had brought a little silver flask of whisky along with her for the trip. She offered me a swallow, carefully replaced the cap, and slipped it back into her handbag. "Has he changed at all?" she asked.

"He still has the China Hall. His parents are both dead, so he's let the grocery business go, though he still wears that apron, you know, with the pens clipped at the front."

It was late afternoon. We were travelling west at the time, I remember, so I was constantly altering the angle of the visor to keep the low winter sun out of my eyes. "And," I added, "he still paints on china. He's an alderman or something now," I said. "Something on the town council anyway. No doubt some day he'll be mayor."

Vivian smiled, then turned her face towards the side window of the car. "Poor George," she said. "Who would have thought that he would ever be grown up enough to be a mayor. Remember how angry he used to be if I danced with anyone else?"

"I didn't think you noticed that."

"I noticed," she said. "In fact, I quite liked it."

We passed through Belleville, then Trenton, then Brighton. I hadn't seen the winter lake since I had been a boy and I had never seen it from this shore. I recalled my mother talking about her skating parties. There was nothing in the ash-coloured ice near the shore that suggested play or laughter, and I wondered for the first time if maybe these outings had been as fictional as our blood kin in their impressive mausoleums.

As we got closer to Davenport, Vivian moved closer to me and touched the sleeve of my coat. "Does George have a woman?" she asked.

I could smell her perfume, recognized it from our night together. "He has a friend, a woman called Augusta. Actually,

I've never been able to interpret their relationship." I was lying, perhaps to myself as well as to Vivian, because even I had been able to understand that the remarkable compassion that passed between them must have been what some people called love. "She's a nurse in Toronto," I said. "Maybe they are just friends . . . I'm not certain. Anyway, he's never married."

Vivian smiled then. "You're certain of this?" she asked in a teasing way, not expecting an answer. She opened her purse and removed the silver flask, which she shook near her right ear. "It's all gone," she said.

"No problem. I've got another bottle in my bag. Augusta might be there," I added. "She sometimes gets the weekends off."

It had already been dark for an hour or so when we drove into Davenport. I parked the Packard in front of George's shop and turned off the motor just as the streetlights switched on. I remember this because there was a strange momentary silence in the car. And since then I have always thought of that pause as a kind of grace note at the beginning of a line of sombre music, a last chance for the theme to move in some other direction. Neither Vivian nor I showed any signs of being eager to leave the vehicle now that the journey had been accomplished. We didn't look at each other, stared instead at the windshield, where large snowflakes were landing and then melting. I remember the way the light was caught on the surface of the empty silver flask Vivian nervously flicked backwards and forwards, and on the hood ornament of the car: a winged woman, her face slightly tilted towards the sky, the wheel of motion held firmly in her hands.

Night in the China Hall is one of my least satisfactory canvases. For it to have been successful I would have had to paint everything I've told you so far, everything Augusta told me, the teeming floral patterns of the china that engulfed us, and the dreadful artificial light raining down on a place in which night was never meant to be witnessed. I would have had to paint Vivian's black mink coat flung over the counter like a wounded beast, Augusta's locket, the cardboard sign that read CLOSED and that George had carefully placed among the cups and saucers displayed in the shop window. I would have had to paint the smoke from my cigarettes that gradually filled the place with a dirty fog, the tassel hanging from the end of the old green blind that George had forgotten to pull down over the glass in the door. I would have had to paint the dining room where we all consumed in silence the simple meal that Augusta hurriedly put together for us, George's homemade wine that we drank with our food. I would have had to paint the look on George's face as

I walked into the shop with Vivian beside me, the bell that hung above the door and that rang too long and too loud in the silence. But, in the end, I painted Augusta talking to me in the shop in the early hours of the morning. Only this. Nothing else.

"Look who's here," I said. "What a surprise, *n'est-ce pas?*"

"What a surprise," George echoed. He stood with a small tube of paint in one hand, the doorknob in the other, and a paintbrush clenched in his teeth. I could not interpret his expression.

"It's Vivian," I prompted. "Or I suppose I should say the famous Vi Desjardins."

George said nothing, seemed frozen.

Then, after several awkward moments, Vivian raised one hand towards George's face, removed the paintbrush from his mouth, and kissed him lightly on the lips. When he didn't respond she took a step backwards and looked at him. "You haven't changed," she said. Silence. Vivian placed the brush in a vase on a nearby shelf, walked past George to the far end of the store, took off her coat, and dropped it on the counter. She stared at each of the three walls in turn. "This place hasn't changed either," she added.

A brief, vivid picture flashed in my mind, a picture of George leaning from the train window. *She crushed it beneath her heel.*

I hoped that Vivian would behave decently towards George's friend. I suspected she was capable of utterly ignoring the presence of another woman in the room.

George didn't answer, began walking down the length of the shop towards Vivian, a peculiar smile on his face. "Oh, I've changed," he said to her. "Everything about me has changed completely."

Vivian tilted her head, looked at him quizzically, then announced brightly, "Not in my view, you haven't."

I looked at the man and woman who stood face to face at the far end of the China Hall. Quite suddenly I knew that in spite of the youthful George's angry misery, a relationship of some kind had developed between them over the course of that winter preceding the war. I found the idea surprising and somewhat amusing. Just as I was smiling to myself about George's romantic past, I heard Augusta call from somewhere in the rooms at the back of the store.

"George," she was asking, "who's in the shop with you?"

It wasn't until after supper, until after I had brought out the bottle of scotch, that George stopped breezily articulating pleasantries. Augusta had excused herself in order to tidy the kitchen, and George had fallen into the kind of quietness that could be mistaken for contentment were it not for the way he stared at the tumbler on the table in front of him, suddenly drained the contents, then pushed it towards the bottle at my end of the table without raising his eyes. I refilled the glass and slid it into his hand. Still, he did not look at me, or at anything else for that matter. Vivian began to relate a long anecdote concerning the unpublished lyrics of a Cole Porter song. George coughed once in the middle of this, shoved his chair back with an abrasive, grating sound, and Vivian paused. But he did not get up from the table and so she continued, her voice rising in pitch. In the middle of a sentence that began with the words, "Then Cole said to me," George said hoarsely, "That's not what we care about Vivian, not what we want to know."

She appeared not to have heard what he said. "What was that, darling?" she asked, leaning her head in his direction.

"Darling," he repeated, still looking at the table, his voice flat. "What kind of a word is 'darling'?"

I could hear Augusta's footsteps in the kitchen, then the sound of running water.

Vivian swallowed. "George," she said, "I wanted to –"

But he interrupted her. "Where did you go . . . darling? Or perhaps we should ask you what you are doing here, what in hell made you come back here?"

Even in the lamplight I could see that his expression was bleak, his face white. The tumbler was shaking in his hand, the ice clinking slightly as if he were drinking on a train. I began to feel uneasy, remembered the day in the shop, George's violent trembling, the lavender paint dripping onto the floor. What was this mood that he had so carefully concealed, hoarding it for three hours, until Augusta was out of the room? It was only in the face of his strangeness that I realized how artificial his previous politeness had been.

Vivian began to recoil from him, but he clutched her upper arm, drew her closer.

"Tell me all about it . . . darling," he said.

She shook him off, smoothed the silk of her sleeve, sat back in her chair, and smiled brightly, first at me, then at him.

"It was Mother," she said lightly. "What else can I tell you? She just wouldn't have it. We left the morning after I told her. She just packed up two suitcases and got us on a train for New York. You must have known this. From there we sailed to Britain. You know what she was like. She wouldn't even consider it."

George remained silent.

"She wouldn't let me write or wire. I just couldn't. I was never out of her sight."

George said nothing.

"You can't seriously believe that it wasn't for the best?" Vivian looked at George with genuine astonishment.

"Best for who?" George angled his upper body towards her. "Best for who, Vivian, darling? Best for me? I don't think so. Best for the boy I was then? I doubt it." A pause, then he added the word "darling."

"But it was all forgotten so quickly. I had my career . . . and then there was the war." Vivian was no longer smiling. She shifted uncomfortably in her chair. "You would have gone to war, George, regardless."

"Yes, I would have gone to war, regardless," he said. He was staring directly at her, his face implacable. "And with any luck I would have been killed . . . is that it?"

Vivian straightened her spine. "Look," she said, "I came here in good faith, to make amends, to explain."

"To explain," George repeated, his voice cold, hard.

"What the hell is going on here?" I said. "What is this?"

"You wait twenty-four years," George said, ignoring me,

"to explain. I don't believe that's why you're here, Vivian. I can't believe that's why you're here. And you," he said, turning suddenly to me. "Is this your idea of a joke?"

I had never heard George speak like this to anyone. "What's the joke?" I wanted to know. "I have no idea what is going on here."

"I didn't tell him," Vivian sighed. "I half supposed he knew. It just didn't come up."

"Knew what?" I looked at each of them in turn and asked again. "Knew what? Will somebody please tell me what's going on here?"

By now the look on George's face was frightening. But I'd seen the expression before, I realized, during dances at the pavilion. In that look all those years ago there had dwelt the man that George would become; the angry man sitting at this dining-room table. "Settle down," I said to him. "We just dropped by to say hello. Vivian wanted to see Davenport again."

George drew back from Vivian. "Jesus," he said. "Jesus Christ." He put his elbows on the table and covered his face with his hands.

He is hiding something terrible, I thought, something he isn't able to remove from the expression on his face. Vivian placed one white hand on the dark wool of his sleeve. "I just couldn't, George," she said softly. "It was one night and then Mother took me away. And she was right. We were just children . . . I was only seventeen and you weren't that much older that winter. I find it touching now that you felt you had to marry me in order to go to bed with me." She laughed. "I certainly haven't run into anyone as chivalrous since."

George raised his head from his hands and looked at her.

"Chivalrous," he repeated, almost as if he had never heard the word before. "We were married," he hissed. "We got married."

I could see there were tears in his eyes, anguish on his face, and felt embarrassed.

"For one night," Vivian said, as if correcting him. Then, when he looked stricken, she repeated, "I just couldn't, George. I was already becoming someone else. You caught me just on the edge of that."

"I suppose you want a divorce," he said. "I suppose that's why you've come."

Vivian removed her hand from his arm, tossed her hair back and laughed. "Not particularly," she said. "Why bother?"

It was then that I saw Augusta standing, shadowed, in the doorway. She was holding a tray on which there were cups, saucers, a coffee pot, and four pieces of cake. Framed by the moulding on the doorjamb, she resembled one of the women in Sargent's full-length, life-sized portraits. She was that frozen, that still. She looked at me, she looked at what she was carrying in her hands, and, for some inexplicable reason, she looked out the side window where not even the wall of the neighbouring building was visible in the dark. Then she turned and quietly carried the tray back into the kitchen.

George had not seen her at all. He had never taken his eyes from Vivian's face.

Augusta made her second entrance into the room five minutes later, after an excruciating period of silence. This time the clatter of the cups on the tray was loud enough that both

George and Vivian turned to stare at her. I couldn't bear to look at her face.

George stood up. "Vivian has to catch a train," he said, "in Toronto. I'm going to drive her there."

"But," I said, "I was going to drive her back to —"

"No," said George, "you told me you were spending the night. You'll have enough driving to do tomorrow. I'll take her there . . . for old time's sake. You stay with Augusta."

I had imagined that he wanted to be rid of her, as quickly as possible. "But isn't there a train from Davenport?" I asked. "Couldn't I drive her to the station here?"

Vivian rose slowly to her feet. She looked preoccupied, distracted, almost middle-aged. Her lipstick had worn off at least half an hour ago and she had uncharacteristically forgotten to reapply it, a strand of her elaborate hairdo had fallen from the pins. "I want George to drive me," she said. "I have to catch the train from Toronto at midnight."

"There is nothing she can take from here," said George, "to get there in time."

"She could take me," I said in exasperation. "I don't see why you should have to —"

"Leave it alone, Austin," George said ominously.

And then there was Augusta, standing, utterly silent, just a few feet inside the door to the dining room.

"I don't know what this means," I said to her. "I don't know why he's behaving like this."

"Let them go," she said quietly. "Just let them go."

The four of us walked, one after another, through the curtain that separated the China Hall from the rest of the house.

Vivian had left her coat and her train case on the counter; this one small piece of luggage suggesting that all along she suspected she would be leaving without me.

Every move that George was making, each gesture – from the way he shook his coat up over his shoulders to the rough manner in which he thumped the cash register to remove some cash for the trip – suggested anger, implacability. Just before he reached the door he stopped suddenly, removed a painted teacup from one of the shelves, and thrust it towards my face. "At least I could have taken some nourishment from this," he said. I could see that his hand was still shaking. "At least I could have filled it again and again with warmth. Can you say the same thing about anything you've done?"

"Leave him alone, George," said Augusta. "This has nothing to do with him."

He swung around then and looked at her, almost with shock, as if he hadn't even known that she was there, as if this was all happening years ago, before they had met. His face softened, but he did not touch her. "Oh, Augusta," he said. "Augusta."

She would not look at him.

To Vivian he said, "That woman . . . Augusta . . . is the woman I've come to love."

No one said anything. This confession seemed ludicrous, trite, as sentimental as the worst piece of painted china in the room. I felt humiliated for him. At that moment not one of us believed him.

George opened the door and Vivian walked out into the snow.

"I'll be back in four hours," he said.

He was speaking to Augusta or to me or perhaps to both of us. Or maybe he was talking to himself. As it was, the sentence hung in the air — a message that hadn't quite reached its destination. The bell on the door rang gaily, inappropriately, for a long, long time after they had gone.

"I'd better go too," I said to Augusta. "I'm sorry about all this."

"No," she said, "don't go yet. I'd like someone to talk to while I wait."

I had no wish to discuss the events that had just passed; George's response to Vivian, the revelation of their ephemeral childhood marriage. I had already concluded that it had been, at least for Vivian, a whim, driven by her need to assert herself in the face of her domineering mother. It probably had very little to do with George, despite his undeniable passion, had been instead a contest between mother and daughter, one which the mother, as is so often the case, won in the end. It all seemed tawdry to me somehow, in ways that a full-fledged adulterous affair might not have. No, I did not want to talk about it — not at all.

As if she sensed this, Augusta clarified her request. "Listen," she said, "I just want to tell someone the story of my life."

And so . . . *Night in the China Hall.*

We did not go back into the rooms of the house, the rooms behind the China Hall. We might have felt that that would have been too confining, too intimate. We were strangers to each other, really, and so I suppose we had no business being alone together at all. I thought Augusta might have felt that way anyway, and so I sat in the captain's chair that George kept behind the counter and she perched on the small stepladder he used when he wanted to reach items beyond his grasp on the shelves. For the first time, I thought about how there were no real doors to George's house, how all exits and entrances were made through this rococo world of tableware, this hall of commerce. And then I thought about the terms "exit" and "entrance" and how suitable they were for the theatricality of the evening, a theatricality I was beginning to believe that Vivian had planned from the moment we entered the taxi to go to her hotel.

Augusta began her story by telling me about her childhood on the farm, about her irrepressible pack of brothers, her stern father and practical mother. I was surprised and impressed by her attention to detail, how she could name and describe the tree nearest each of the windows of her girlhood home and how each of the baby boys had looked when he was six months old. She told me about Decoration Day in the village graveyard, about her Sunday-school cards, and her brief months of outdoor play. The snow house. The grey girl. Often she laughed – at herself, her father, her brothers. Hours passed while she explained this world to me, its rituals and eccentricities. Hours passed as she took me on this tour of her girlhood, her young womanhood. Yet I knew that the journey she was taking me on would eventually reach its destination and that that destination was going to be the war – the war and her alliance with George.

"There was always a fresh wind from the sea," she said when it became evident that she was ready to reveal this part of her story.

Always a fresh wind in this place in France called Étaples. Thousands of Allied soldiers were billeted at one time or another in camps there. And thousands more were freighted in on hospital trains; these two cargoes passing each other on the tracks that led to and from the front. As it turned out, George had been one of the many with minor wounds who had spent only a day or so in the hospital before being sent back into action.

"George told me that you got to know him there," I said.

"Only a little, not much," she said. "Only enough to discover that we were from the same county. But I was a farm girl and he came from Davenport. I remembered him because of the China Hall, this China Hall. My grandmother's good dishes had come from there – from here. Blue birds with pink ribbons in their beaks were painted on them, and as a child I would have loved that. The thought of those dishes there in Étaples made me briefly homesick, but just briefly. There was no time for homesickness or anything else. So many of them were dying right before our eyes, and there was nothing we could do."

She told me then about her uniform. She still had one, she said, hanging in a closet somewhere, probably at the farm. It comprised a grey-blue worsted skirt, with a cotton blouse of the same colour. The latter garment had the word "Canada" embroidered on the shoulder. There had been a white apron, starched white cuffs, and a white veil. It sounded nunlike to me, and would have seemed slightly absurd in the chaos of a room filled with men who were ripped to pieces. Calm female donors kneeling at the edges of sixteenth-century altarpieces — altarpieces featuring horrifying last judgements — came to mind, but of course I didn't mention this to her.

Augusta walked around the China Hall now as she talked. Everything about her was small and neat, her hands and shoulders, for instance. And then there were her eyes, large and dark in her pale, heart-shaped face. Sometimes she picked up a piece of Spode or Limoges for no apparent reason, took it on a tour of the room, then placed it carefully back on the shelf in the spot from which it came. True to her word, she didn't make any reference to Vivian, didn't mention her at all. It was at first as if Vivian had never made an entrance into the building, as if I had come to Davenport as I usually did, alone.

She spoke for some time about Étaples, describing its physical setting so vividly that now, years later, I can still picture it despite the fact that I've never been there and have no wish to conjure up the place.

I had been concerned with the granite shore of Lake Superior, had painted it for such a long time I became fascinated by the idea of the gentle approaches to water she described: estuaries, tidal flats, the soft curve of the dunes folding down to the sea. While Augusta talked about this landscape, she moved her hands and arms as if she were spellbound simply by the act of remembering it. She said that scrub pine grew there, and that in late spring quite suddenly the dunes would be covered by a profusion of wildflowers; poppies mostly and some blue-and-yellow flowers I've forgotten the name of.

"You have no idea what the light was like," she said. "It was like nothing else I've ever seen."

When she spoke about the light, she was carrying a small porcelain pitcher in her hands, a pale-yellow vessel with gold-leaf bands on the handle and base.

"The light was muted," she said, "fragile, as if the world were one large watercolour. Sometimes in the summer, between battles, we were given leave to go to Paris Plage for a swim and we would stay to watch the sunset. Then we would walk back over the dunes, which were rose-coloured and mauve. The clouds were sometimes yellow-coloured – like this."

She held the pitcher out in front of her for a moment, then turned it over and read the bottom. "Sèvres," she said. "George ought not to import it. It's too costly. No one here will buy it."

It was getting very late, was by now one o'clock in the morning. An uncomfortable silence followed the mention of

George's name; it seemed we were both terribly aware of the time that had passed since his departure, though neither of us would say anything.

"I'm sorry," I eventually muttered. "I'm sorry I brought her here. I didn't know."

"Neither did I." Augusta laughed a little at this, then placed the Sèvres piece on the counter. "Though so much of everything," she said, "is unexpected, isn't it? Accidental — even if it's hard to believe that. Still, it's almost impossible to believe the opposite — that everything is planned. Overseas at the hospital so many of the men spoke of their wounds as if they were avoidable mistakes, talked about being 'caught,' as if the whole war were a natural phenomenon and if only you took proper care it wouldn't harm you. A lot of them talked that way when they were dying . . . insisted that it was their fault, the result of some carelessness, some clumsiness on their part." She paused. "But none of us wanted to acknowledge the random cruelty of the thing, did we? Otherwise . . ." She stopped speaking then and looked at me, remembering, I suppose, that I had experienced neither battles nor casualties.

I was becoming more and more conscious of the oddness of this situation, alone, as I was, past midnight, in an over-lit China Hall with this dark-haired, delicate-looking woman I barely knew. And she speaking of twenty years ago as if it were last week; her lover off with his recently rediscovered wife. I wondered about George, his anger, his insistence on delivering Vivian back to her world, a world he knew absolutely nothing about. I wanted him to come back, wanted him to comfort this thin stranger who was pacing the boards of his store. I myself wanted to cross the lake, to return to my own country, my studio.

Augusta began to talk again. "Number One Canadian Hospital grew and grew," she said, "all over the sand dunes. Battles and battles and battles. Huts and tents springing up like mushrooms. The graveyard doubling, then tripling in size." She sat on the stepladder, looked at me and smiled. "I won the egg and spoon race," she said, "and Maggie won the hundred-yard dash, on Easter day."

I was mildly shocked to hear that they had played games in such a place and under such conditions, imagining, in my ignorance, that a kind of sobriety would have always been enforced in the face of repetitive tragedy. "Who was Maggie?" I asked.

"My friend, she was my best friend there."

There were no passersby on the street at this hour, but if there had been, how strange this one lit window would have seemed to anyone looking in. Augusta, who had risen from the stepladder again, was walking back and forth. The china remained stupidly colourful in all the artificial light. Yet neither Augusta nor I would suggest that we move into the privacy of the house.

"Sometimes when things were really desperate, Maggie and I would serenade the patients. I suppose that's what George remembered." Augusta stood in the centre of the floor, folded her hands in front of her stomach, and sang, "There are rats, rats, as big as alley cats in the china dealer's store."

"Augusta," I began, "he was young and —"

"You'd like a drink," she cut me off. "I know you would and so would I. Wait here and I'll fetch the scotch."

I was exhausted. I wanted to leave the place. But failing that, she was right, I wanted a drink.

When Augusta was in the back rooms, I looked at the vase George had been painting before Vivian and I had so carelessly interrupted the work period he kept for himself at the end of each afternoon. I lifted the object from the turntable and rotated it in my hands. George had become much more skilful over the years, particularly when rendering trees. This forest scene, I couldn't help but admit to myself, was beautifully composed, the foliage a sort of sweep of motion towards the right side of the oval that contained it, the clouds in the sky luminous and plentiful, yet not overstated. I thought of the day I had seen a younger, slimmer George packing away his brushes, one by one, just before he went to war, and I realized abruptly that he would have been already married at the time; married and then almost instantly abandoned. So this painting, these smooth forms, the brushes he handled with such care, would have been his only comfort, for I knew instinctively he had told no one of his humiliation. His secret marriage in the winter of 1914 would have been, to his parents and friends, simply a weekend away in the city. For Vivian, the whole catastrophe would have been merely an adventure. How many weeks would have passed before he permitted himself to accept the brutal truth that she would live the rest of her life without a backwards look? I remembered how adamant he had been about not seeing her when he went overseas. There had been that anger then, that passion.

And now this fractional glance cast over her shoulder towards the past. And me, the stupid facilitator of the whole unfortunate reunion.

Augusta returned with the half-bottle of scotch. She took two Blue Willow teacups from a shelf on the opposite side of the room, brought them to the counter, poured a couple of inches in one of them, but left the other empty. Then she sat on the stepladder and looked down at her hands. I noticed that she wore no jewellery.

I heard a motor car in the distance and lifted my head to see yellow light entering into the otherwise empty street.

"He won't be back tonight," Augusta said, observing the direction of my glance. "You can leave now if you like. He won't be back."

"He'll be back soon," I assured her. I glanced at my watch. "It won't be long now."

"He's still in love with her."

"Augusta," I argued, "he could hardly wait to be rid of her. He was tremendously angry."

"Nevertheless," she said, "I saw his face. He won't be back until morning."

There was a listlessness about her I couldn't interpret, a limpness that seemed to suggest she didn't care much one way or the other.

"He'll be back," I said. "In the meantime, I want to stay. I want to explain."

"What is there to explain?" Augusta was holding her empty cup, turning it around and around in her hands. "Everything seems perfectly clear," she said. "Now." She placed the cup on the counter. "I knew he didn't want marriage . . . or children, but I thought it was because of the war. That hideousness." There was a vacancy in Augusta's expression, but she was still smiling. "It is astonishing to me," she said, "how a world — a complete social system — can be constructed and then dismantled, just like that." She snapped her fingers in the space between us.

"Nothing has been dismantled," I said, believing she was speaking about her liaison with George.

Augusta appeared not to be listening to me, but then she said, "That's not what I mean. It's those dunes, those huts, and all those men, all of us. The trains passing over the estuary on that bridge. Everything was assembled, then dismantled. Even the pain and the death, even that was constructed, or at least planned on paper. That place was the whole world once, and it's all gone. Taken apart. If you went there now, there would be only a graveyard. Maggie and I knew everything about each other." She looked around the China Hall. "But she knows nothing about all this."

"Your friend," I said. "Are you in touch with her now?"

"She's dead." Augusta stood, walked behind the counter, opened the glass-fronted cabinet, and began to remove the china figurines that George kept there — certainly not Meissen or anything like that, but some of the things he felt ought to be protected, locked behind glass. She placed several of these pieces one by one on the counter. A ballerina, a lady of the court, a top-hatted dandy, a shepherdess, and two china birds – pigeons. She was trembling slightly and I could see sweat glistening on the palms of her hands.

"Have a drink," I said.

"She's dead and I'm alive and that is the way it is. They bombed us, the patients too. They unravelled everything we had stitched together. I was out on the dunes at the time, but Maggie was in the nurses' quarters. Only three of the nurses died. She was one of them." Augusta glanced at me and smiled in that odd, distant way that I had noticed before. "The Americans had been in Europe for a year or so then. You had already arrived."

"I never went to war."

"I meant your country."

To the tune of "Mademoiselle of Armetiers," Augusta sang absently:

"The Yankees think they won the war, *parlez vous.*
The Yankees think they won the war, *parlez vous.*
The Yankees think they won the war,
But we were there three years before.
Inkey Dinkey, *parlez vous.*"

She told me that schoolchildren had chanted this taunt at recess while skipping rope, well into the early 1920s in Canada. I was reminded of Rockwell bellowing German lieder from the steps of his house overlooking Brigus Cove in Newfoundland, how he had been run off the island for that. And now this woman twenty years later singing a variation of an old war song while small breakable figures stood lined up on a flat surface in front of her.

I saw that she was unconsciously separating the male and the female figures.

"How did you come to know him . . . George, I mean? How did you come to form this . . . partnership?"

"I'll tell you," she said. "I'll tell you everything." Augusta reached for the bottle and poured another inch or so into my Blue Willow cup.

Hers remained empty.

There was nothing I could do but listen. George had not returned.

Augusta did not remember, would never remember, returning from overseas. It wasn't until she had been back in Canada for a month or so that she was able to recall the war, Étaples, the broken men, the beautiful dunes she had described, her friend Maggie. She said it was as if she, who had been trained for it, had discovered a way to anesthetize herself, to put herself into a great darkness, a dreamless sleep. Her return to the world, she told me, was like a return from diethyl ether, but more gradual, more prolonged.

The first thing she became aware of was the colour green: flat, unobtrusive, all-pervasive. This brought with it, in time, memories: the shelf paper in her mother's pantry, a pinafore she had worn as a child, and the soft pods of milkweed plants in the meadow. The green was a painted wall in the Ontario military hospital in Davenport that had recently been adapted for the treatment of shell-shock victims.

Augusta was the only woman there. She was given a room of her own.

The night after the first bombing raid and Maggie's death, everyone who could be moved slept in the scrub pine woods on the opposite side of the River Canche. Sometimes, even now, more than twenty years later, Augusta dreamed of moonlight and poplar trees, fire and noise, for the bombing had occurred again. On the third night of moonlight and bombs, poplars, sand, and fire, and surrounded by men who were howling in fear and anger, Augusta showed signs of neither fatigue nor fright. Instead, she spent the whole night quietly laughing, and talking to her brother Fred.

Fred was not there. He had been reported missing and presumed dead at Passchendaele.

"They didn't know what to do with me," she said. "Shell-shocked nursing sisters were a rarity. But I came from Northumberland County and they had opened the hospital by then. So I was brought here, to Davenport." Augusta was silent for a moment, then she said, "There are none of us still there now, none of us left from the war. But the hospital remains. Those of us who didn't recover were sent to asylums closer to our homes." She smiled. "I suppose if I hadn't recovered I'd still be there, at the neighbourhood funny farm. It is close, after all, to the place I used to call home."

But she did recover, she assured me. Her first real perception, after the green, was of a series of shadows tumbling across her lap in a more or less irregular way. These dark shapes, she came to realize, were the shadows of pigeons. She had been taken by an orderly to one of the upper-storey screened porches on a warm day in early spring; a warm day, but one still cool enough that they had dressed her in a scarf and mittens and had placed a pale-blue blanket over her knees. She had seen the shadows on the blanket.

The pigeons were busily nesting in the eaves around the porch. Augusta had spoken the word "pigeon" aloud, and after that she had heard flies buzzing, drowsily coming to life after a winter sleep. She panicked then because she had no idea how long she had been gone. Her whole life might have passed — she felt the way she had imagined an old woman might feel — but when she removed one mitten she saw with relief that the skin on her hand was smooth, young.

The first few days of reawakening were really quite wonderful; the world was so fresh and new. "It was on parade," she said, "and I was like an infant. A fir tree, a cloud reflected in the window across the street, a squirrel leaping from one branch to another — all of this delighted me. But, of course, this couldn't last."

She remembered that Fred was gone.

She remembered the war and her time at Étaples.

She remembered how Maggie died.

After she told me about Maggie's death, I searched her face for signs of guilt. There was only grief there. While she wept I fumbled awkwardly around in my pockets for a handkerchief until I was thoroughly convinced I didn't have one. Then Augusta said something I will never forget.

"What were any of us to do with the rest of our lives anyway? After all that. We were only in our early twenties and our lives were finished. And yet here we are, George and me, right in the middle of the aftermath. What makes it just continue and continue?"

I had no answer for this.

"Sometimes," she said, "George and I were given leave to walk from the hospital down to the beach where you had your summer place, down to the lake."

"George visited you in the Davenport hospital. He told me something about carolling."

Augusta looked up abruptly from the figurines with which she was still toying. Her eyes were wide with surprise. "George had been in the hospital for eight months when I arrived."

"In the hospital? As a patient?"

She nodded.

I thought of my art-school days, how involved I had been with the bohemian life I had chosen, how I had assumed George was overseas during all that time. I had simply been too preoccupied to continue to write to him after the first year or so. "I never knew," I said to Augusta. "He never told me."

"He was sent there after Passchendaele."

Augusta looked towards the dark, still-empty street. "Where Fred was lost; a battle with a beautiful name. But it wasn't the battle, though I suppose those who invalided George thought it was. He told me that after the battle, in some village or other that had been left in ruins, he found a piece of porcelain: a figurative group. Children playing with birds near a tree.

It was all smashed and he couldn't find all of the pieces and he refused to leave until he did. When they tried to force him to leave, then . . ."

I couldn't understand it. There had been all this death and then this one broken piece of china.

"He would hate it if he knew I was telling you this," Augusta said. "But it was the end of the world for him, the smashed porcelain. He still had one of the children's little white hands with him at the Davenport hospital. I wonder how he managed to keep it with him. It was only about this big." Augusta raised her hand with thumb and forefinger half an inch apart. "I wonder where it is now, what ever became of it?" She twirled one figurine slowly on the counter. "That little hand was another of the first things that I saw, then George behind it, showing it to me. I didn't remember him, of course, but he remembered me. Later I recalled that he was the Northumberland boy I had met in Étaples."

I reached for the bottle, secretly glancing at my watch as I did so.

"He should have told me about her," said Augusta. "He should have told me right away. We were that close."

"Perhaps it wasn't important," I said.

Augusta kept twirling the shepherdess. "It was important," she said.

I had never even considered marriage, could not imagine domesticity, the contractual companion, household chores. I was dependent on being single, wanted to avoid the daily structure that a constant woman guaranteed. There was no real relevance to this past, this moment, that had so disturbed George. I was convinced of that. Too much had happened in the meantime for it to have really stuck. Painful at first to the boy he had been then, it could only have become, with time, a minor wound, a barely discernible scar. By now it could not possibly have damaged much more than his pride. I could not take it seriously. He was reacting to the surprise of Vivian's sudden appearance, I decided. He would be over it in a week.

"It was important," Augusta repeated. "I saw his face."

George had been a pigeon dispatcher as part of his duties during the war. It had comforted him to hold the warm, smooth bellies of the birds in his hands, and it pleased him to watch them rise and carry something as beautifully constructed as a sentence above the turmoil of the battle. Language was never ordered, he claimed, in the front lines. Expression was limited to commands, curses, cries. So a sentence, regardless of its subject, a sentence being taken to its destination was, to his mind, a rare and wonderful event.

At Passchendaele, however, the confusion was so desperate, the noise so deafening, that the birds would not fly, clung instead to the sleeves of his uniform or fluttered helplessly around the tank from which they were being released. It was then that George knew that language in all its forms was becoming irrelevant, that nothing in the mayhem around him could or should be documented.

After the war, he often painted pigeons on china, and he encouraged children in the town to collect them as figurines. The birds were precious to George. There was a war memorial, he once told me, erected in honour of these feathered messengers, somewhere in Belgium. He himself had wanted to write a book entitled *Birds in War*, which would celebrate the role of the homing pigeon in the madness of the battles, but, as far as I knew, he had never started it.

That night in the China Hall, Augusta told me that her first conversation with George in the Davenport hospital had involved homing pigeons; the same pigeons whose shadows she had seen on the blue blanket. Each day George came to the sun porch to watch the birds return to the eaves where they lived and to listen to the creatures speak to one another. Their song was full of pleasure, he informed Augusta, because they had come home, to domesticity, to familiarity. He who had fed them in cages, who had stroked their feathers and tied announcements and requests to their bodies, had never until his time in the hospital witnessed the moment of arrival. He said that in the sounds they made there was a pure expression of devotion and reunion. "They mate," he told this woman who sat with the blue blanket over her lap, "for life."

Augusta rose from the stepladder and placed the figurines and china birds back in the cupboard. Then she closed the door and turned the small brass key that always remained in the lock. "I don't know why I took them out," she said. "I don't know what I wanted them for."

"For a while," I told her, "I thought that Passchendaele was two words. 'Passion' and 'dale.'"

It was almost four o'clock in the morning, but it was winter and dawn was a long, long way off.

"Did you know," Augusta asked, "that there was a small girl who lived in Davenport in the 1820s whose name was Jane Eyre?"

She spoke then about her tonsillectomy, about how she had hallucinated the girl's story.

"It was my first taste of the anesthetic that I had used so often on others. It might have caused a kind of madness in me. And me, a trained anesthetist."

It was not, however, her first taste of morphine.

She confessed that she and her friend Maggie had "borrowed" the drug occasionally when they felt that otherwise they might collapse because of the fatigue. Some of the surgeons, she said, had used it as well, but no one ever spoke of this.

I looked at Augusta now and saw that she was very pale.

"Why don't you lie down, go to bed?" I said. "I'll wait for George."

I had at last given up the charade that he would, at any minute, appear at the door.

"All this waiting," Augusta said. "I feel as though I've always been waiting for something, but I've never known exactly what it was. Maybe it was tonight I was waiting for all along."

I could think of nothing to say to her.

Augusta stood up and smoothed out the wrinkles on her dark skirt. "You should sleep too," she said.

"I'll wait up for George."

She shrugged and turned towards the curtained door at the end of the shop. Then, without looking at me, she asked, "What's it like to be famous?"

"It's like nothing," I said, knowing this to be an evasive answer.

"Nothing," she repeated without turning around. She stood absolutely still for a moment. Then suddenly she was beside me, her hand on my arm. She looked at me as if she were filled with curiosity, and I thought she might, at this late hour, begin to inquire into the facts of my own life. But, instead, she had one last thing to tell me.

"When we were still patients and given leave to walk on the beach, do you know what George would say to me? He would say that there was no place in such a beautiful world for unhappiness such as ours." She paused, ran her hands over the top of her head as if tidying her hair, then closed both fists. She lowered her arms until they were stiff and straight at her side, tilted her head back slightly as if she were about to take an oath. The tendons in her neck were taut, exposed. "But it was my unhappiness," she declared passionately, "mine that there was no place for. In the end, I saw that our grief was self-contained, separate. Look at these unruined towns, these tree-lined streets, that lake out there with perfect flakes of snow falling on dark waves. There is no place at all for unhappiness such as mine in a world as beautiful as this. I belong with mud, stained bandages, moaning soldiers. I thought that George and I . . . that we shared the permanent misery of that war. But he is perfectly at home here. In the end, we each held our own unhappiness, as distant, as far away from the other as possible."

I didn't understand, didn't know what she was saying. "Augusta . . ." I began.

But she had already disappeared. At the far end of the China Hall, a place of entrances and exits, the curtains fell easily back into place after Augusta had passed through them.

I have almost always slept alone. A few nights here and there, yes, but even then the presence of another body often caused me to sleep fitfully and rise early. I have almost never, since early childhood, been awakened by another person. That morning I was awakened by George.

Slumped in the chair behind the counter, I dreamed I was trying to take a picture of my mother. I was watching the camera, which she had snatched from my hands, slowly tumble towards the rapids of the Genessee River when George shook my shoulder.

"Is Augusta still here?" he was asking. "Is she still here?"

"Of course," I said. "She went upstairs, she went to bed." I put my hands on the counter and pulled myself out of the chair. "Where the hell have you been?"

He didn't answer at first. His face was grey, his eyes bloodshot. "Why did that woman come here?" he asked. "What reason did she have for coming here?"

"I don't know," I said. "She didn't tell me."

"I couldn't want her," he said. "I don't even know who she is." He was looking at the curtains at the end of the room, the curtains through which Augusta had passed. "I never knew who she was. God, the nights I spent inventing her, trying to work out what had happened."

"It doesn't matter now," I said. "Now she's gone for good."

"Gone for good." He looked at the two Blue Willow cups. Then suddenly his face changed, turned paper white. He staggered a bit and then steadied himself on the stepladder on which Augusta had been sitting. I saw he was beginning to tremble dangerously. "Augusta," he whispered.

"What is it?" I asked. "What's the matter?"

"She didn't drink anything," he said.

"No, I drank it all. What's wrong?"

"Did she talk . . . did she talk about the war?"

"Yes," I admitted. "Quite a lot. She talked quite a lot."

"She never drinks, and she goes on and on about the war when . . ." Suddenly he swung away from me as if he sensed something menacing behind him. He looked around in an unfocused, almost desperate manner, then bolted from the room, through the curtains, and up the stairs.

I felt wretched. The dawn was weak and grey and it was still snowing. I wanted my studio, the pale geometric shapes I had been working with, their emptiness. The China Hall was crowded with colour, with subject matter. I found myself staring at a row of ridiculous tankards from England: square, arrogant faces whose smirking expressions infuriated me. The whole breakable business infuriated me – all the flowered tableware destined to carry bad food and encourage idiotic conversation at dinner parties. I was on my way to the door when I heard George yell.

I had never heard a sound like it before. It was almost musical, almost like song.

One cry. That's all. A held note. Crescendo. Diminuendo. Then silence.

I have often, since then, thought about Augusta's claim to unhappiness, her insistence upon the exclusivity of its owner-ship. "My unhappiness," she had asserted. "Mine!" The fierceness with which she identified the singularity of her emo-tions, her state, is something that has preoccupied and perplexed me for the remainder of my life, for there had been a sense of triumph in her declaration. Each of us wants something that is ours alone, I suppose, some idiosyncrasy of character, some carefully maintained victory or sorrow. Augusta had her dead friend, the war, her drift towards morphine. Certainly she could have allowed George his neophyte failed marriage, his passion, his anger concerning Vivian.

I've come to believe there was something twinlike about George and Augusta, their shared war, their shared recovery, their knowledge of this for all the years after. Was Augusta defining herself in the face of partnering by clinging to memo-ries of grey girls and hallucinations of lost children? Was she laying claim to sorrow? Or was it simply that by walking out the door with Vivian, George had broken the partnership?

But what did I really know of them? Augusta, as I've said, was almost a stranger to me. Perhaps George was as well. He had thrust the painted cup in my face, in the face of the life I had chosen to live, the art I had chosen to make. How long had he held all of this, held me in contempt?

Now, as an old man, I ask myself: How long did I refuse to look at George, to learn him, to come to know him?

I was about to leave.

I placed my hand on the doorknob, which I noticed for the first time was porcelain and covered with small bunches of painted violets. This pointless decoration sickened me. Someone I couldn't see was shovelling the snow from a nearby sidewalk; a harsh, scraping, rhythmic sound. Through the glass panel of the door I noted one lone figure heading for Victoria Hall. He crossed the street at an angle, his head bent into the wind, his hand on his hat. I wanted to be that figure, walking away from the scene that I believed was unfolding upstairs; George's yell, the inevitable quarrel. *We were that close*, Augusta had said. *That intimate.* And intimacy, I had always suspected, was one long argument. Still, I drew my hand away from the porcelain knob, from the delicate flowers I so despised. I was going to wait it out, speak to George when he descended the stairs. It was Monday morning. No matter what, he would have to be in the shop. As I walked back towards the chair in which I had spent the night, I heard the sound of breaking china. Despite her previous calm, I concluded, Augusta must have been enraged.

At 9:30, two delivery men arrived with a shipment of dinnerware. I thanked them, signed for the crates, watched them drive away. About fifteen minutes later a customer appeared and asked for George. I told her I was minding the shop, said she should return in an hour.

At 10:30, I called both their names from the hallway of the ground floor. I waited for five minutes for an answer. Then I climbed the stairs.

There are a number of formal things that one has to do after death enters a house. Someone has to be called: a policeman, a coroner, an undertaker. I am nothing if not efficient when it comes to formal things.

That night when Augusta told me she had sometimes used the drug, she had referred to it as "morphia" and I remember thinking that the word had a lovely, open, feminine sound to it. I thought about how George had said that he wished she had been involved in a less dangerous profession. Only after I had climbed the stairs did I understand that the danger in nursing lay, for Augusta, in the easy access it provided to the needle, the easy access it provided to the end of the story she had been telling me all night long.

But it was all hers, wasn't it, this addiction, if that is what it was? A gift from the war.

I think. But then, as I've said so many times before, what did

I know, what do I know about George, about Augusta, about myself?

They looked like children who had been playing and who had been overtaken suddenly by sleep. George hadn't even removed his coat, though his hat lay where he dropped it on the floor and there were a number of dark spots on the carpet where the snow he had tracked in from the street and up the stairs had melted and been absorbed. I thought of the Nordic sagas that Rockwell so loved. I remembered him telling me how Burnt Njal and his wife lay down in the midst of fire on a nuptial bed wreathed in smoke, glowing beams falling on them. The pain. I thought of those old ballads of partnered death where roses and briars entwine on freshly dug graves. On the bedside table were the needle and the small, now empty, bottle.

The rose. The briar.

There was no note; no testament to the sequence of events that had led this woman and this man to the brink. I still believe it possible that Augusta's death may have been a mistake, one last injection beyond the limit. But there was no mistaking what had happened to George. And he had left a personal message for me: the shards of his china collection were strewn like petals all around the room.

This was my first inheritance.

I remembered how he had showed his few purchases to me before he left for the war, my trivialization of them, his defence. I remembered that, since then, whenever I had seen him, he had assured me that I was still to be the beneficiary of the collection, including the newer pieces he had added. Now I understand that until that dreadful night he had clung to the belief that I might come to have some affection for the small, the delicate, the fragile. At the time, I remained staring stupidly at the mess on the floor, this reprimand spelled out in shards, which told me that George believed that I had never understood, that I was responsible, that the scene that greeted me in this boyhood room had been created by me as surely as if it were a painting I had completed with my own hand. It told me he was convinced that what had transpired was a deliberate act of cruelty on my part.

But it was much worse than that. It was an act of carelessness.

After the men had taken George and Augusta away, I returned to the China Hall, where I carefully unpacked the new shipment of dinnerware, making a display of a complete setting in the window as I had seen George do in the past. Then I tucked a broom under my arm and hauled the empty crate up the stairs. There I removed dustpan after dustpan of fragments from the floor. I washed the shelves where George had kept the collection and dusted the top of the dresser with a damp towel I had found in the bathroom. I shook a small braided rug out a window I had forced open and pulled the still-wrinkled coverlet tight across the bed. There were indentations in the pillows where their heads had rested and I couldn't bear to touch them. "No, sir," the coroner had assured me, "you won't be needed. Mr. Kearns has a brother in Brockville."

The older brother whose education was paid for.

The room was beautifully clean when I had finished with it. Getting the crate into the Packard was difficult, but I managed somehow to wrestle it into the back seat. I slammed the rear door, opened the front, and climbed in behind the wheel.

On my way out of Davenport I stopped at the telegraph office in order to wire Silver Islet. I knew what I was going to do. I was going to follow the old King's Highway to Port Hope and make a right turn at Highway 28. Sara once told me that in winter there were no roads to Silver Islet, told me how she would sometimes ski across Thunder Bay to the small city of Port Arthur, often for something as simple as writing paper or to buy a book. I had no experience with skis, no experience with frozen lakes, but I could steer the Packard. I knew exactly what I was going to do. I was going to drive north.

3

ONTARIO LAKE SCENERY

Two and a half years before – the last time I had been in a room with her – Sara was no longer a young woman. Though in certain lights and from certain distances she could still be taken for one, mistaken for one because of her slimness and the fact that her hair showed no traces of grey. She wore her hair in a braid that hung down her back, or sometimes she wound it around her head as if it were a crown. Or a serpent. She wore it like that when she was swimming. Only very occasionally did she let it hang free, after she washed it and was letting it dry, or now and then when I asked her to.

She was, as I've said, no longer a young woman – maybe forty, or forty-five – but I can't say for certain because she'd never told me her age and I'd never asked. We had regarded each other, Sara and I, from the opposite ends of a room I knew so well I could have drawn it, could still draw it, in my sleep. Have I mentioned her eyes? They were quite unusual, grey mostly, but with a yellow sunburst at the centre when the pupils were small.

The last time I stood in a room with her, the pupils were large, the eyes wide open, as if she wished to absorb the most minor details of the visual information surrounding her.

It had been her father's room, and everything that was beyond the windows was, as she had pointed out early on, her father's view. I had told her that it couldn't possibly be the same view that her father had seen since the mine on the small offshore island, the island for which the settlement was named, was in a state of collapse. The superstructure had been slowly pried apart, year after year, by storms and the lake, ever since my father abandoned it in 1920. Sara believed that there was still silver there and she may have been right. But in the last year of its operation a half-dozen otherwise rational men from good American families had lost their fortunes to my father's obsession, his certainty that something continued to glitter under the water. And then in the end, all my father's money, all of the shareholders' money, was washed away by the superior lake.

Sara had said that her father's view had included more than Silver Islet Mine. It had included the lake, the landscape, the sky; especially the sky, which was precious to him because he had spent so much time underground. He had loved the surfaces of things, she said, rock, bark, water. He had loved light. In that way, she said, he was like me, for I was a landscape painter at the time and undoubtedly talked about colour and texture and light at great length, even though I don't remember doing so. I do remember speaking to her about the working class, about strikes and unions, working conditions and social injustices. I thought I was interested in the working class, had seen in Sara the embodiment of all that, and so I lectured her on the rights and privileges that, in my opinion, her father ought to have demanded from various bosses. Lectured her until one day she rose from her chair, walked across the floor, opened a cupboard door, and pulled out his last weekly two-pound supply of candles.

"These are what my father carried with him into the dark," she said.

She was angry with me then, and she had every reason to be. The ignorance. The condescension.

The small log house where she lived was filled with lamps and lanterns. All of the miners' houses had been, Sara told me, because the men so loved light. One of their great pleasures when emerging from the mine in the evening was to see the settlement lit like a locomotive along the shore. In the winter, of course, daylight would be lost to them, their shift being twelve hours long. One of Sara's great pleasures as a child was to imagine the miners' lanterns coming to life on the winter island, then moving slowly towards the log houses as the men made their way across the ice. The candles, she told me, had been stuck on the miners' hats to help light the rock faces of the tunnels under the lake, tunnels which had been flooded ten years before her birth.

How sad to have been Owen Pengelly, to have been Sara's light-loving father. At the age of seventeen he had walked away from the only map of the world he knew, a map comprising footpaths over fields, engine houses looming awkwardly on precipitous coastlines, the shafts and passageways and caverns under the sea, and the wretched rows of grey houses. He had walked with three of his friends, away from the weeping mothers of the village of St. Just, eight miles to the port of Penzance and to a ship headed for Canada and another set of shafts and tunnels and caverns; this time under the greatest of lakes: Superior.

How is it that this ordinary boy, who became an ordinary man, this man I never met, occupies my thoughts when I can barely call up the features of my own father's face? Of course, I never really knew my father, could only guess at what moved him to search for wealth, for social standing. Him and his money. Sara, on the other hand, learned her own father, stayed close to him until his last rattling breath. She wanted to be known by me as she had been known by him and so handed me her father's story as if it were a gift. I have not yet used it in my work, though there is still time.

It was only very recently — just a few weeks ago — that I pulled the atlas from the shelf and looked at the claw-shaped land that Owen Pengelly sailed away from. I was examining Belgium, France — Étaples, Ypres, Calais — and all those other godforsaken places that I have kept so unfortunately close to me, when I noticed Cornwall at the bottom of Britain. It looked like the back paw of a beast, extended as if attempting to grasp something in its talons. Familiar names came into focus under my magnifier. St. Ives, St. Just, Lizard, Ludgvan, Botallack. Suddenly I recalled a pair of mining overalls hanging from a hook on the back of Owen Pengelly's cupboard door, my drawings of them.

The last time Sara and I spoke we had been alone in her father's room and she had said to me, "I have neither the strength nor the shallowness . . ."

She didn't finish the sentence, didn't tell what she had neither the strength nor the shallowness for. I remember once, long ago, reading a book by a classics scholar who had spent much of his life decoding fragments of Greek sentences. The tone of the book was one of frustration, of desire rarely satisfied. "Would that we had the subject of that verb!" the scholar exclaims in an uncharacteristically personal way about halfway though the book. There were nouns and a verb in that partial sentence of Sara's, but over the years its fragmentary nature has been a source of discomfort for me.

Cornwall, according to the *Encyclopaedia Britannica*, which I consulted after I was finished with the atlas, is a peninsula seventy-five miles long by forty-five miles wide. The climate is mild and by British standards quite sunny. In fact, its coast is often referred to as the English Riviera. Palm trees flourish there. None of this would have made much difference to Owen Pengelly, who spent most of his boyhood under the ocean in the hellish halls of the tin mines, learning in the darkness to love light.

In the beginning I had decided to work in Owen Pengelly's room because of the view and for the light. Sara led me into her father's room and watched as I looked out each of its three windows in turn. She removed the curtains. She removed the curtains and sunlight filled her father's room.

Fifteen summers had passed. The last time I had seen her, Sara and I stood facing each other at opposite ends of Owen

Pengelly's room, me leaning against the interior wall, she a dark figure framed by the south window. I had been walking back and forth over paint-spattered pine flooring. She had remained entirely still. As I approached the east window, the hotel at the Landing became larger. As I approached the west, the beach flung itself into my line of vision like a small white scythe. I did not want the details of these things, the hotel's unpainted clapboard, the sand backed by dark pines, but they pressed themselves upon my attention as I spoke. I no longer wanted any details, the objects I had drawn so fastidiously: lamps and washstands, suspenders, boots and overalls, candleholding hat, her father's stories, her mother's death, the sharp sun in the sky above the lake, the grotesque gestures of north-shore pines. I no longer wanted sentences leading to narrative. Sara had taken me from the mine that we could still see bits of out the window all the way back to Cornish labyrinths under heaving oceans. I didn't want sweating rock lit by lamplight, and I didn't want exaggerated light raking the surfaces of objects locked in rooms.

I have neither the strength nor the shallowness . . .

I stopped pacing and leaned against the wall. "It has nothing to do with you, Sara. I'm not talking about character."

"Fifteen years," she said.

"Fifteen summers," I corrected.

She stared hard at me then. The sunbursts in her eyes had been swallowed by her pupils. I was angered by the shame I felt under her scrutiny.

We were both silent.

"I'm sorry," I finally said, though I wasn't at all at the time. "I'm sorry, but this is an aesthetic not an emotional decision."

Sara stood at the south window, blocking the view of the sun-drenched lake.

"I'm sorry," I said again, with all of the coldness I had in me then. "I've painted you enough."

I left Davenport on the King's Highway Number Two. I made a right turn at Highway 28. I drove north.

As I manoeuvred the Packard over icy highways, past frozen rivers, I concentrated on the wire I had sent, imagining its strange route across the ice of Thunder Bay to Silver Islet Landing – the place to which no roads led. I could see the telegraph office in Port Arthur, the yapping dogs of the mail sled, the arrival of the message, Sara opening the envelope, reading the words. Otherwise I focused on the weather. Sometimes the snow was so heavy I was completely disoriented. Had it not been for the white banks the plough had left on either side of the road I might have lost my way altogether, the way one loses the thread of a conversation late at night, or an idea that has come to one shortly after waking. I don't remember where I slept at night, one northern town or another. Parry Sound or North Bay. Sudbury, perhaps. Wherever it was, I sent another telegram from there.

I checked into the Prince Arthur Hotel in Port Arthur on Wednesday evening, collapsed fully clothed onto the bed in a room on the fifth floor, and slept for fourteen hours. The next morning I rose, opened the curtains, and was confronted by the piercing light of the sun on the snow-covered ice of Lake Superior. The cloudless sky. The blinding view. The huge man made of rock slumbered now on a smooth white sheet, not on the textured dark bed of glimmering water I remembered from my summer arrivals. A thin mist covered his body. Everything else was clear, precise, and painful to look at under that light that revealed, then blinded. Even when I turned my back to the bay the brilliance persisted, breaking through the large window and into the room. Nothing in my experience of the north shore had prepared me for this season's lucidity. My age was written all over my face in a ruthless hotel mirror. I barely recognized my own hands.

After breakfast I walked on squeaking snow up and down Cumberland Street, in and out of stores until I came across a pair of binoculars in a junk shop. They were well worn, had belonged to a soldier of the Great War, and still housed in their leather case the original instructions for their use in that night-mare. But they were in perfect repair.

The shopkeeper told me that the temperature was thirty below zero. But the sun, the white blaze, was everywhere and so the chill seemed irrelevant. I wanted to believe in a new, clean light, wanted to believe that it would banish forever the dark rooms behind George's China Hall. The examined past.

I returned to my room with the binoculars in a brown paper bag and began to wait.

Almost immediately I pulled the desk chair towards the window. I was determined to face that which was coming towards me. My eyes watered constantly for the first hour, until finally I was able to look at the radiant bay without wincing or weeping, my face tightening under dried salt. I would gaze through the binoculars, bring the stone giant closer to me for four or five minutes, then let him recede again into the distance. I knew that when Sara appeared — I was certain she had received at least one of my telegrams and that she would appear — she would come into view from around the head of The Sleeping Giant.

Sometimes I read the Bible I had found in the desk drawer. I read the instructions in case of fire on the hotel door. I read the admonitions on the yellowed piece of paper in the binocular case. Every line seemed portentous, charged with meaning. "Try to avoid the reflection of enemy flares in the lenses." "Proceed in an orderly fashion to the stairwell or the fire escape." "How sweet are thy words unto my taste, yea, sweeter than honey to my mouth." The rest of the time I looked out over Thunder Bay — either with the binoculars, or without.

Because I had spent only the summer months at Silver Islet, and had taken the steamer there as soon as I could after stepping from the train, I had come to know this bay only superficially during my trips back and forth over the water. Sara had taken me to the top of the stone giant I could now see from the window. She had forced me to look over its edge, thirteen hundred feet down to dark water, but I had resented the effort and rejected the view, though I had allowed some of the surrounding rocks and trees to leak into a painting I completed a few months later. My father, I recalled, had been impressed by the cliffs, the heights, the legend of the native warrior turned to stone for revealing the secret location of silver to the invading Europeans.

Drawn in his more reflective moments to the romantic side of this particular brand of capitalism, he was charmed in the end by the conviction that some extraordinary power had prevented his success. And this belief protected him, at least in his own eyes, from the banality of a lost fortune, a pointless endeavour. It was the shape of The Sleeping Giant I wanted to fit into one of my paintings; neither its natural nor its supernatural history interested me. My father and I both had exploited this landscape – differently, it's true – but we had exploited it nevertheless.

By late afternoon I had stared out into the bay for such a long time I was beginning to suffer from snow blindness. I had seen clouds shaped like peninsulas float across the sky, blue shadows move under these across the white plain of the frozen lake. I had seen light unfurl like sheets of delicate yellow paper behind the slumbering stone man. But nothing in me wanted to reach for a pencil, a brush, a tube of colour. My hands held only the binoculars, the distances and intimacies they were creating. The long white surface. The reclining granite figure.

At 5:30, I left the hotel for the streets, where I bought a quart of whisky. I ate in the hotel dining room with my back to the bay. I returned to my room. The white had vanished, was replaced by a deep shade of blue. A star appeared over the ribcage of the stone man, then another near his foot. And another. My face, the bed, the dresser were reflected in the window. I closed the curtains and poured myself a drink.

I ask myself: What has your life been? You have used everything around you. And for what? An arrangement of colours on a flat surface. "At least I could have taken nourishment from this," George had shouted, holding a teacup at the end of the arm he thrust towards my face. "At least I could have filled it again and again with warmth."

Shards all around him and both of them gone.

With the white hope out the window shadowed by night and the curtains closed, scenes from the previous Sunday presented themselves like photographs in a grim family album, everything fixed and still, terrible and permanent — the whisky cranking open the part of my brain where these tableaux were printed. Augusta's pale face, George's hand on her dark sleeve, the sound of breaking china, the inexplicable carefulness with which I swept the room the following morning. Vivian's head thrown back in laughter, the dull eyes of the fox she wore around her neck, her black mink flung over the counter. And now the woody taste of the same scotch I drank that night present on my tongue.

I'd heard of men who had locked themselves into hotel rooms, drinking quart after quart of whisky, and were found by the house detective days later having choked to death on their own vomit. Now it came to mind that there would have been windows in the rooms where these tragedies took place, and beyond the windows a view. What had these desperate men looked at before the event they were courting overtook them? I wondered if men had died drunk in this hotel, whether their last registered image was that of the stone man sleeping or whether they were on the other side, the city side, where the colourful mass of clapboard buildings climbed up the hill. *Brilliancy is moving towards colour, not towards white.*

I'd heard of men who shot themselves in hotel rooms. I poured myself another drink.

I awoke with the buzz in my head of a mild hangover. I washed, ordered breakfast, and ate without opening the curtains. Then I placed the chair in the correct position, reached for the binoculars, and took up my post. Again the dazzle, the watering eyes, the ice and sky and sun. No misty bedspread for the giant. No clouds at all.

She would come today.

There were three or four ice fishermen a hundred yards or so off the ends of the piers. One had miraculously built a hut early in the morning while I was still sleeping. The others were unsheltered. I tried to compare their patience to my own but knew I had failed when the chambermaid knocked and I was forced to stand in the dark hall while she moved a carpet sweeper back and forth across the room. I wanted her out of there. I wanted to be at the window, alone, when Sara rounded Thunder Cape. I wanted to see her sixteen miles away, then twelve, then eight. . . .

She would come today and I would come to love her. My atonement would be in that love. Augusta, George, would be vindicated. Every broken piece of porcelain would be mended, the China Hall swept clean. I would see Sara's eyes when I closed my own, not George's, not Augusta's.

"Feel the dignity of a child," Robert H. had once said. "It is a dignity of innocence." Sara was the only innocent person I knew. There had never been, would never be, children in my life. She, her clarity and lightness, would be a kind of childhood, would allow the atmosphere of childhood, at least, to enter my rock heart. In that wild, uncultivated place she would be like a bush garden.

In the end, I was, of course, unable to see her from sixteen miles away. Not even the binoculars could accomplish that. She would have been ten miles from Port Arthur, I suppose, when she appeared in the centre of the circle the lens made — a black dot on that vast white sheet. She had to be far enough out on the bay to become visible. She had to be completely surrounded by white. Otherwise she simply disappeared against the landscape of The Sleeping Giant. Now she was like a fugitive cell that had broken loose from the stone architecture of his body. A grain of sand. I was relieved by my belief in her.

An hour later I could see her with the naked eye. "The naked eye," I said aloud, testing the phrase. The eye unassisted, uncovered. But it made no difference; she was a tiny spot on the retina. It would still be hours until her arrival. How small and insignificant she looked. How unprotected, exposed.

I watched her inch towards me for the next hour. The wind had picked up and often she would vanish into white. But always she re-emerged unchanged; small and far away. I knew the limbs that crossed the ice so well I could have painted them blind-folded. I had seen, and recorded, the changes time had made from year to year. No one, I was certain, had ever scrutinized Sara with such voracious intimacy or, I could admit now, with such coldness.

I had been examining distance for two days. Sara's moving body could have been misinterpreted as a flaw on the white skin of the bay, the white skin of distance. I knew this vista was beautiful now, more beautiful, perhaps, than it had been in the summer when it was all dancing and stars. The clean sheet, the new leaf, unscarred by experience. The clarity of the north that Rockwell raved about. Brigus Harbour. Greenland. Boreal. How he would have loved this bay. And how he would have loved the man mountain with all of winter spread out around him.

I could see that everything that had passed between Sara and me until this moment had been an approximation. Mere subsistence. I, who had previously been so restrained, would now engage in such blatant exposure that when I was finished she would have the entirety of my life in her possession: the Rochester ravines of my childhood, the nonsense of The Art Students' League, Rockwell, Robert H., the self-conscious salons and soirées that had been my winter life since. I would place the facts of George, Vivian, Augusta, the China Hall at her feet, tell her how everything had smashed up. She would look at it all with the opalescent view of an innocent. She would forgive me and I would be exonerated.

All this was very clear and very real to me. I sat in a room blade-bright with sun. Prisms angled towards me from the bevelled edges of mirrors, and anything made of metal — the lamp base, a caster on the foot of the bed, my Zippo lighter — glared.

Things could not have been more transparent than they were in that light. Each thought that entered my mind was sharp, well defined. And out on the ice, the woman I had decided to want, moving slowly towards me.

How to explain what I did?

There are certain moments in a man's life that demand and deny response at the same time. I spotted her through the binoculars at eleven o'clock in the morning, this woman I had not communicated with for two and a half years. I might have seen her earlier, but I had begun to play those games one engages in when waiting – setting limits, making rules. I wouldn't let myself pick up the binoculars except on the hour and the half-hour. Earlier in the morning, I had taken the mirror from the wall and had stood with my back to the window, superimposing my own head on the giant's prone body in the glass. None of these games were games of skill, but they probably caused me to miss the exact moment of her materialization.

Watching the small approaching figure, I recalled that when I was younger and studying art history I had realized that medieval pilgrims would still have had a full day of walking ahead of them after they had glimpsed in the distance the spires of Chartres or Compostela; they who had already come so far. After that there could only have been anti-climax. I had always wondered what it was that continued to drive them forward. I had assumed, you see, that the perfection of the destination they had built in their minds during the journey could only fade or tarnish as they drew nearer. And then there would be the beggars on the steps, the hawkers, the pickpockets, the corrupt clergy.

Yes, I remembered this as I sat in the radiant room.

I imagine you will judge what I did to be an act of cowardice – and perhaps you are right. I had come to the very edge of a moment, the moment when it might have been possible to remove the cloak of fear that had protected me all those years. But after all was said and done, the flesh beneath was too white and weak to be exposed. Is there really any one among you who in the face of such grief would not panic at the approach of happiness? If Augusta had waited, George would have returned to her whole, his emotional history utterly exposed, his love for her intensified. Could it have been something as banal as a wedding certificate that killed her? They had made their own marriage, after all, a pact based on sorrow, conceived in the halls of an asylum. And now that pact had been destroyed. The partnership might have cast off the mud of Flanders, the knives of the surgeons, the hoarded passion of a betrayed heart. Had Augusta glimpsed happiness, the banality of *that*?

As Sara moved closer I was able to see that she was wearing her father's old overalls. She was coming steadily towards me across a pristine whiteness where everything shone. Behind her the stone man slept on, unmoved by her journey, his body hard and rigid and unchanging.

Heart of granite. Bed of ice.

She must have been less than a mile from the shore when I decided to leave Port Arthur, remove myself finally and permanently from Sara's life. How could I break into her innocence with my own corruption? In all fairness, ultimately, I could not bear to pollute her strength with my own damaging weaknesses. I panicked in the face of the possibility of happiness.

As I followed the highway along the curving shore of Lake Superior, I watched the hotel where we were to have met diminish in size in the rearview mirror. I imagined Sara asking for me at the desk.

Over one hundred and fifty years ago in England, a Stafford-shire potter was thinking of Upper Canada, a huge tract of land stolen for the Empire from a continent he had never seen, would never see, except in his imagination. Perhaps he was bored with repetitive calls for views of Niagara Falls and its attendant Terrapin Tower and Table Rock, wanted to explore instead the Great Lake towards which the waterfall hurled itself. Or perhaps he had read the journals of Samuel Champlain, where the foliage of the north shore of the gleaming ocean of fresh water is described as being almost ornamental in its beauty. Whatever the case, the title he gave to the landscape he composed – Ontario Lake Scenery – is so ambiguous that I spent the better part of the morning trying to determine whether it was all the lakes of Ontario or the Great Lake Ontario that he had in mind. For my own comfort I decided on the former inspiration, wanting, I suppose, to believe that both of my own north shores are memorialized by the last piece I place upon my shelves.

For I am pleased to be able to tell you that the huge task of reassembling the collection is completed. Completed as successfully as an old man can ever complete the task of piecing together all that has been broken. Some of the tinier fragments were impossible to place, and who knows how many hills and streams, birds and flowers were shattered beyond recognition or exploded into powder as they smashed against the floor. By pure coincidence this porcelain view of Ontario lakeside landscape emerged from the final small, sad pile of shards at the bottom of that crate I removed from a Davenport bedroom forty years ago. And yet the scene, which is now fully glued back together, has nothing to do with what I learned when I visited the shores of that northern country. As I pieced this painted terrain – my last jigsaw – together, I held elegant ladies, a ruined castle, several mountains, and East Indian tents in my old gnarled fingers. The Staffordshire china painter had created a theatrical mirage, a fantasy, then printed the words "Ontario Lake Scenery" on the reverse side of the plate.

But how much different is this from the complicated preconceptions I have carried with me? Had the potter visited Ontario, would he have been able to see past the fog of his fantasy straight through to the reality of swamp and muskeg, blackflies and bad weather? Would he have believed, as I believed, that nothing important would ever happen to a young man who sat in an apron behind the counter in a Canadian China Hall? Would he have valued the vulnerable skin of the art he created, and the real world that composed the earthenware ground on which it was based?

Would he have been able to accept the approach of happiness, of love?

Or would the elegant ladies, the romantic ruin, the nonexistent mountains have persisted, blocking his view, keeping him distant from his own life?

Despite the clear January weather that followed me south all the way to New York, my withdrawal from the north shore of Lake Superior was one of the most fatiguing journeys I had ever made. When the exhaustion became unbearable I would pull the Packard over to the side of the road and stumble into the winter woods, regardless of my stupid city shoes and the deep snow that often reached my knees. I would then become almost immediately alert because of the cold, and because I was so afraid of becoming lost in the forest. It says something about my state of mind, I suppose, that I had made at least a half-dozen forays before realizing that to return to the car I would only have to follow my own tracks.

It was on the second or third of these treks that I disturbed a deer that had been lying in the snow. She rose slowly, unsteadily to her feet and stared at me in terror. She was so thin her ribs were shadowed on her hide and her ears looked too large, too cumbersome on either side of her narrow face. Then, with a startling burst of speed, she pivoted and leapt away from me into the trees, clouds of powdery snow rising in her wake. I looked for some time at the soft shape her body had pressed into the snow, the steam of my own breath filling the space where she should have been permitted to remain.

I went back to the car. I wept.

Because, you understand, Sara had told me about winter-stricken deer, had described the delicate balance that keeps them alive when the season is unusually harsh. They have endured so much already, she had told me, so much scarcity and hardship, that their metabolism slows down to allow for survival. Any interruption of this, any sudden spurt of energy, causes damage.

"Don't run," I had shouted at the fleeing deer. "Please, please don't run." I stood yelling in the forest, causing the animal's flight to intensify. Faster, farther, causing more harm.

"Often it is their last run," Sara had told me. "This one final rush of adrenalin – no matter how minor – is just too much for them; the system can't cope. You can see a serious amount of deterioration in a week. More often than not, after two weeks, they are dead."

She had added that sometimes, walking in the woods in springtime, she had found carcasses.

I put my head on the steering wheel. I wept.

I live in this great white barn of a house with its sparse furnishings and few souvenirs. The current canvas leans against the wall, stretched and primed and ready for the hand that holds the brush. It is a flat white rectangle resting inside the walls and floors and ceilings of a cube, which is itself part of a series of cubes – the rooms I walk through, their generous allowance of natural light, their views of sorrow.

I remember that Rockwell, who loved the Nordic sagas, told me that Njal and his wife lay down on a bed in a burning house and covered their bodies with the skins of animals. The beams above them burst into fire and their enemies cheered beyond the blazing walls. Njal's life had been one of frenzied transition; a history driven by wooings, slayings, voyages, and battles. His existence had been vehement, rough, and brief; there had been no passivity in it. Now with the hides covering him on the bed, he allowed experience to visit him for the first time, lay down with the bride of his heart to welcome it – this wild brightness, this burning, this atonement. There was one son called Kari who leapt from the roof of his father's flaming house, his hair and clothing ablaze, and ran through the night to quench the fire he carried with him in a snow-filled valley he had played in as a child.

"There is not a trace of the house of Burnt Njal," Rockwell told me. "Of course there is not a trace of that left. But to this day there is a ravine in Iceland called Kari's hollow."

A place to quench fire, lust, thirst: a place of rest. A valley in a northern country. A white canvas rectangle. A window overlooking a frozen Great Lake. All these views of snow.

Tonight I will begin *The Underpainter*, the last canvas of the series, a portrait of myself. In it, I will carefully detail both of my inheritances. Every piece of reconstructed china on the shelves that mar the famous modernist architect's cold and empty walls. Each object and all the histories contained by Sara's house.

The views of the lake outside her windows. George's treasured pigeons locked behind glass. I will add my mother's mausoleums, her fictional skating parties, her music box, the look on my father's face the afternoon he knew that he was disappearing into wealth, Augusta's grey girl, snow house, mauve dunes. Her glorious brothers, radiant in fields of golden hay, Sloan's Bar, Rockwell's laughing face. I will even add Vivian, the boats on which she twice sailed effortlessly, brightly away from tragedy.

I will paint Sara's skin glowing in the yellow light emanating from a thousand autumn birch leaves. Then I will paint myself with the love I could not accept coming towards me, despite my cloak of fear, the implacable rock man, the miles and miles of ice.

It will be full of beautiful dark shorelines, this painting, full of all the possibilities that we believe exist in alternative landscapes, alternative homelands. Hills and trees, gold-leaf birches, skies and lakes and distances. I am old, it is true, but I know that I will be able to finish it. And when it is finished, I will want to keep it close to me so that I may look at the images there, from time to time.

Acknowledgements

This book could not have been written without the encouragement and help of many people. I am most grateful for the information and advice given to me by Katherine Ashenburg, Mieke Bevelander, Nick Carter, Anne Hart, Stuart MacKinnon, Émile Martel, Ian Munro, Amy Quinn, Roseanne Quinn, Helen Quinn-Campbelle, Diane Schoemperlen, David Staines, Ken Snyder, Tony Urquhart, Bernie Weiler, and my mother, Marian Carter. At McClelland & Stewart, thanks to Heather Sangster and, as always, especially to my editor, Ellen Seligman.

Several books were important for research and inspirational purposes. Among these I would particularly like to mention *Let Us Remember*, a collection of letters from Northumberland County boys involved in the First World War, edited by Percy Climo; *Nineteenth Century Pottery and Porcelain in Canada*, by Elizabeth Collard; *History of Number 1 Canadian General Hospital, 1914-1919*, by Kenneth Cameron; *The Materials of the Artist*, by Max Doerner; and Rockwell Kent's delightful autobiography, *It's Me O Lord*. Some, though not all, of the statements made by Robert Henri can be found in *The Art Spirit*, a collection of his lectures, notes, and letters.

Although Robert Henri, Abbott Thayer, and Rockwell Kent did in fact exist, their characters are used in the text in a purely fictional manner, as are certain recognizable places and events, some of which have been altered slightly to fit the shape of the narrative. All other characters and events are fictional.

Conceived during a residency at Memorial University of Newfoundland, *The Underpainter* was completed at Massey College while I was writer-in-residence at the University of Toronto. My heartfelt thanks goes out to both of these institutions.

Finally, a special thank you to Robert Gardner.

Jane Urquhart was born in Little Long Lac, Ontario, and grew up in Toronto. She is the author of three books of poetry, *I Am Walking in the Garden of His Imaginary Palace*, *False Shuffles*, and *The Little Flowers of Madame de Montespan*, a collection of short fiction, *Storm Glass*, and three previous internationally acclaimed novels, *The Whirlpool*, *Changing Heaven*, and *Away*. Her fiction has been translated into numerous foreign languages, and has earned her awards and honours, including the Trillium Award, the Marian Engel Award, Le prix du meilleur livre étranger (Best Foreign Book Award) in France, and, for her bestselling novel *Away*, a place on the shortlist for the prestigious International IMPAC Dublin Literary Award. In the fall of 1997, her fourth novel, *The Underpainter*, was published to wide critical acclaim internationally, won the 1997 Governor General's Award, was shortlisted for the Rogers Communications Writers' Trust Fiction Prize, and became a long-time national bestseller. She was recently named a Chevalier dans l'Ordre des Arts et des Lettres in France.

Urquhart has received two honorary doctorates from Canadian universities and has been writer-in-residence at the University of Ottawa and at Memorial University of Newfoundland, and, during the winter and spring of 1997, she held the Presidential Writer-in-Residence Fellowship at the University of Toronto. She has also given readings and lectures in Canada, Britain, Europe, the U.S.A., and Australia.

Jane Urquhart lives in southwestern Ontario.